SHUTOUT

Sylvester Cole leaned into my shoulder and spoke in a soft voice. "Do you mind if I ask you something, Mrs. Fletcher? You're an artist, a writer. You must be a sensitive woman. Am I imagining it, or are you picking up the same negative vibes I'm getting?"

"I'm not sure I know what you mean."

"The atmosphere in this room and on the team. I've been around plenty of conflict in locker rooms and at team dinners, but nothing like this." He faked a shudder, and rubbed his arms as if he were cold.

All evening, I'd sensed the tension flowing between Ty Ramos and Junior Bennett. The conflict between the manager and the owner was no secret either, with the two men seated at either end of the dais and seemingly intent on avoiding any attempts to bring them together—or to get them to smile. At times, the foul mood in the room seemed as thick as the Arizona air outside, and I'd contemplated escaping the ballroom for a breath of fresh air.

"Well, I have to admit there is a certain level of discomfort this evening," I said.

Three Strikes and You're Dead

A Murder, She Wrote Mystery

A NOVEL BY
JESSICA FLETCHER & DONALD BAIN

Based on the Universal television series created by
Peter S. Fischer, Richard Levinson & William Link

AN OBSIDIAN MYSTERY

OBSIDIAN

Published by New American Library, a division of
Penguin Group (USA) Inc., 375 Hudson Street,
New York, New York 10014, USA
Penguin Group (Canada), 90 Eglinton Avenue East, Suite 700, Toronto,
Ontario, Canada M4P 2Y3 (a division of Pearson Penguin Canada Inc.)
Penguin Books Ltd., 80 Strand, London WC2R 0RL, England
Penguin Ireland, 25 St. Stephen's Green, Dublin 2,
Ireland (a division of Penguin Books Ltd.)
Penguin Group (Australia), 250 Camberwell Road, Camberwell, Victoria 3124,
Australia (a division of Pearson Australia Group Pty. Ltd.)
Penguin Books India Pvt. Ltd., 11 Community Centre, Panchsheel Park,
New Delhi - 110 017, India
Penguin Group (NZ), 67 Apollo Drive, Rosedale, North Shore 0745,
Auckland, New Zealand (a division of Pearson New Zealand Ltd.)
Penguin Books (South Africa) (Pty.) Ltd., 24 Sturdee Avenue,
Rosebank, Johannesburg 2196, South Africa

Penguin Books Ltd., Registered Offices:
80 Strand, London WC2R 0RL, England

Published by Obsidian, an imprint of New American Library, a division of
Penguin Group (USA) Inc. Previously published in a New American Library
hardcover edition.

First Obsidian Printing, September 2007
10 9 8 7 6 5 4 3 2 1

Copyright © 2006 Universal Studios Licensing LLLP. *Murder, She Wrote* is a
trademark and copyright of Universal Studios. All Rights Reserved.

OBSIDIAN and logo are trademarks of Penguin Group (USA) Inc.

Printed in the United States of America

Without limiting the rights under copyright reserved above, no part of this pub-
lication may be reproduced, stored in or introduced into a retrieval system, or
transmitted, in any form, or by any means (electronic, mechanical, photocopy-
ing, recording, or otherwise), without the prior written permission of both the
copyright owner and the above publisher of this book.

PUBLISHER'S NOTE
This is a work of fiction. Names, characters, places, and incidents either are the
product of the author's imagination or are used fictitiously, and any resemblance
to actual persons, living or dead, business establishments, events, or locales is
entirely coincidental.

The publisher does not have any control over and does not assume any
responsibility for author or third-party Web sites or their content.

If you purchased this book without a cover you should be aware that this book
is stolen property. It was reported as "unsold and destroyed" to the publisher
and neither the author nor the publisher has received any payment for this
"stripped book."

The scanning, uploading, and distribution of this book via the Internet or via any
other means without the permission of the publisher is illegal and punishable by
law. Please purchase only authorized electronic editions, and do not participate
in or encourage electronic piracy of copyrighted materials. Your support of the
author's rights is appreciated.

For:

My grandfather, Cornelius "Con" Daily, whose career as a major-league baseball player spanned thirteen years (1884–1896). Primarily a catcher, although he also played other positions, he had stints with teams in Philadelphia, Boston, Indianapolis, Brooklyn, and Chicago.

His older brother, Edward "Ed" Daily, an outfielder who also did a little pitching for teams in Philadelphia and Washington. His professional baseball career lasted seven years (1885–1891).

My father, George Sutherland Bain, who signed as a pitcher with the Dodgers in 1916 but fell off a roof shortly after signing, broke his shoulder, and never had the chance to play professionally.

And my grandson, Alexander Bain Wilson, a future major-leaguer, to be sure.

Donald Bain

Chapter One

"**W**e're down to the Rattlers' last out, folks, and the tension is thick in Thompson Stadium—bottom of the ninth, the score three-two, with the Texons on top, two outs, and the tying run on base. If the Rattlers fail to pull it out here, it will be back to the showers and another year before they get a chance to win a league championship and bask in the glory."

"Shortstop Junior Bennett, number fourteen, is up next, Ralph, but he's oh-and-three for the day against this left-handed pitcher. Think they'll leave him in?"

The camera focused on a heavily perspiring young fan wearing a number 14 Rattlers jersey over a Hawaiian shirt. He held up a sign that read, JUN-IOR FOR MVP. Ralph Trienza checked the TV monitor before lifting his red-and-green ball cap to wipe his brow with a handkerchief. "Wishful thinking on the part of that young man, don't you think, Doug?" he said, as the camera swung back to the two announcers. "Junior's been in a slump for a month, and

Washington's been trying to let him play through it. But there's a lot at stake today. If I was a betting man—and I am—I'd have to go with a right-handed pinch hitter here."

"I'm with you, Ralph. Washington has Ty Ramos on the bench. Ramos has had a good year. He's batting three-ten, three-twenty-five against left-handers. That's a pretty convincing argument."

"Might not be enough to satisfy H.B. though. Ty's got that strained hamstring that kept him from starting today. But Washington said in the pregame that Ty's available for pinch-hitting." Trienza looked into the camera. "You're watching KRM-TV, and I'm Ralph Trienza with Doug Worzall coming to you from Thompson Stadium in Mesa, Arizona, with the score three to two and a lot of folks wondering what manager Buddy Washington will decide to do. We'll find out in a minute, but first a few words from our sponsor."

"Who's H.B.?" I asked my friend Meg Duffy as the bright light trained on the announcers was switched off and the monitor reflected a commercial for Thompson Tools and Hardware. With our seats next to the broadcast booth behind the visiting team's dugout, we could watch the game and listen to the local station's play-by-play at the same time.

The organist struck up "Take Me Out to the Ball Game," and a dozen cheerleaders ran out on the field behind the first-base foul line. They performed an acrobatic dance routine that ended with each cheerleader holding up a letter on a card. All the cards together spelled out THOMPSON TOOLS.

I was in Arizona visiting an old school friend, Meg Hart Duffy, and her husband, Jack—Judge Jack Duffy to his legions of fans *and* detractors in the Family Division of the Superior Court, Hudson County, state of New Jersey—who had invited me to join them in Mesa, where they'd rented a house for the baseball season. The Rattlers were a Double-A team in the Pacific West division, and we were rooting for them to win. But even more, we were rooting for Ty Ramos to get to play on what was the final day of the season for the Rattlers. Ty was the Duffys' foster son.

"H.B. is Harrison Bennett, Sr., the team's owner," Meg said in answer to my question.

"Is he related to the shortstop?"

She nodded and her eyebrows flew up. "Junior is his son. And you can see why it's been hard for Ty to get time on the field when they both play the same position. Buddy Washington tries his best—he knows Ty's the better player—but the orders come from above and Junior gets preference. It's been very frustrating."

"I imagine it would be."

"Jack won't come to watch the game if Junior's playing. He even did some research to see if Bennett's actions were a breach of league rules, but there's no regulation about an owner's conduct if he has a son on the team. It may be unethical, and certainly not good for the team, but it isn't illegal. Too bad for us."

It was late afternoon. The Arizona sky was a clear

blue, the sun still high enough to heat the stadium to a constant simmer. Summer in my home in Cabot Cove, Maine, is plenty hot, but it never reaches the extremes of the Arizona desert.

"Couldn't Ty play another position?" I asked, fanning myself with the program.

"The manager uses him in the outfield every now and then to keep his bat in the lineup, but the regular outfielders complain when they have to sit one out. No one wants to miss a chance to play. Besides, Ty likes the action at shortstop. It's a busy position and he thrives when there's lots to do."

"I guess he'll have to learn to be patient, then."

"Not for long. At least I hope not." Meg lowered her voice and leaned closer to me. "We heard there was a scout from New York down here last week talking to the manager about Ty."

"So he has a good chance to move up to the major leagues?"

"Most likely Triple-A first. The Rattlers are in the Chicago Cubs' farm system. They have a good Triple-A team here in Arizona, too. Of course, there's always the possibility of a trade to another major-league ball club. It doesn't matter who he ends up playing for as long as he makes it to 'the Show.' That's what the kids call the majors—'the Show.' That's what we're all praying for. Everyone tells us how talented he is. All he needs is a little more experience, and he'd get it on a Triple-A team once he's out from under Junior and Harrison Bennett. If he does, it could be less than a year before he gets called up."

"Does he have a say in who he wants to play for?"

"He'd be happy with any team, I'm sure. He loves the Cubs and their history." She laughed. "Everything except their inability to get to the World Series. Naturally, his heart's set on playing in New York, for the Mets or even the Yankees." Meg shivered despite the heat. "To be candid, I kind of hope he'll get to see another part of the country—San Francisco or Tampa or St. Louis, rather than New York."

"But wouldn't playing for a New York team bring him closer to your home in New Jersey? You're only across the river from the city."

"True, and we do love to attend his games. But New York is a big city with big-city temptations, and it's too close to Jersey City, where he had all that trouble when he was younger. I'd like to see him stay away from those kinds of influences. He's still so young and impressionable."

Ty Ramos had been only eleven years old the first time he was brought up before Judge Duffy on a charge of juvenile delinquency. His mother, who lived in the Dominican Republic, had sent him to live with an uncle in New Jersey, hoping to give her only son the benefits and opportunities of a life in the United States. Instead, the uncle, who worked two jobs to support his own children, had little time to watch over yet another youngster. Ty was left to fend for himself in a school where he didn't speak English and where teachers were overwhelmed by a student body with myriad problems. Outside, on the streets, was no better. The young boy learned to endure beatings from older bullies, most of them gang members, who demanded his jacket and gloves in the winter, his baseball cap in the summer. He hid his lunch money in his shoes until they took those from him as well.

Homesick and angry, he was a magnet for trouble, fighting in school, staying out all night, stealing change from his uncle's pockets and fruit from the corner grocery. He joined the gang that had tormented him; carried a knife in his boot; and earned money by warning the drug dealers when a police car turned the corner, and by delivering messages for the owner of a local bar, a low-level mobster who liked it that his errand boy didn't understand enough English to testify against him. That wasn't really true anymore, but Ty let him believe it was.

Judge Duffy watched as an innocent first-time offender began to develop the makings of a hardened career criminal, and he felt he had to intervene. Ty's situation reminded the judge of his own childhood in a poor neighborhood in Trenton, where he had to fight hard for respect and even harder to finish his education. Sending Ty back to the Dominican Republic was not an option. His mother had moved, and no one could locate her. Sending him back to his uncle would only perpetuate the problems. Foster family after foster family rejected the boy as too disruptive to keep. But Judge Duffy saw a spark in Ty that the others had missed. Beneath the shield of resentment that the teenager wore like armor, the judge recognized a yearning to fit in, and he thought he might be able to reach Ty Ramos.

The first couple of years with Ty at the Duffys' sprawling suburban New Jersey ranch were daunting. More than once Meg thought Jack had taken on more than they could handle, but through a combination of love and discipline, they began to see a change. Ty's transformation was helped by a new high school away from his old friends and enemies, one with strong academics and an even stronger sports program. Ty blossomed once he joined the baseball team, first as a catcher—the only boy willing to catch the streaking fastball of the team's star pitcher—and later as a first baseman. But he was to shine brightest at shortstop, the perfect position for his quick moves and uncanny ability to read the batter accurately.

There was no question of college when Ty graduated from high school, although not due to lack of achievement. He wasn't an honors student, but he'd acquitted himself well academically, passing all his tests with respectable grades, even the English literature exam, on which he'd scored an 89. But Ty had found his home in baseball, and an offer from the Cubs to join its Rattlers farm team had sealed his future—at least the immediate future.

"We're back, and Buddy Washington is in the dugout talking to his shortstops."

Ralph Trienza peered into the monitor as the camera trained its lens on the manager seated in the dugout. "Okay," Trienza said, "he's given the signal. Ty Ramos will pinch-hit for Junior Bennett."

A round of cheers greeted Ty as he climbed the stairs from the dugout, picked up two bats, and swung them, choosing one and dropping the other before taking his place at home plate.

"There's no love lost between those two," Doug Worzall said into his microphone. "Ramos and Bennett have been battling all season for a permanent slot at shortstop. They're not exactly friendly competitors, according to people close to the situation. That was a tough call to yank Junior."

"But a good one for the team, Doug. It's hard going up against Evans, a left-handed pitcher. Now, we'll see if Ramos can pull it off. A hit here would put the winning run on base and bring up Carter Menzies, who's three for three today. But if Ramos fans, it's the end of the season for the Rattlers. Tough position to be in. There's a lot riding on those shoulders."

A chorus of boos swelled up from the vicinity of the left-field fence. Meg took my hand and squeezed it.

"Those boo-birds out there are from San Pedro," Doug Worzall announced as the camera panned a contingent of Texon fans wearing yellow-and-red shirts, the team colors, and waving WE'RE #1 foam hands.

"Here's the first pitch. It's a swing and a miss. That ball was outside, out of the strike zone. Looks like Ramos might be a little anxious."

"That corner is the pitcher's favorite, Ralph. Evans has left a lot of Rattlers swinging at that curveball."

"C'mon, Ty," Meg whispered, watching her foster son intently. "You can do it."

"Here's the windup. It's outside. One-and-one."

Ty used his bat to knock dirt from his cleats and twisted his right foot into the batter's box. He nodded to the umpire and squinted at the pitcher, taking a practice swing.

"Ramos is an interesting guy, Doug. He was born in the Dominican Republic. That country has baseball in its blood. It's the national passion. They've contributed more ballplayers to Major League Baseball than any other nation outside our borders, and with a population of less than nine million. Amazing, isn't it?"

The next pitch was low and outside, a ball.

"Those population numbers are almost the same as New Jersey's," Trienza said. "And don't forget, that's where Ramos was raised. He was an all-star on his high school team, took them to the state championships."

"He's looking to take the Rattlers to the league championships now. Here's the pitch. Ooh, he fouled that one off his instep. Got to sting. Two-and-two."

The pitcher took off his mitt and rubbed the new ball between his hands, pinching the top with his fingers as if he wanted to smoothe out the leather. He stretched, put the glove back on, leaned over, and stared at the catcher, shook his head, then nodded and threw the ball. Ty jumped back as the ball whizzed by close to his head. He stepped out of the batter's box and swung his bat twice.

"That was a close one, Doug. Evans was giving him a warning there—don't crowd the plate. It's a full count, folks, in the bottom of the ninth with two out. This next pitch could decide the game."

Worzall laughed. "I'm feeling nervous myself, Ralph," he said. "Imagine what Ramos must be feeling now. The whole team is counting on him. That's a lot of pressure for a young player."

"But he's poised, Doug. Mature for his age. Let's see what he does with this pitch."

Ty tapped home plate with his bat, tugged on the peak of his cap under the batting helmet, and stole a glance at Meg. A small smile played around his lips. He adjusted his hips, swaying from side to side, lifted one shoulder after the other, then settled down into his batting crouch and waited. The pitcher wiped his lips, set the ball at his waist, reared back, raised his right leg, and hurled the ball toward home plate.

Ty swung. There was a loud crack as his bat connected with the ninety-mile-an-hour fastball. The crowd rose to their feet, and Meg and I joined them to watch the ball sail toward the right-field wall. The Texon outfielder skipped backward, keeping his eye on the ball, then turned to watch it clear the fence and bounce on the street outside the stadium.

"Home run! The ball game's over. Ty Ramos hits a homer to end the game. The Rattlers have won the championship, with Ramos's long ball bringing in two runs for a four-three victory over the San Pedro Texons. Here come the tying and winning runs down the third-base line. The San Pedro Texons will have to wait another year. The Mesa Rattlers are the Pacific West Double-A champions!"

Meg gave me a hug, tears streaming down her cheeks. "Oh, Jessica. He did it! He won the game! I'm so excited. I'm so proud. I knew he could do it."

"Congratulations, Meg. What a wonderful day for you and Jack."

"Oh, I know Jack saw this. He's watching our boy on TV."

Around us, fans were jumping up and down, screaming and laughing, giving each other high fives. The cheerleaders bounced onto the grass, doing back flips and somersaults. The team mascot, an oversized character in a carpenter costume, wiggled his hips and pumped his fist in the air. Ty's teammates poured onto the field to greet him as he crossed home plate.

With one exception. Junior Bennett spat on the ground, threw his glove across the dugout, and stomped off toward the locker room.

Chapter Two

Ty whooped and shivered as the ice from a bucket of Gatorade was spilled down his back. The floor was flooded. Whatever liquid was available—water, soda pop, juice, rubbing alcohol, and a few smuggled-in bottles of beer—had been used to anoint the team members, and not a few of the guests who'd been intrepid enough to enter the locker room and join in on the postgame festivities. Meg and I had congratulated Ty, who'd ushered us to a bench away from the melee. "You'll be safer here," he said, grinning. "And drier."

"I almost took Jessica's hand off when you were at bat," Meg told him. "I squeezed it so hard."

Ty smiled at me. "You okay, Mrs. Fletcher?"

I waved my hand in the air. "It still functions," I said. "What an exciting game! I'm glad I got a chance to see you in action. Very impressive."

"I was just happy I got to go in," he said. "I would've hated sitting on the bench the whole game." He glanced back at the sounds of cheers and whistles.

"You go on and celebrate with your teammates," Meg said. "We'll see you later at the dinner."

"No, no," he said. "Wait for me. I'll only be here a little longer. I want to stop home to see the judge."

"He called us on my cell phone right after the game," Meg said, tearing up. "He's just bursting with happiness. You make him so proud."

Ty turned a pink bright, enough to be discernible against his naturally dusky complexion. "I like making the judge proud," he said. "You stay right here, okay? Don't leave without me."

"We'll be here," I assured him.

Rattlers manager Buddy Washington was soaked from the top of his bald head to the bottom of his cleats. He wiped away rivulets of moisture from his face with his hand as a female reporter in a bright red suit with dark wet patches, testifying that she hadn't escaped the celebration, shoved a microphone at his mouth. Behind her, a cameraman flicked on a light and aimed his lens at the manager.

"Buddy Washington, manager of the Mesa Rattlers, that was quite a nail-biter in the ninth inning, but your guys came through. You've been around a long time, but this is your first championship. Did you ever think this day would come?"

"We've got a great team, Karen. These kids are great. I've known we had a winning team ever since spring training. I had confidence in them."

"And you kept it through that seven-game losing streak in July?"

Washington winced at the reminder. "Sure I did.

Every team has its ups and downs. That was just a temporary hitch. You've got to play through it. And we did. We've got the basic talent here to be champs in any league, any league at all."

Meg and I watched the interview and laughed along with Washington as Ty, egged on by another teammate, poured bottled water over his manager's head.

The reporter turned to Ty.

"Ty Ramos hit a homer to win the game and seal the league championship. You're the game's most valuable player, Ty, and there's talk you'll be named MVP of the season. Tell the people how it feels to be the hero of the day."

Ty pulled over another player and wrapped his arm around his teammate's neck. "Carter here got three hits today," he shouted into the microphone. "And our pitchers kept the Texons to only three runs. We got a great manager in Buddy Washington, who had faith in us even when we sucked. Can I say 'sucked' on TV?"

"You just did," Carter said, laughing and taking a slug from a bottle of beer.

"Then I guess it's okay," Ty said.

"I can edit it out later, if the station objects," Karen said. "Keep talking."

"Where was I? Oh, yeah, like Buddy says, this is a great team, with great team spirit."

Someone shouted from behind him, "Rattlers forever!" and let out a loud war cry that left my ears ringing.

"See what I mean?" Ty said, looking over his

shoulder. "When you got a great team, everyone contributes. It isn't one guy or two. It's all of us."

"You tell him, captain," Carter said, grinning.

"That's a her, not a him," Ty said, pointing his empty bottle at Karen, whose figure beneath the suit said loud and clear that she was indeed a "her."

Carter guffawed and covered his mouth with his hand.

"Even Junior Bennett?" Karen said. There was a skeptical note in her voice.

"She's baiting him," I said to Meg.

"He can handle it," she replied.

"Junior's a great player," Ty said. "Where is he? I haven't congratulated him yet." Ty craned his neck, peering around the chaotic locker room, then caught Meg's eye and winked at her before turning back to the microphone. "Right now," he said, raising his empty water bottle, "we're the best team in baseball."

Another reporter with a pad and pen stepped in front of Ty and Carter. "Can I get a comment from you for the *Gazette*?" he asked.

"Sure, Franco," Carter said. "What would us to say?"

"Tedeschi, you stepped right into my shot," Karen said, a frown marring her pretty face. She moved sideways to get the unrepentant newspaperman out of the picture. "We'll have to edit. Keep rolling." She adjusted her expression and continued. "This is Karen Locke in the Mesa Rattlers locker room, where good fellowship prevails—for now—and the celebration continues. Back to you in the studio."

The cameraman flicked off his light and looked to Karen for guidance. "You want more?" he asked.

"Yes. I need some B-roll for tonight's wrap-up," she said, popping a piece of chewing gum into her mouth. She looked past the *Gazette* reporter and the two ballplayers and cocked her head at her cameraman. "I see team owner Harrison Bennett, Sr., coming in," she told him. She lifted a foot off the wet, sticky floor and shook drops of moisture off her shoes. "Let's get a comment from him and then get out of here before we're all electrocuted."

Ty spotted Junior Bennett and broke away from Carter and Franco Tedeschi to approach him. "Hey, buddy," he said, grinning and raising his hand for a high five.

Junior ignored the gesture and pushed past Ty, shouldering him aside.

"Junior, Junior. We're the champs," Ty said to his teammate's back. "Doesn't that make you happy?"

Junior swung around, his expression furious, his hands fisted by his side. "You just love to be in the limelight, don't you?"

"Sure, especially when we win," Ty said, working to keep the grin on his face.

"You think you're such a big shot. Anyone could've got a hit off that pitcher. He was slowing down."

"Maybe he was. So what? The thing is we won."

"So that was my hit. I should've been the one at bat."

Ty held his hands up, palms out. "Hey, buddy. Not my call. Can't you just be grateful we're on top?"

"Don't preach to me, you dirty sp—"

Buddy Washington grabbed Junior's elbow and stepped between him and Ty. "Back off," he growled. "I don't want to hear that stuff. Grow up, Junior. He did what I wanted. He got the job done."

"I could've done the same."

"Maybe, maybe not. But I make the decisions around here, not you."

"We'll see about that," Junior said. "You were supposed to leave me in. You're not long for this job."

Several team members nearby turned to listen in on the conversation.

Junior looked around sheepishly.

Washington stroked his chin and peered at Junior from under bushy eyebrows. "I'm not? Really? You got some inside knowledge, Junior? Your father consulting you now about his plans for the team?"

Junior had the grace to blush. "No, um—I just think—" he stammered and fell silent.

"Yeah, well. Confine your thinking to how you're going to work on improving your batting average in the off-season. And in the meantime"—he glanced at Ty, then back to Junior—"keep your disagreements private. The press is swarming all over the place. I don't want to read any negative comments tomorrow or see anything but smiles on the news tonight. Understand?"

Junior gave a quick nod and hurried away.

"Don't look at me," Ty said to his manager, his hands in the air. "I was just tryin' to congratulate him." The grin was back on his face.

Washington scowled at him. "I got no patience for grandstanding," he said, pointing his finger at his star player. Then his expression softened. He gave Ty a soft punch in the arm. "Good job today, son."

"Thanks, Coach."

"Yes, congratulations, Ramos," a deep voice said from behind Ty.

I saw concern flash in Washington's eyes and just as quickly disappear as the manager gave the owner a hearty smile, and said, "Congratulations to you, H.B. I told you we had a winning team."

Bennett rested a hand on Ty's shoulder. "Leave us alone, boy."

"Sure thing, sir," Ty said, looking to Washington, who waved him away.

"I don't like it when my orders are ignored," Bennett said.

"Shouldn't we discuss this in your office?" Washington said softly, his eyes on the television reporter across the room. "We don't want to be overheard."

"Don't tell me where I can talk. This is my team and my locker room. You're my employee, and don't forget it."

Washington shrugged, but even from a distance away I could see a vein beating in his temple, a sign of the tension he felt. "Suit yourself," he said, feigning nonchalance.

"I do suit myself. And so should you if you know what's good for you. Didn't I tell you to leave him in?"

I noticed that with all the Gatorade, beer, and soda

flowing, no one in the locker room had dared pour a drop over Harrison Bennett, Sr. He was immaculately dressed in a gray sharkskin suit, a white shirt, and a tie patterned with little baseball caps of red, white, and blue. He was a tall man, broadly built, with a receding hairline camouflaged by a buzz cut that gave him the appearance of someone in the military.

Washington plucked at his damp jersey and weighed his words. "Junior hadn't connected all day," he said slowly. "The Texons had a leftie on the mound. We needed a good bat against a left-handed pitcher. Ramos was that bat." He locked eyes with Bennett, his lips a tight line.

"I don't pay you to second-guess my instructions."

"But you do pay me to win," Washington said. "And that's what we did."

The *Gazette* reporter, pretending not to listen, was inching toward the two men, and across the room Karen Locke strode in their direction and beckoned to her cameraman, who switched on the light on top of the camera.

Bennett squinted in the glare. "Turn that off, and get it out of here if you want to keep your locker room privileges."

"But, H.B.," Karen said, smiling sweetly, "the people in Mesa are always interested in what you have to say."

"I already gave you a quote. I said turn it off."

Karen gestured to the cameraman, who extinguished the light.

"Now get out of here," H.B. said. "And that goes

for you, too, Tedeschi. Put that notebook away. You print anything I didn't tell you directly, the *Gazette* will never get another interview with a Rattler. Do I make myself clear?"

The locker room had fallen silent, all signs of celebration suspended. Meg gripped my hand again.

I watched, fascinated, as the reporters retreated from H.B. Obviously, freedom of the press was not honored here. It was more important to maintain access to the team than to challenge its owner in public. But I wondered why in the midst of a celebration of his team's victory its owner would reprimand the man responsible. It obviously had to do with the manager's decision to use Ty as a pinch hitter for the owner's son. I'm not a big baseball fan, although I do enjoy following the trials and tribulations of the Boston Red Sox, and I'm certainly not knowledgeable enough to second-guess a manager's decision to use a pinch hitter. But it seemed to me that, personal considerations aside, what should have mattered at that moment was winning, regardless of who got the winning hit.

Oh, well, I thought as Meg and I left the locker room and waited for Ty by the players' entrance, *it will all be forgotten in the glow of victory.*

At least I hope it will be.

Chapter Three

"**I**'d also like to offer up a big thanks to the Dominican Republic for their number one export to the U.S.—baseball. Amazing how a tiny, poor country can manufacture such incredible talent. It's a great way to climb the ladder. Let's give it up for our neighbors south of the border—um, south and east of the border. They produced a helluva shortstop."

A discernible hush fell over the already quiet room, only to be interrupted by the shuffling of feet and nervous repositioning of bodies on chairs, myself included. Ty slapped his hands together and shouted, "Yeah, let's hear it for the D.R., baby."

The room responded with tepid applause.

At the microphone, Theo Thompson, owner of Thompson Tools and Hardware and corporate sponsor of Thompson Stadium, looked down at a lady who was pulling on his sleeve. "What? What'd I say wrong?"

"Not the most politically correct speech," I whispered to Sheriff John Hualga, seated to my left.

Hualga shrugged, brow furrowed. "He means well. Theo puts his foot in his mouth sometimes," he whispered back, "but this team would be playing on a Little League field without him. He built that stadium with his own money, gives away tickets to the kids who can't afford them. He's one of the nicest fellows you'll ever meet."

The same could be said of John Hualga. Before I'd left Cabot Cove for Arizona, our sheriff and my friend, Mort Metzger, had urged me to look up Sheriff Hualga, whom he'd met at a forensic conference in Salt Lake City years ago. "Terrific guy," Mort had said. "You'll love him."

It was pure coincidence that I ended up at the table with him, and I quickly saw why Mort held him in such high regard. Despite his formidable appearance—he was short and solidly built, muscular arms protruding from the sleeves of his tan uniform shirt, cheeks slightly pockmarked, made more evident by the oily sheen of his face, shaved temples next to a crop of coal black hair on the top of his head that seemed to protest whatever he might do with a comb—his most striking feature was his laugh. It came easily and bubbled up from deep within. Well read and well spoken, he had a keen sense of humor. A most likable man. Before Theo Thompson had commandeered the microphone, the sheriff and I had been discussing the origins of names.

"*Hualga* means 'moon' in Mohave," he'd said. "Mohave is a Western Arizona tribe, one of twenty-one tribes in the state. Have any idea what your name means, Mrs. Fletcher?"

"As a matter of fact, I do," I replied. "*Fletcher* means 'maker-of-arrows' in Middle English."

"Mort tells me you're straight as an arrow," he said. "Do you always hit your target?"

"I try to, but I'm afraid, like everyone else, my aim isn't always perfect."

He chuckled. "That's not what I hear."

Seated across from us at the table were Jack and Meg Duffy, who'd communicated their reaction to Thompson's remarks with grimaces and raised eyebrows while clapping politely. Meg, perfectly coifed with her Anna Wintour haircut and minimal but deftly applied makeup, looked across to me. She gently shook her head and smiled. Jack was fond of casual dress when not on the bench, and tonight was no exception. His ten-gallon hat sat on the empty chair beside him. He wore a colorful Southwestern-inspired shirt with green cacti, a light brown snake-skin belt with a giant turquoise buckle, and dark brown tooled-leather cowboy boots. All this on a six-foot six-inch frame graced by a full head of white hair. Judge Duffy was no wallflower—on or off the bench.

Meanwhile, Theo still droned on. "The Rattlers are lucky to have the MVP of the season and of the game, Ty Ramos, here in Mesa. Helluva shortstop. It's a tough position. Requires agility and . . ."

I glanced over at the adjacent table, where Ty sat with about half the team's members. He was clearly uncomfortable that he was still the center of the attention coming from the podium. The MVP trophy, awarded earlier, sat next to his untouched plate of food. When his teammates had razzed him about winning the award, he'd plucked some of the flowers from the centerpiece to fill the cup at the top of the tall trophy. "Come over later and I'll fill it with Gatorade for you."

Carter had smirked. "I'd rather have beer."

"You'd end up on the floor."

"It ain't that big of a cup."

Junior sat at the next table with the other half of the team. His sullen expression was matched by those of his friends, who squirmed at the praise Theo was heaping on Ty, their eyes darting from Junior to the ceiling to the tabletop, trying to avoid looking as if they were listening to anything Thompson was saying. As the host clapped his hands, trying to start another ovation, Junior pushed his chair back with a jerk, stood, and marched toward the door. When he passed my seat, it sounded as if he muttered an ethnic slur under his breath before storming out of the room into the lobby.

Had he really said that? It was sad if he had, but I feared it was true. I may be getting older, but all of my senses work quite well, including my hearing. I looked at Hualga to see if he'd heard what I'd heard, and his scowling countenance confirmed it.

Upon witnessing Junior's defiant departure, Thompson backpedaled a bit with a couple of "ums" before finally saying, "But let's face it, there is no 'I' in the word 'team,' and this whole team, each and every player, is to be congratulated for an incredible season. Best of luck to all of these fine young men. And God bless."

He started to step away from the microphone— and not a moment too soon—but grabbed the mike again and said, "Ladies and gentlemen, ladies and gentlemen, please. One more thing." He waited while the buzz in the room quieted. "Thank you. I almost forgot. Please join me in a big round of applause for the Mesa Hilton for donating this wonderful hotel facility to the Rattlers for this marvelous dinner."

The crowd applauded once more, as much in gratitude that Thompson had finally left the stage as in appreciation for the meal and the venue.

I was sitting between John Hualga and a man who'd been introduced to me as a baseball agent. Sylvester Cole was a handsome fellow in his thirties who I'd been told had played in the major leagues for the Seattle Mariners before a nagging groin injury sealed his fate. If a seductive personality and a killer smile were all it took to stay in the Big Show, he'd surely still be there, whether his bat was connecting or not.

He leaned into my shoulder and, when I turned toward him, looked deeply into my eyes and spoke in a soft voice. "Do you mind if I ask you something, Mrs. Fletcher?"

"Not at all. I'll be happy to answer if I can."

"You're an artist, a writer. You must be a sensitive woman. Am I imagining it, or are you picking up the same negative vibes I'm getting?"

"I'm not sure I know what you mean."

"The atmosphere in this room and on the team. I've been around plenty of conflict in locker rooms and at team dinners, but nothing like this." He faked a shudder and rubbed his arms as if he were cold.

All evening, I'd sensed the tension flowing between Ty Ramos and Junior Bennett, and the teammates who seemed to have lined up behind one or the other. The conflict between the manager and the owner was no secret either, with the two men seated at either end of the dais and seemingly intent on avoiding any attempts to bring them together—or to get them to smile. At times, the foul mood in the room seemed as oppressive as the Arizona air outside, and I'd contemplated escaping the ballroom for a breath of fresh air despite the heat. A Maine gal through and through, I don't mind occasional exposure to the Arizona heat, although I never could live there. My blood is too thick from all those Yankee winters.

"Well, I have to admit that there is a certain level of discomfort this evening," I said.

"You're being diplomatic," Sylvester said, flashing me his most captivating smile. "I should have expected that, of course. This place is churning with 'discomfort,' as you put it." He shook his head. "I want to get Ty out of this environment as soon as I can. It's not good for his psyche. He's a street-smart kid, thanks to his early years, but even that couldn't prepare him for the animosity swirling around him. I've never seen anything like it, and I've been in this game a while. I don't want it to poison the well, so to speak."

"I don't believe his psyche has suffered," I said, thinking of all the praise that had been heaped on Ty earlier. I watched him interact with his teammates at the next table. He didn't look unhappy, although he did glance at his watch a few times. I cocked my head at the agent. "Besides, the season is over, isn't it?" I said. "He'll be out of this 'environment' relatively soon, I imagine."

"When he signs with me, he will." He lowered his voice. "I don't want it to get around yet, but I've been working on his future already. Got connections here in Arizona, and in California, too, and I've been talking with some higher-ups in the Chicago organization. Together, we'll get him into the majors in no time at all. I think we'll make a great team, Ty and me."

"Do you have many players under contract?"

"Not exactly what you'd call 'many.' I've always been choosy about who I take under my wing." He chuckled. "There are quite a few fathers calling me, but I only want the best, the guys who can go the whole way."

"And you think Ty can?"

"Oh, yes. Have you ever gone fishing, Mrs. Fletcher?"

I was a bit startled by his change in subject, but I went along with him. Smiling, I said, "It's one of my favorite pastimes."

"Ah, so you'll understand my reference when I tell you Ty's a keeper."

"A fish you're not going to throw back."

He grinned at me, his eyes lighting up. "I expect he'll make my career as much as I'll make his."

"It's nice when it works out well for everyone," I said.

"Exactly."

"I've known Ty for quite a long time," I said. "He's a very talented athlete and an upright young man. I wish you both well."

"You're obviously a fan. The judge tells me that Ty thinks the world of you, too. He says that if he doesn't make it as a ballplayer, Ty wants to be a writer just like you."

"The judge has told me that before, and whenever I've been with Ty, he expresses interest in writing. It's very flattering."

The waitress snaked her arm between us as she removed empty dishes from the first course—tequila-battered shrimp. "That was marvelous," Cole said, switching his charm to the young woman who took his plate. She blushed as if he had paid her a personal compliment.

The atmosphere at the dinner may have been strained, but the food was excellent. For my entrée I'd chosen spice-rubbed rotisserie chicken, and for dessert vanilla ice cream with hot-fudge. I may never acclimate to the brutal desert heat, but I've become a fan of Southwestern cuisine.

Someone must have told Junior that dinner was being served, because he came back into the room on cue and took his seat. I watched as Ty, seated at the table next to Junior's, made momentary eye contact with the owner's son. Junior looked away immediately. Ty smiled to himself, shook his head, and began talking to Carter.

Ty and Junior were such different physical types. I'd noticed when Ty came up to bat that he was tall and sinewy, with not an ounce of extraneous fat on his frame. For some reason, I always thought of outstanding hitters in baseball as more on the stocky side, compact, with low centers of gravity. But then I remembered the great Ted Williams, known as the "splendid splinter" because of his long, lanky physique. Seeing Ty at the table without his baseball cap, I had a better view of his face. His black hair was short and neatly trimmed, his face a series of sharp angles. A handsome young man by any definition.

Junior Bennett, while as tall as Ty, had the more typical baseball physique—square and solid. His looks were all-American, right down to the freckles across his pug nose, his blue eyes, and the floppy blond hair that covered the tops of his ears and the back of his neck. He didn't have an all-American disposition, however. I had the feeling he wasn't used to smiling, and that when he did, it was more of a sour grin than a genuine appreciation of something humorous. Having a father like H.B. must have made his life difficult.

Cole was also keenly aware of the exchange between the two young men. He leaned close to my ear again and said, "I think it's time to make my pitch." To the rest of the table: "Please, keep eating. Don't let it get cold." He excused himself and went over to

Jack Duffy, who was getting drinks from the bar. I could see from the expression on Jack's face that he was surprised to find Cole accosting him. After a few seconds of conversation, Jack left his drinks on the bar, and the two men exited through the same door Junior had used to reach the lobby.

"Delicious, isn't it?" Meg asked from across the table, indicating her dinner. I was happy to have the conversation turn to food and away from the conflict, which had seemed to occupy too much attention.

"Wonderful," I agreed.

My friend's eyes went to the doorway through which her husband had just left, and then to the table where Ty and his teammates were enjoying their main dish. It was evident that she was concerned about the tension, too, and the possibility that some sort of confrontation might take place. As long as I've known Meg, she's always been one to avoid controversy whenever possible. Some people thrive on confrontation, people like the team owner, Harrison Bennett. Others, like Meg and me, shy from it. Of course, there are times when it's impossible to turn your back on it, to pretend out of self-preservation that it isn't there. I just hoped this night wouldn't turn into one of those situations.

A few minutes later Cole and Jack came back into the room. Their collective mood seemed decidedly more upbeat. They were smiling and patting each other on the back. They took their seats, and the waitress placed the main course in front of them.

"Great," Cole said. "I was hoping I hadn't missed my meal."

He was still eating when a hand appeared on his shoulder. It belonged to Harrison Bennett, Sr.

Cole stood to greet the team's owner. "Hey there, Mr. Bennett," he said. "Congratulations on a great win."

"Thanks, Sylvester," Bennett said matter-of-factly. "We need to talk."

"Okay," said Cole, "but I'm having my dinner right now."

"How about a drink in the Atrium Bar following dinner?"

"Sorry, sir, but I won't be able to do that," Cole said. "I have another engagement this evening."

Bennett cleared his throat. "All right," he said. "We'll meet for breakfast."

"No, sir, afraid I can't do that either," said Cole, wiping his mouth with a napkin. "I'm leaving for Phoenix later tonight. Gotta catch a flight to L.A. first thing in the morning. Sorry."

"Seems you are one *helluva* busy guy," H.B. said sarcastically. "Let me just say this, then: You're making a mistake, Sylvester. It'll come back to eat you." He forcefully patted Cole twice on the shoulder, walked away from the table, and disappeared into the lobby.

Cole sat down. "He wants me to sign his kid," he said to me in the conspiratorial voice to which I'd become accustomed. From the way he had brushed off Bennett, I assumed he'd already made up his mind not to sign Junior, but I might have been wrong.

"I'll let him dangle a while," Cole said.

I was thinking a breath of fresh air might be nice, and glanced toward the ballroom doors just as a voice boomed over the microphone: "I hope you are all enjoying your dinner. I just wanted to get in a couple of words, if that's all right with you."

It was Buddy Washington at the podium, and the crowd quieted immediately. Washington had earned the respect not only of his players and their families but of the fans and, from what I could see, the media as well. Sadly, the same could not be said of his team's owner.

"The boys at those tables are probably thinking I'm going to remind them to come in tomorrow and clean out their lockers—and they're right. I am," he began. "You wouldn't believe the kinds of things they leave in there at the end of the season—half-eaten sandwiches, barbells, comic books, love letters, water pistols, not to mention dirty socks. A guy's whole life is in his locker. Once, I even found a live turtle in a bowl of water."

There were smiles all around the room. "But we'll get back to that," he continued. "I have something else to say." He held up one hand. "I know it sounds like some sorta cliché, so you gotta forgive me, but I've coached a hell of a lot of teams, from Little League to high school, and right on to here coachin' the Mesa Rattlers Double-A team, and I can *honestly* say from my heart that I have never—let me repeat that—*never* met a finer group of young men. I love them like family. They are the sons I never had."

It was apparent that Washington had downed a drink too many. He didn't slur his speech, but his emotions had bubbled up to the surface and were beginning to spill over. He wiped tears from his face with a napkin, pumped his fist in the air, and said, "To the team. Thanks for the sweat, the tears, and for saving me from the nervous breakdown I was on the brink of havin' when we were on that losing streak."

A wave of laughter swept through the room. Washington threw back his head and gave out a contagious guffaw that kept the crowd laughing, too.

"Bud-dy, Bud-dy, Bud-dy," a couple of players started to chant, and others joined in.

Embarrassed, Washington waved his hands to try to quiet them down. When the chants faded, he continued: "I would like to thank so many people. But most of all I'd like to thank my wife, Teddy."

The audience responded with another burst of applause.

"As some of you know, Teddy couldn't be here tonight because she's not feeling well."

Cole whispered to me, "Cancer, but most of the guys don't know that's what it is."

Washington paused, took a deep breath, looked to the ceiling, and continued. "Teddy has put up with me and with all of my boys, who became her boys when it was time for a hot meal, a couple of dollars, or a shoulder to lean on. In fact—and I won't single anyone out, but he knows who he is—Teddy was even called on by one of the players to deal with a scorpion that had invaded his room."

The two tables where the team members sat erupted with laughter, the first time that evening I'd seen all the Rattlers smiling.

"We won't mention names, now, will we, men?" Washington said.

"Scorpions aren't the only poisonous things around here," yelled Junior.

Another player punched him in the arm and the two of them laughed. Smiles faded on the faces of others at the table. I saw Ty's brows fly up and he looked to the ceiling, shaking his head. His buddy, Carter, slapped his arm around him and whispered something into his ear that made Ty chuckle.

Washington continued, ignoring the horseplay between the friends of Junior and Ty. "Teddy is a surrogate mother to many of these kids, and I want her to know that the Rattlers could not have clinched this title without her. Thanks, Teddy. We love you." He blew a kiss to the room, as though his wife were there. "And that's all I have to say, except this: Clean out your lockers."

Washington sat to a standing ovation from his players, and most of the other people in the room. Junior remained defiantly seated, even though his teammates urged him to join them.

Yes, a breath of fresh air was definitely in order. I excused myself and walked to the door to exit the room. It flew open as H.B. pushed through it.

"Mr. Bennett," I said, thrusting out my hand. "We haven't been officially introduced. I'm Jessica Fletcher, a friend of the Duffys. In fact, I'm staying with them."

"I know who you are, Mrs. Fletcher," he said, accepting my hand and giving it a brief shake. "Enjoying yourself this evening?"

"Very much. This is a lovely affair, wonderful food. And of course the game was such a delight. It's always fun to be on the winning side. You must be especially enjoying this victory, Mr. Bennett."

"Yeah, well, there are pluses and minuses in everything. We had a good season despite some rough patches. However, our *star* player"—he said "star" as if there were a bad taste in his mouth—"may just get brought up on charges one of these days. Nothing you should mention, by the way."

"Really?" I asked. "Charges? Against whom? For what?"

"I'm not naming names. No, you didn't hear that from me. I can't talk about it yet, but suffice it to say some of the boys have brought their suspicions to me."

I had a feeling "some of the boys" meant Junior.

"Suspicions aren't proof, Mr. Bennett. I hope you're not drawing conclusions based on rumors."

"I'm not concluding anything, Mrs. Fletcher. But I do have the league looking into his activities."

Rather than seem upset by the possibility of trouble for one of his players, he seemed pleased, even excited.

"I can't get into it right now," he said, "but I would like to make a suggestion for your next book."

"Which is?"

"How about a sports agent gets murdered? I'd really enjoy that plot." With that he brushed past me.

I left the room and walked through the lobby, a soaring atrium studded with towering cacti and statues of coyotes. The walls were draped in murals depicting desert scenes. The space was at least twelve stories high, and I spotted the Atrium Bar that H.B. had mentioned earlier. *Nice spot for a quiet drink,* I thought.

Outside, in the still Arizona night, the temperature must have been in the hundreds, but it actually felt good. The ballroom inside was excessively air-conditioned. I walked over to the side of the entrance so that I would be out of the way of the hustle-bustle of people coming in and out of the hotel.

I took a couple of deep breaths and admired a pot that held an unusual and especially colorful bush, something I assumed was indigenous to this neck of the woods since I'd never seen it before. I made a mental note to ask Meg if she knew what it was.

Out of the corner of my eye, I spied a shadow and heard the muffled voice of someone speaking into a cell phone. *How our lives have changed,* I thought, *with the advent of that little device.* I had declined to carry one when they first came out, thinking it wasn't necessary to be reachable at all times of the night and day. But eventually, good friends—Seth Hazlitt, in particular—had persuaded me that it was prudent to own one. Seth is an old-fashioned country doctor and one of my best friends. He's usually the last to accept modern conveniences, unless they have to do with medicine. Then he's off to a medical conference to learn all he can about them.

I hadn't meant to eavesdrop on a private conversation, but I couldn't help hearing the man on the phone.

"Yeah, I lost a bundle on that game. Wasn't supposed to happen. Stupid kid. The boys upstairs are not gonna be happy." There was a long pause. "I'll let him know. You ever get ahold of that woman? Ramos said he'd get me the money later. Don't sweat it. Tell her she'll get it. Tomorrow. Peace out."

I turned. The voice belonged to a slight man nervously pacing back and forth. He was wearing a tan plaid jacket over a brown shirt and tie, and flourished a white handkerchief with which he continuously mopped his brow. He disappeared as quickly as he had appeared. I don't know if he saw me, but if he did, it seemed of little relevance to him.

Dessert will be served soon and I should get back inside, I thought. But it was nice to bask, even momentarily, in the peaceful evening. Peaceful, that is, until I heard the tinny notes of a snippet of one of my favorite songs, "Stompin' at the Savoy." It was my own cell phone ringing. I dug the jingling instrument out of my purse and checked the screen for the name of the caller. It was Mort Metzger, our sheriff in Cabot Cove.

"Mrs. F! How're you enjoying Arizona?"

"Just fine, Mort. Is everything all right? It's late back home. We're three hours earlier out here."

"I know. I know. That's why I figured it was okay to call. Not too late for you. There's nothing wrong. We're great. So how's everything going out there?"

"Everything is fine. In fact, I'm enjoying a dinner with your friend, Sheriff Hualga. What a delightful gentleman. He speaks so highly of you."

"He's a great guy. Please send my best."

"I already have."

"By the way, Maureen and I would like to ask you a favor. I hope it won't be a problem. We don't want to make anything more difficult for you. If you don't want to do it, please tell me. We won't be offended. We understand that it's your vacation. It's just that—"

"For heaven sakes, Mort, what is it?"

"Maureen was wondering if you could bring her back a jar of that sauce—what's it called, Maureen?"

I heard Maureen talking in the background.

"She's writing it down for me. Okay, here it is. Chipotle sauce? It's some kind of Southwestern sauce she needs, and Graham Feather down at the market doesn't stock it."

"I'll be happy to look for it," I said.

"Maureen has been watching Bobby Flay again—you know, the chef who has the cooking show?"

"Yes. I've heard of him."

"She's into grilling now. Doesn't want me eating anything fried. Anyhow, we've got good weather for it, so she wants to try one of his recipes."

Maureen, Mort's second wife, was an enthusiastic, if not exactly gourmet, cook, always trying out new dishes on him, some successful, some less so. She was also vigilant about watching Mort's weight and keeping him on a healthy diet, although she hadn't been able to break his love of sweets. There was always an open box of Charlene Sassi's doughnuts sitting on the counter down at the sheriff's office. Charlene's bakery had managed to survive the competition from both Dunkin' Donuts and Krispy Kreme. Her doughnuts were still Mort's favorites.

"I'll ask Meg," I said. "She'll know about it, I'm sure. How many jars does Maureen want?"

"One is fine. We don't want you to have to carry back anything heavy. Besides, we don't even know if we'll like it."

"Mort, as long as you've called, I have a question for you."

"Shoot."

"I know that betting goes on in horse racing. In jai alai, too. But is there a lot of betting involved in baseball games?"

"Not legally anywhere other than Nevada, but I'm sure it still takes place, even though the Pete Rose scandal sent it underground for a long time."

"I'd forgotten about him. Point well taken. Thanks."

"I'll give you a tip, Mrs. F."

"A betting tip? From a law enforcement officer?"

"You wouldn't turn me in, would you?"

"What's your tip?"

"The Red Sox are looking good this year. Now, why did you ask me about betting and baseball?"

"Oh, idle curiosity."

"Uh-oh. I'd better warn John Hualga to watch out. I know what happens with your idle curiosity." He laughed and I joined him.

I saw H.B. leave the hotel with a woman whose face I couldn't see, and realized I'd been gone from the dinner too long. I didn't want Meg and Jack to think there was anything wrong.

"I have to run, Mort," I said. "Thanks for the tip."

"Not so fast. Who won the big game that your friends' kid was playing in?"

"My friends' team won, and their 'kid' hit the winning home run in the ninth inning."

"Wow! Will we see him playing for the Red Sox next year?"

"I'm working on it," I said. "Good night. Best to everyone."

Chapter Four

"**W**henever I go to the supply store in town, Jess, and tell them what I need for my swimming pool, they always insist on calling it a *shpool*. That's the term they use for a small pool. This may not be Olympic size, but it's a swimming pool nonetheless. *My* swimming pool!" He chuckled and paddled away.

I laid my head back on the baseball glove–shaped raft in the backyard *shpool* of Jack and Meg's Mesa home and looked up into the starry Arizona night. When it's 110 degrees in the day and not a lot cooler at night, a pool is a pool, no matter what its size.

Meg came from the house with a pitcher of decaffeinated iced tea, which she poured into two plastic glasses for Jack and me. She makes hers the same way I make my tea in the summer. Her secret recipe: She brews the tea bags in water heated by the hot Arizona sun, leaving it out for several hours before chilling it. She handed us our glasses and descended the steps into the pool to join us. The raft had a handy cup holder, in which I placed my glass.

"Ty sure has come a long way, hasn't he?" I said.

"I think he always had a good heart," said Meg. "We just needed to help him remember that."

"It's the old nature-versus-nurture argument, Jessica," Jack said. "Sure, nature has something to do with it. But at the end of the day, I believe, it's nurturing that'll make the difference. That boy wasn't getting the nurturing he needed. He could have all the God-given talent from his genes, but it was being tossed out the window because that youngster was on a destructive path to nowhere."

"How old was he when you took him in?" I asked.

"I plucked him out of the Jersey City Detention Center when he was twelve going on thirteen," Jack said. "He'd already come before my bench several times, and I figured if we didn't get him out of that poisonous environment pronto, he'd be a lost cause. This was a kid who had so much potential, but he could never benefit from it. He was involved in a gang. He would probably have ended up dead, or wasting his life on drugs, and in and out of jail."

"Jack used to talk about him all the time, used to say that Ty reminded him of himself at that age."

"It was Meg who saved him."

"No, Jack. It was you."

"I'd come home and talk about Ty, frustrated that the system wasn't following up, wasn't taking care of him. Then, one night at dinner, Meg turned to me—

I'll never forget it—and she said, 'Jack, bring him home.' And I did."

"We had to wade through a lot of red tape, and the first couple of months were rough," said Meg, "but what I realized was that Ty didn't need discipline as much as love. Pure, unconditional love. Boy, did he respond to that. It was sad, Jessica, how much he craved it. He must have missed his mother so much."

"What happened to her?" I asked.

"No one really knows," Meg replied. "She sent him off to her brother, and then disappeared. He never talks about her, but I know he hasn't forgotten her."

"Once he began to turn around, it was an about-face," said Jack. "A quick and sudden change. Like Jiffy Pop popcorn. Pop! One minute you're a kernel, next you're a popcorn." We all laughed at the comparison. Jack was known on the bench for his colorful analogies the way Yogi Berra was known for his Berra-isms.

Meg splashed her husband gently, and he in turn threatened to overturn her raft.

"You know, Meg," he said in a sad voice, "I have an overwhelming fear that Ty needs to be rescued again. It's the same sensation. The tension at that game celebration was as thick as my waist," he said, patting his considerable girth. "If Ty doesn't get called up to the majors soon, he may never make it there. H.B. has it in for the kid because Ty's been upstaging Junior all season."

"If he doesn't like Ty, why doesn't he just trade him?" I asked.

"He doesn't want to look foolish to the league. Everyone here knows Ty's the better ballplayer, and so do the scouts and agents. Bennett knows it, too. If he trades Ty away, he'll lose face, as the Japanese say."

"You mean he'll look like he doesn't know his business?" I said.

"That's it. I really believe he'd rather thwart Ty's future success, make the kid look bad, which was why he didn't want Buddy Washington to put Ty in to pinch-hit for Junior. It's ironic, really. Makes me wonder if he cared at all whether the Rattlers won tonight's game or not. But I know one thing. He sure as hell didn't want Ty to get the winning hit."

"Is that what you were talking about with Sylvester Cole tonight, when you so rudely abandoned my drink at the bar and left the ballroom?" asked Meg.

Jack smiled. "My apologies to both you ladies for my abrupt but temporary absence. And the answer to your question is yes, Miss Manners. That's what Cole and I were discussing. Cole says he's meeting with someone in Phoenix and Los Angeles about Ty. He said he'd call tomorrow. I hope something works out to get Ty away from Mesa and the Rattlers. Bennett will stifle his opportunities and spirit here. I want him gone to another team."

I certainly understood Jack's feelings. Without the support of the team owner, it would be difficult for even a gifted athlete like Ty to continue to develop his skills and to mature into a responsible adult. Harrison Bennett was so unlike Jack Duffy. Bennett championed his son's future through intimidation and jealousy. Jack, on the other hand, was a positive force in his foster son's life, encouraging him without criticism and setting a sterling example that the young man seemed eager to emulate.

I remembered what Sylvester Cole had said to me—that Ty wanted to be a writer if he didn't make it as a major-league baseball player. So many talented young men never do. If Ty gave a thought to a future career without baseball, he was wise beyond his years.

I looked up at the twinkling stars, squeezed my eyes shut, and wished that Ty would be signed by another team and forge the sort of success in baseball that he was capable of, without the unwanted negativity of men like Harrison Bennett.

"Does anyone know what time it is?" I heard Meg ask.

Sitting up on my raft, I checked my waterproof watch. "It's after midnight, way past my bedtime."

"The coolest part of the day in Arizona," Jack said.

"Past my bedtime, too," Meg announced. "Come on, Jessica. I'll get you settled in your room. The AC works fine, thank goodness."

I said good night to Jack and followed Meg inside the house, where the blast of refrigerated air hit me like a giant fan.

"It feels cold now," Meg said, opening the door to my room, "but you'll appreciate it once you get acclimated. There are extra covers in the closet if you need them. And you can always open the sliders and let in some warm air. Jack loves it out here, but I have to admit, I'm not crazy about the weather. I'd like to be back in New Jersey before the leaves fall. I don't want to miss the changing seasons."

"I like them, too," I said. "Autumn is my favorite. Of course, I change my mind every spring."

It was a two-story house and my bedroom was at the back, with sliding doors leading to a small balcony. I went through my nightly ablutions, slipped into a lightweight nightgown and a powder-blue cotton bathrobe that I always travel with, and sat outside the sliding doors for what seemed a very long time, looking out into the darkness and reflecting on what had transpired that evening. I thought of the epithet Junior Bennett had uttered as he passed my chair, and of the cell phone conversation I'd overheard outside the hotel. The man had said that "Ramos" would pay the money. The only Ramos I knew was Ty Ramos. What money? To whom?

None of my business, I told myself as I closed the drapes over the doors, dropped the robe on a chair, and climbed between the delightfully cool, fresh sheets.

In my dream, I was being chased by a dozen giant scorpions wearing cowboy boots, the spurs jingling. Away from home and in a strange bed, I was groggy trying to fend off the scorpions. I reached for a button to shut off the ringing alarm, but the clock didn't have one. I had awakened confused, until it came to me that it was the sound of a telephone that had stirred me from my sleep. After three sequences, the ringing stopped and I realized where I was.

"We'll be right there," Jack said outside my door. Meg and Jack spoke in hushed tones. I glanced at the clock: 4:06 A.M. I put on my robe and slippers and walked cautiously into the hall, where Meg met me.

"Jessica, I'm so sorry we disturbed your sleep."

"Don't even think about it," I said. "What's wrong?"

"It's Ty. He's—he's been arrested."

"Arrested? For what?"

"We don't know. Jack's getting dressed. He's going to the jail. I'm going with him."

"I'd like to go, too, if you think it's all right."

"Of course it's all right, but only if you want to. I don't want to put you out."

"I'll get dressed right away," I said. "I'll only be a minute."

We spent most of the thirty-minute car ride to the jail not speaking. It was one of those times in life when you have so many questions but are afraid that to ask them would be inappropriate, considering the shock my friends were suffering. Jack's face was set in stone, eyes focused on the road, his square jaw in motion as he chewed on his cheek.

Meg and I stared out our respective windows and watched as Mesa began to stir. It was already in the eighties, and the horizon grew lighter as the desert sun promised to peek through within the hour. We passed several strip malls, a school, and a succession of neighborhoods.

"Jack phoned a lawyer friend of his in town and asked him to meet us at the jail," Meg finally said.

"That's good," I said, "although hopefully it's all been a mistake and an attorney won't be needed." While my words were positive and meant to comfort, my inner feelings didn't match them. Somehow, this was no mistake. I could feel it in my bones, and in a stomach that had been churning ever since Meg told me that Ty had been arrested.

"I pray that you're right," Meg said.

"What's the drinking age in Arizona?" I asked.

"Twenty-one," Jack growled, never taking his eyes off the road.

"Is it possible that in the midst of the celebration, Ty might have had a beer or two and has been taken in for driving while under the influence and for being underage?" I asked.

Meg sat straighter and brightened. "I'll bet that's it," she said. "Boys that age do so many silly things."

"I wouldn't call that silly," Jack said, taking a corner too fast and pressing me against the door.

"You know what I mean," Meg said. "Maybe 'foolish' is a better word." She turned to me. "We bought Ty a used Jeep Wrangler, one of those small ones with a canvas top. First-year ballplayers make so little money. Jack said he'd heard that Ty drove too fast when his teammates were with him. I hope he hasn't been in an accident."

"I spoke with Buddy Washington about it," Jack said as we turned into the police headquarters parking lot. "I suggested he have a talk with the players about responsibilities *off* the field as well as on. He said he intended to do that, but— Damn it!"

"What's wrong?" Meg asked.

"Look," Jack said. "The press is already here."

A television news van was parked outside the station, its floodlight lighting up the lot like a Hollywood set. I recognized the reporter, Karen Locke, from the locker room at last night's game. She was leaning against the van, her arms crossed. Another female reporter, a pretty black woman, stood next to Locke, primping in one of the van's side mirrors. Jack got out of the car first. When Locke recognized who it was, she alerted the cameraman and they rushed toward us. Ms. Locke shoved a microphone into Jack's face and asked, "Judge Duffy, how do you feel about your foster son's arrest for murder?"

Chapter Five

As the early morning grew warmer, thanks to a bulbous sun that began to appear above the horizon, the media frenzy outside the jail began to swell. A shaken Jack had brushed off questions from Locke and other reporters and led us inside, where an officer at the desk told us to wait. Sheriff Hualga was unavailable and would get in touch with us later.

After what seemed an eternity, the three of us were escorted down a narrow hallway to a small, inadequately air-conditioned room in which Ty sat with Jack's lawyer friend, David Pierce. In his mid-forties, with broad shoulders and a thick neck, Pierce looked more like a football player than any lawyer I knew. He had a healthy head of wavy black hair and a closely clipped goatee. Even though it was so early in the morning, he was dressed in a beautifully tailored navy blue suit, a crisp white shirt, and a red regimental tie. When he stood to greet us, it was apparent that he was a man who'd once been an athlete and who probably devoted a good part of each day to staying fit.

By contrast, Ty looked exhausted, his eyes half closed, his body language testifying to his fatigue. An orange jailhouse shirt hung loosely from his lanky frame, and his shoes were missing. He still wore his own jeans and socks, now dusty and soiled from his ordeal. As we made eye contact, I smiled, silently reminding myself that he, like every other person charged with a crime in America, was innocent until proven guilty. His eyes flitted back and forth between Meg and me, but their expression was vacant. Up until that point, he hadn't looked at the judge, his foster father.

Pierce and Ty sat on one side of the wooden table, the three of us on the other, with Meg in the middle, between Jack and me. The police officer who had escorted us stood near the door with a second officer who had been in the room with Ty and Pierce when we arrived.

"Ty, you look awful. Are you hurt? What happened?" Meg pleaded. "Tell us."

Tears tumbled down Ty's face and he buried his head in his hands. Jack took Meg's hand and asked Ty's lawyer, "What's the charge, David? A reporter outside said it was murder."

Pierce placed his elbows on the worn table and winced. He didn't have to say a thing. His face confirmed the bad news. "That's right, Jack. He's being charged with second-degree murder."

Meg gasped, "Oh, my God." She began to cry and I put my arm around her.

"Who?" Jack bit out.

"Junior Bennett."

Jack muttered a curse.

"Junior was found bludgeoned to death," Pierce continued. "They haven't told me if they found the weapon yet."

"I don't believe it. You didn't kill Junior, did you, son?"

Ty swallowed hard, his Adam's apple bobbing up and down. "No, sir," he said in a hoarse voice. He turned to Meg. "I swear I didn't do it." He pounded his fist on the table. "Someone has to believe me. I didn't do it. I know I didn't."

Meg reached across the table and placed her hand over his fist.

"Take it easy, son," Jack said. "I want you to take a deep breath and tell us exactly what happened, everything that you remember."

"That's the problem," Pierce put in.

"What's the problem?"

"He doesn't remember—at least he doesn't remember everything."

"What's that supposed to mean?" Jack said, his voice rising, his face getting red. He was holding in his temper, but the effort was taking its toll.

"Why don't you tell us what you *do* remember," I said, drawing Ty's attention away from his foster father.

Ty closed his eyes, and then slowly opened them, looking at me. "I went to the Crazy Coyote with a bunch of guys after we left the hotel dinner—

Nassani, Murph, Wilson, and Bobley. I drove my Jeep. Carter was driving some of the other guys and we were going to meet up there."

"Okay, stop," said Jack. "Where is this place?"

"It's out of town on the road to Apache Junction."

"What time did you leave the hotel?"

"I don't know, sir. Maybe a couple minutes after you did. Sylvester wanted to talk to me before I left, but it wasn't long. He was meeting someone for a drink in the bar."

"Go on," Jack said.

Ty shrugged. "That's it. We left the hotel, changed our clothes in the parking lot, and drove to the Coyote."

Jack interrupted. "You changed clothes in the parking lot?"

"We didn't want to wear suits to the Coyote. We get hassled enough as it is in there. So I'd thrown a pair of jeans and a T-shirt into the trunk so I could change, and the other guys did, too."

"Why aren't you wearing your T-shirt now?" I asked before Jack could interrogate him about the decision to use the parking lot as a changing room.

"The police made me take it off."

"Apparently there was blood on his shirt," Pierce said. "They took it for evidence."

"Your shoes, too?" I asked Ty.

He looked down at his feet under the table, as if he hadn't realized his shoes were gone. He nodded. "I guess."

"What kind of shoes did you have on?"

"Nikes. Sneakers."

"How long did it take to get there?" asked Jack.

Ty looked confused. "Where?"

"To the Coyote."

Pierce interrupted, "Listen, folks, I think we should let Ty tell the story his way first, details later."

Jack put his hands up in defeat and mumbled, "Okay. Proceed."

"Where was I?" Ty said, picking up a pencil from the table and tapping it on his thigh. "Oh, yeah, so we went to the Coyote. We had some beer. Look, I know what you always told me, I know I'm not supposed to be drinking, but we were celebrating and I thought it couldn't hurt."

Jack cut him off. "What happened next?"

"Nothing. We just had a couple of beers."

"That's all that was on the table, beer?"

"There might have been a couple of Jell-O shots, too."

"What's a Jell-O shot?" Meg asked.

"Who knows?" Jack growled, "But they can't be good."

"They're shot glasses of Jell-O made with vodka or other liquor in place of water," I said. "Isn't that right, Ty?"

He nodded, his gaze on the pencil he now twirled in his fingers.

"You're not old enough to drink in Arizona," I said. "Who bought the drinks for you?"

Ty's eyes met mine and then he looked down again. "Carter went to the bar first. There was a Diamondbacks game on, so I don't think the bartender was paying much attention."

"He'll pay a lot more attention when I have him hauled into court," Jack said. "Who else was there besides Carter?"

"Just the guys on the team and some people."

"Some people?" asked his lawyer.

"Some girls and stuff."

"Did you know these girls?" Pierce asked.

"Sure. They're nice girls; they work up at the Biltmore spa."

"Can we get to the point, please?" Jack said. "I want to know what happened."

Ty heaved a sigh. "We were just sitting around, hanging out. Next thing I know, Junior comes in with some guy I don't know. He's not a player. That reporter was with them."

"Which reporter?" I asked. "One of the ones from the locker room?"

"Right. You know—Karen. Miss Locke."

"She was with Junior and this friend of his?" Jack asked.

"Yeah, only she spent most of the time in the bathroom. I heard Junior say she didn't feel good."

"She probably drank too much," Meg said.

"Yeah. Maybe."

"The answer isn't 'yeah,' Ty, it's 'yes,' " Jack said sternly.

"Sorry, sir."

"And speak up, Ty, don't mumble."

"Jeez, Jack," interrupted Pierce. "Cut him some

slack. He's not in a courtroom yet. Let him speak. He's tired. This is not an interrogation. Not yet, anyway."

Jack got up from his chair and leaned against the wall. "You're right," he said. "Sorry."

"Go ahead, Ty," Pierce said.

"Well, Junior starts giving it to me. You know, telling me that I suck and stuff like that. Then he said how my mother was a Latina—only he said it real snide—and how she didn't want me and . . ." His voice trailed off and he squeezed his eyes shut.

Everyone gave him his moment of silence. Without further prompting, he continued, but there was a quaver in his voice. "Then—then I began to feel kind of sick, like the room was moving a little. But I was mad, really mad that he'd said those things to me about my mom. I know she loves me—" He started to sob. "I know she loves me."

Meg went to where he sat, put her hands on his shoulders, and rested her cheek on the top of his head. "Your mother loved you very much, Ty," she said. "She did the best she could, and she wanted you to have a better life here." Her voice trailed off, and I knew what she was thinking, that the life he was living at the moment—one of sitting in a jail, accused of having murdered someone the night before—was not the life his mother in the Dominican Republic had envisioned for him.

I felt terrible for Meg. She'd done the best she could do for Ty. She and Jack had given him the love and direction he'd needed. Despite their admirable efforts, it appeared something out of their control had gone terribly wrong. I ached for them.

"What happened next?" Pierce said.

Meg gave Ty's shoulders a squeeze and returned to her chair. Ty pressed the heels of his palms into his eyes to wipe away the tears. He shuddered, pinched the end of his nose, and sniffed sharply. "Okay. What was next? I swear I wasn't dead-drunk or anything, but I remember feeling woozy and I was having a little trouble standing. The guys were egging me on, telling me to shut Junior up, to give him a lesson he wouldn't forget. Even Junior's guys, the ones on the team who always side with him, were telling me to take him out. They were so disgusted with him. I went outside and Junior was already there. He started in on me again, talking in a fake Spanish accent."

Ty's anger was palpable as he recounted the insults he'd suffered from Junior Bennett. Meg mouthed "Calm down" to him from across the table.

"He said I should go back where I came from. I told him to shove it, that the whole American and National Leagues were full of Dominicans and Mexicans and Venezuelans, and if we all went home, there wouldn't be anyone left in baseball for him to play with. That's not exactly so, but I wanted to make my point. Then he started in on my mother again. He called her a *puta*, a whore, and that's when I punched him in the nose." His voice dropped. "I might have broken it. He started to bleed, I know that." Ty shook his head, as if to rid his brain of the image. He looked down at the knuckles of his right hand. They were swollen and cut. He sighed and blew out a long puff of air. "That's all I can remember."

"The police told me they discovered Ty asleep in Carter's car," Pierce said. "They gave Ty a Breathalyzer test and, according to the police, he failed. Junior's body was found in the parking lot, a couple of hundred feet from Carter's car. Carter was nowhere to be found."

"What happened to *my* car?" Ty asked.

"All three cars were impounded," Piece replied. "Yours, Carter's, and Junior's."

"When will I get it back?"

"There's no telling."

"You'll get it back when the police release it," Jack said. "It's not important right now." Despite his tanned complexion, all the color had faded from Jack's face, his pallor a sign of his drained emotions. He looked over to Pierce. "Maybe this whole thing was an accident. Can we plead down to involuntary manslaughter?"

"It's a little early to talk about pleas, Jack. Let's start by trying to get him out on bail. That's a problem with homicide cases."

"Jack, you have to make them let him out," Meg said. "I want to take him home. He needs to be home."

Ty was mumbling to himself, "I don't remember seeing Carter outside. I don't know how I got into his car."

"You were drunk," Jack said, his disgust clear. "The drinking age in this state is twenty-one. There's a reason for that. How did Carter get the beer?"

"Everybody goes to the Coyote because they know they don't card kids. Carter wasn't the only one. I got some of the beer myself. I ordered it from the bartender and paid her."

"So now it comes out."

"But I got it for the guys. I swear I didn't have that much to drink."

Jack uncrossed his arms and approached his foster son, then squatted by his side. He put his arm around Ty's shoulder. "You may think so, but how do you explain not remembering what happened after you punched Junior? How do you explain being found in Carter's car, asleep, with blood on your clothing, and a Breathalyzer test that indicates you were legally intoxicated? If you can't remember, how do you know you didn't kill Junior? How do you know you didn't pick up something in anger and hit him?"

"Jack!" Meg was begging him to stop.

Ty looked up at Jack and didn't answer, his large, dark eyes seeking understanding. Finally, he dropped his head, slowly shaking it, and said in a barely audible voice, "I was really pissed, but even so I would never do that. I would never kill anyone, no matter how much they made me mad, no matter how drunk I was. I wouldn't. I swear to you." He lifted his head. "But it's true I don't remember what happened, sir. I only wish I did."

Jack stood and turned to Pierce. "Was anyone else around when they discovered Junior and Ty?" he asked the attorney.

Pierce answered, "There were a lot of people in the bar, but no one admits to being out in the parking lot. The sheriff said they got a call from that reporter, Karen Locke from WXYK."

"Why was Karen Locke hanging out at the Crazy Coyote?" Jack asked.

"Maybe there was a television camera crew with her outside the bar," Meg said, hope in her voice. "Maybe they have on tape what really happened to Junior." She looked around the room at each of us, and the hope faded. "I know, that's not very likely," she said.

"It's unlikely the press would have filmed the murder," I said, "but the bar might have had surveillance cameras in the parking lot. That's not out of the realm of possibility." I turned to the lawyer. "Do you know if they did?"

Pierce shook his head. "They have cameras, inside and out. Unfortunately, they don't bother to keep them maintained. Neither one was working last night."

"What about the pizza place next door?" said Ty. "Maybe they had one."

"There's a pizza place next door?" asked Jack.

"Yes, sir," Ty replied. "I had a slice before we went to the Coyote."

"But you had just come from a big dinner," Meg said.

"I didn't eat that much at the hotel dinner. I was too nervous. I felt like everybody was watching me. Especially Mr. Bennett." He paused and hung his head. "Maybe Junior was right. I should have stayed in the Dominican Republic. Or even Jersey City. This never would have happened."

Meg began crying again, and Ty immediately grabbed her arm across the table. "No, please—I didn't mean that I don't want to live with you. But here—here there's so much hate and jealousy. They want me to fail. And now they got their wish." He released his grip on her and sat back. Shoulders hunched, elbows on his thighs, he stared down at the floor. "But I swear to you that I didn't do what they say I did. I could never do that. I just couldn't."

An officer opened the door, and Pierce tapped Ty on the shoulder. The lawyer signaled to Jack. "Why don't you go home, rest, get something to eat. I'll meet you at the arraignment this afternoon."

As Ty shuffled out the door, he glanced back at Meg. She started to reach for him, then withdrew her hand. "It's okay, Ty," she said. "It will work out. The truth always prevails. Have faith. We're here for you and always will be. We love you and believe in you. Remember that. We believe you."

And so did I.

Chapter Six

The moment Jack's BMW turned the corner onto Hedgehog Court, where they lived, the media circus began. Television satellite trucks choked the street, making it impossible for Jack to navigate his way to the house. He threw the car in reverse, made a U-turn, and we sped off—to where, I wasn't sure. I don't think he knew either.

"My God, Jack," Meg said, "what are we going to do? They're all hungry for a piece of Ty. Where can we hide? They're not going to leave us alone."

"I'd like to drive all the way back to Jersey, but we can't leave Ty here to face it alone. We have to stay until this nightmare is over." He peered into his rearview mirror. "Bloodsuckers," he said.

"Will they allow Ty to be released on bail?" I asked, afraid I already knew the answer. It was a rare judge who would grant bail to an accused murderer, although it wasn't out of the question, particularly considering Ty's age and the fact that he lived with a respected member of the bar, who also happened to be a judge.

"We'll see this afternoon," Jack said. "I know the judge who's scheduled to preside over Ty's hearing, knew him back in New York before he pulled up stakes and headed west. These Southwestern states are crawling with former judges and lawyers from back East. They come out here, ostensibly to retire, and end up sitting on the bench again. If the judge does grant bail, they'll yank Ty's passport and stipulate that he not leave Mesa for any reason. Looks like we'll be here a lot longer than we'd planned."

The Duffys had intended that once baseball season was over, Jack would spend weekdays in Jersey City and commute back to Mesa by air for a few weeks before they packed up and drove cross-country to their home in New Jersey. The Arizona house rental was up in a few weeks. Now it looked as if they'd have to extend it if they could. Fortunately, Jack was semi-retired and able to choose which cases he presided over.

Jack suddenly accelerated.

"Jack, slow down," Meg said.

"Look behind us," Jack said, his eyes darting from the road ahead to his rearview mirror. "Those damn reporters are on our tail."

Meg and I turned to see what appeared to be a caravan of media.

"Why are we running?" Meg asked. "Actually, I'd like to speak to the press to tell them that Ty is innocent. The boy needs a voice, someone to champion him. This story is probably all over the news, and not only locally." She spoke as though reading from an article: "Young baseball star, on the brink of being called up to the major leagues, sits in an Arizona jail accused of murdering a competitor—who also happens to be the son of the team's owner." She smashed her fist on the dashboard. *"Stay tuned!"*

Jack took a sharp right, onto a narrow two-lane road.

"Where are we going?" I asked.

"Back to the jail," Jack announced. "There's a restaurant next door where we can get something to eat, and there's always plenty of cops around to help fend off the press. You must be famished, Jessica."

"Don't worry about me," I said.

"We sure haven't been," Jack said. "Some host and hostess we've turned out to be."

"My only concern is not to be in the way."

"You're not. I'm so grateful you're here," Meg said. "I need all the moral support I can get."

"I can't think of anyone I'd rather have with us at this time, Jessica," Jack said. "I hope you'll stay and give us the benefit of your experience."

"You know I'll help however I can, Jack. You don't need to ask."

We pulled up in front of the restaurant and Jack let out a short laugh, more of a snort. "House Arrest," he said, pointing to the sign that hung over the restaurant's front door.

"Clever name for a restaurant located next door to a jail," I said.

"The owner's a former New York City cop."

"Obviously one with a sense of humor," I said.

Jack opened the car door for me. "Maybe you can use it in your next book."

"I just hope it's not nonfiction," Meg said quietly. "I've had enough reality today to last me a lifetime."

Jack took his wife's hand as she exited the car. She had aged years since the phone call early that morning. The color in her face was gone. Even her lips were colorless, and dark circles shadowed her blue eyes.

"Judge Duffy," a woman called. It was the TV reporter, Karen Locke. Despite being up most of the night herself, she appeared, as news reporters always seem to, perfectly coiffed and ready to go.

"How's Ty doing?" she asked. The question was innocent enough, except that a microphone was simultaneously shoved in front of Jack's face.

"No comment," Jack said firmly. He grabbed Meg's arm as well as mine and hurried us toward the restaurant's entrance.

"End of his baseball dream, wouldn't you say?" Locke asked loudly, with what could be characterized as a smirk on her face.

Jack stopped in his tracks and spun around. I could feel him shaking with anger. He started to respond but stopped in midsentence and said to us, "Let's go inside before there's a second member of this family charged with murder."

The restaurant's owner greeted Jack warmly and had seated us at a booth in the back where we could have some privacy when my cell phone rang. I peered at the tiny screen. Caller ID told me it was Mort Metzger on the other end.

"If you don't mind," I said to Jack and Meg, "I'd like to take this call." I pressed the TALK button.

"Mrs. F, I just heard on the news about your friends' kid being accused of killing another ballplayer. How are they taking it?"

"Please hold on a moment, Mort." I excused myself and slipped out of the booth to go outside. Not only did I not want to disturb anyone by talking on my cell phone—I find it exceptionally rude when people speak on a cell phone in a restaurant or other public place—but I didn't want Meg or Jack to know that the news of their son's murder charge had already traveled all the way to Cabot Cove, Maine.

As I opened the restaurant door to go outside, I saw Karen Locke heading straight for it. I quickly retreated and went into a small, dark hallway that led to the restrooms to continue my conversation. Ms. Locke entered the restaurant and was hurrying in my direction. I faced the wall outside the ladies' room, hoping she wouldn't recognize me. She forcefully swung the ladies' room door open, bumping into me as she did, but she looked to be in too much of a hurry to apologize. Not that I would have expected it from her. Karen Locke didn't strike me as being the most polite of women.

Mort must have heard the commotion on the other end because he asked, "You okay, Jess?"

"Yes, I'm fine, Mort," I whispered. "It's tough for

me to talk right now. I'm in a restaurant and the place is buzzing with media and Lord knows who else."

I was afraid to continue, fearing that Ms. Locke could hear my conversation through the wall. "I'll have to call you back," I said.

"Sure, no problem. Call me whenever you can."

"Thanks for understanding, Mort. I'll speak to you later. And by the way, I don't think Ty Ramos murdered anyone. Good-bye."

Knowing Ms. Locke was in the ladies' room, I debated going in. But she'd been at the Coyote last night. What did she know about what took place there? I braced myself and pushed through the door, expecting to see her in front of a sink, perhaps preening for her next on-air moment. But the bathroom was eerily quiet, and for a moment I wondered whether she had magically slipped past me, or disappeared through the exhaust vent like an apparition. But my escape-artist suspicions were lifted when I heard the sound of someone being sick.

I remembered what Ty had told us about the Crazy Coyote, that Locke had been sick last night, too. *That's quite a hangover,* I thought. Or perhaps she had the flu. In good conscience, I couldn't leave her alone. I scanned the openings beneath the stall doors. There she was—her red slingback shoes gave her away.

"Are you all right?" I called. "Do you need any help?"

"No, thank you," she replied. "I'll be okay."

She flushed the toilet and emerged, pale and perspiring.

"Too much partying?" I said, hoping to raise the topic of the Coyote.

"I don't drink," she said as she washed her hands and checked her face in the mirror. "Had some bad clams last night. That's the last time I eat in that restaurant." She took a piece of chewing gum from her pocket and gave me a wan smile.

"Ms. Locke, I'd like to talk to you if I may."

"No time. Sorry. I'm on a hot story." She brushed past me and left the ladies' room.

And you're part of that story, I thought. *But what part?*

Chapter Seven

"**M**r. Ramos, do you understand the charges against you?"

"Yes, sir," Ty replied. He spoke softly and tentatively, like a little boy caught by the school principal.

"How do you plead, Mr. Ramos?"

"Not guilty, sir."

"It's my understanding that you reside with an officer of the court, Judge Jack Duffy."

"Yes, sir, I do."

"I've taken that into consideration regarding whether to grant you bail. The district attorney, as you've heard, has asked that no bail be granted. Under ordinary circumstances, I would support the prosecution in the matter of bail. But considering your young age, and the fact that you've not been in trouble with the law since moving here to continue your baseball career, I'm going to have you post bail at two hundred and fifty thousand dollars. You'll surrender your passport to the court clerk and must understand that you are not to leave Mesa until this matter has been fully adjudicated. I'm also ordering that you be under house arrest and wear an ankle bracelet to monitor your location for the duration." The judge, an elderly gentleman with wispy rust-colored hair and a ruddy complexion, smiled at Ty. "Congratulations on winning your game with that home run. I was rooting for you to do it." Realizing he might have gone too far, he cast an embarrassed glance at the prosecutor and announced in his best stentorian voice, "Court adjourned." The gavel came down hard on the bench and he strode from the courtroom, black robe trailing behind him.

Naturally, I was extremely pleased with the judge's decision, as I knew Jack and Meg were. But I also realized that, as restricted as it might be, Ty's getting his freedom because of connections Jack might have had would become added fodder for the media. *A great sidebar story.*

Meg and I waited in the hall while Jack arranged for Ty's bail, putting up his house back in New Jersey as collateral. A policewoman, who looked to be over six feet tall, waited with us for security purposes. I smiled and thanked her for holding the door for us. She did not return the smile nor acknowledge me in any way. An imposing lady, not one you'd want to come up against.

Given the original media interest in the story, I feared reporters would hound everyone involved, day and night. We'd be beset by TV stations and other media competing for viewership and readership, which translated into ratings, which further translated into higher advertising revenues. The story of Junior Bennett's murder, and the accusation that Ty had committed the crime, was "hot," as Karen Locke had said. How frightening it must be for celebrities to be relentlessly pursued by paparazzi. I thought about what Ty had said, that people wanted to see him fail. How sad that he thought that, and even sadder that it might be true. He was a young man who'd had the world by the tail—with brains and talent and good fortune. From the depths, he'd been singled out of the crowd and given a chance to succeed. That he had succeeded inspired admiration, but it also engendered jealousy. A tough lesson for any young man. For superior athletes, it starts early.

Jack, Ty, and Ty's lawyer came down the hall, escorted by two policemen.

I didn't know who appeared to be more exhausted, the father or the son. In contrast, David Pierce was as immaculate as when we'd first seen him, not a wrinkle in his suit or shirt. Ty and Jack had five-o'clock shadows, and Ty's eyes were practically swollen shut, a combination of that fatigue and the effects of weeping.

When Ty reached us, Meg gave him a kiss on the cheek. He tried to smile at her, but it came out more like a grimace. He seemed too tired to try again.

"Sheriff Hualga said we can leave by a back door," said Jack, familiar with the need for behind-the-scenes routes in courthouses. "David was able to arrange with him for a police guard at home to keep the press away from the front door."

"Please thank the sheriff for me when you see him again," Meg said to Pierce.

"I'll do that," he said, ushering us down a hall to a metal door with a push bar. "My car is parked a few rows down. Wait here and I'll drive up to the door. I'll honk once when I get there."

"What about our car?" Meg asked after Pierce had left.

"I'll come back for it tonight or tomorrow," Jack replied.

It was one of those infrequent times when I wished I had a driver's license. I could have driven Jack's car home for him and perhaps served as a decoy for the pursuing press. Ironically, I do have a private pilot's license, and had hoped to get in some flying hours while in Arizona, where the weather is perfect for it. But I doubted I'd find the time to rent and fly a plane, or to do much of anything personal.

I sat next to Ty in the backseat of the car. Thankfully, the press hadn't caught on that we had left the courthouse, and there were no suspicious-looking vehicles following us. Ty sat stiffly in his seat and stared out the window. The air outside was oppressive. You could see the heat in the shine on people's faces, feel it reflected from the stucco walls of the squat buildings we passed. You could sense the landscape baking under the hot desert sun. It drew out our energy and replaced it with lassitude. We were too weary to talk, too hot to sleep.

David Pierce was smart enough not to play the radio, sparing us from news reports of Junior's murder and Ty's arrest, lest they further sour what was already a bleak atmosphere. Meg, who sat up front with the lawyer, leaned back against the headrest and closed her eyes. I'm sure Jack would have liked to do the same, but he sat stoically next to me in the backseat, his expression a mirror image of his foster son's.

The silence was uncomfortable. I wondered briefly if I should leave, move into a hotel. What would they prefer? This was a family matter. A legal matter. Not the place for a visiting friend with a reputation for snooping and sleuthing. But as much as I wanted to stay out of this family's sudden troubles, I knew that Meg and Jack needed me. And I would do what they asked of me.

"I'm going take a shower and try to get some sleep," Ty said as the car rounded the corner to Hedgehog Court—and once again faced a clog of media vehicles. "I can't believe this," he said. "This is a nightmare."

Several television station vans were in front of the house, along with two police cars, their red lights flashing. An officer backed a patrol car away from the entrance to the driveway and waved us in.

Pierce pulled up to the garage, and we hurried out of the car and into the house. I watched him back out of the driveway with almost reckless abandon and wondered whether he would have taken pleasure in running over the few reporters who jumped out of his way. He didn't hit anyone, though, and I breathed a sigh of relief.

Ty went straight upstairs. Meg, Jack, and I headed for the kitchen, which was flooded with sunshine, a welcoming contrast to the bleak emotional day it had turned out to be.

Jack walked around closing the blinds to shield us from cameras with telephoto lenses. "I wouldn't be surprised if they bribed my neighbors into letting them shoot pictures from their bedroom windows," he said. He went to the bottom of the stairs and called up to Ty to close the drapes.

"Here, Jess, have a seat on the window bench," Meg said. "I'll put on a pot of coffee. Or would you prefer tea?"

"Whatever you're having is fine with me."

Jack excused himself, saying, "I want to talk with Ty some more."

"Maybe it's best to leave him alone," Meg suggested.

"No," Jack said, "I think it's a good time to follow up with him, while what happened is still fresh in his mind. I won't be long."

"How are you holding up, Meg?" I asked when he was gone.

"I'm worried sick, Jessica. I don't know what to do. Jack has experience with the legal aspects of this. He knows what we're up against. I believe Ty. I really do. But unless there are witnesses to come forward and back up his story, I don't see how he stands much of a chance of being exonerated."

"Have you had any messages from Buddy Washington?" I asked. "Or from anyone else affiliated with the team?"

"Not that I know of," said Meg. She walked to a small table in the kitchen on which there was a telephone and an answering machine. "Full," she said, shaking her head. "The answering machine is filled with messages. I'd better wait until Jack comes down to listen to them."

The phone rang. Meg looked at the caller ID. "It's Sylvester Cole," she said nervously. "I'm not up to speaking with anyone."

"Want me to talk to him?" I asked.

She nodded and handed me the phone.

Sylvester's hello was friendly, almost too cheery considering the situation. Surely he knew what had happened. "I have to speak with Jack right away," he said after acknowledging me. I told Meg, and she went upstairs to get him.

"Sylvester, while you're waiting, let me ask you. What have you heard? What has been reported?"

He answered with confidence. "I just saw Karen Locke's live report on WXYK. From the preliminary results of an autopsy, it appears now that Junior Bennett was bludgeoned to death and died from a brain hemorrhage."

"Anything else? We haven't had time to watch the news, for obvious reasons."

"Ty's arrest for Junior's murder is all over the tube, but there's also an unsubstantiated report that the police are now interested in speaking with someone else who was seen hanging around the hotel during the time the team dinner was taking place, and who evidently showed up later at the same bar where the murder occurred."

I immediately thought of the man I'd overheard speaking on his cell phone outside the hotel's entrance, the one who said that Ramos would pay someone money. But there were so many people at the hotel, between its guests and those who attended the team dinner, that it was silly of me to speculate about one man.

"Has Harrison Bennett or anyone else associated with the team been quoted on the news?" I asked. "Have you spoken to any of the players?"

"Spoke to Matt Muscarel, one of the guys on the team whose father is a pain in the butt, always insisting that I sign him. Matt's a good kid, but he isn't going anywhere. I ran into him this morning at Scorpions. Only news he had—and it's just scuttlebutt from him—was that the TV reporter, Karen Locke, and Junior Bennett had a big fight last night and broke up."

"Broke up?"

"Yeah. According to Muscarel, they had just started dating. It was a big secret because Junior didn't want his dad to know because—well, the old man isn't fond of reporters. Besides, the players were discouraged by Buddy Washington from having girl-friends during the season." He laughed. "Seems old-fashioned in this day and age, but Buddy is an old-fashioned kind of guy. He sees girlfriends as a threat to a player's commitment to the team." Another laugh. "Buddy means well, loves his players like they were his own kids, but preaching celibacy is a bit much."

"And Scorpions?" I asked, remembering my nightmare. "What is that?"

"A local breakfast and lunch place. Kinda like a New York diner, I guess, except no egg creams."

"Was his father with him?" I asked. "Was Muscarel with anyone?"

"Didn't see his dad. And believe me, if he was there I would have known it. That guy is always in my face. No, Muscarel was there alone."

Jack and Meg came downstairs. I handed the phone to Jack, who opened the sliding glass doors off the kitchen that led to the enclosed patio and pool—his *shpool*.

"Ty's in the shower," Meg said. "He and Jack had a talk. Jack told me that he's one hundred percent convinced that Ty had absolutely nothing to do with this. He said he could see it in Ty's eyes more than anything."

Meg seemed relieved, calmer than I'd seen her all day, obviously relieved to have Ty home again. It must have been dreadful for her to think of him sitting in a jail cell.

As we sat and sipped our coffee, I watched Jack through the sliding glass doors, pacing back and forth while speaking on the phone. He'd changed into a pair of khaki shorts and a green-and-blue-striped polo shirt. Eventually he came into the kitchen and put the phone back onto its base. "I spoke to Buddy Washington," he said. "He says they're planning a memorial for Junior at the stadium."

"Washington?" said Meg. "I thought you were on the phone with Sylvester."

"I was. He was at Washington's house. Buddy got on the phone."

"I thought Sylvester was going to L.A.," I said.

"Must have changed his mind," said Jack.

Meg excused herself and went upstairs, returning a few minutes later to say that Ty was already asleep.

The three of us went into the den, where I sank into a buttery-soft, ivory leather couch. Jack sat in what he called his "Archie Bunker chair," worn around the edges but his favorite nonetheless. Meg curled her legs beneath her on the matching ivory leather love seat. The plasma-screen television set was too much of a temptation. Jack took the remote and hit the buttons until he got to Channel 5, WXYK. A commercial for the Arizona Diamondbacks played. It was interrupted by a blue screen that read, BREAKING NEWS. And there stood Karen Locke, in front of Jack and Meg's house, right outside the front door.

"This is Karen Locke reporting from the rented home of Judge Jack and Meg Duffy, foster parents of Ty Ramos, who has been accused in the murder of teammate Junior Bennett. We've learned that Ramos was released on two hundred and fifty thousand dollars' bail by a local judge with reputed ties to Ramos's foster father, himself a judge in Jersey City, New Jersey. The animosity between these two players, Ramos and Bennett, was well known. Both were shortstops. Some fans I've spoken to say that Junior was the more talented of the two but that Ramos was poised to make a jump to the major leagues ahead of Bennett."

The picture switched to a fan in a Rattlers cap giving his opinions. With the camera back on her, Locke turned and indicated the house. "Ramos and the Duffys are holed up inside, obviously avoiding the press. Meantime, Junior Bennett's family are planning their son's funeral. Friends say his father, Harrison Bennett, Sr., who owns the Mesa Rattlers, is devastated. When I spoke with him earlier today, he told me that Ramos is a troubled young man with a criminal past, and that his past has caught up with him. Our hearts and prayers go out to the Bennett family. That's it from here. I'm Karen Locke with WXYK."

"The more talented of the two?" Jack said. "She's got to be kidding." He went to a window next to the television, lifted the checkered curtain, and peeked out. "There she is," he said, letting the curtain swing back into position.

"Jack, did you know that Junior had a girlfriend?" I asked.

"No," he said.

I cocked my head toward the television. "I was told that she was dating Junior Bennett," I said.

Meg and Jack looked at me and then at each other. "Who are you talking about?" Meg asked.

"The reporter, Karen Locke."

"How do you know?"

"Sylvester Cole told me. Didn't he mention it to you?" I asked Jack.

Jack stroked his chin. "No, he didn't. She's older than he is, for God's sake."

"That's not important," I said. "I doubt her station knows, or they wouldn't have let her cover the story. At least I hope they wouldn't."

"These days the news desk might think it's just another interesting angle," Meg put in.

"They might," I replied, "but I don't think Ms. Locke is playing straight with them. It makes me wonder what else she isn't telling."

Chapter Eight

"The guy's a dweeb," said Ty. "Got these thick Coke-bottle glasses and greasy hair and he wears tourist kind of clothes. You know, Hawaiian shirts and stuff."

I was glad I hadn't packed mine.

"He's at most of the games," Ty continued. "He thinks he knows a lot about baseball, but he's no expert in my book."

Ty was speaking unfavorably of the self-appointed president of the Rattlers Fan Club. Jack, Meg, Ty, and I sat inside at the kitchen table. A rare rainstorm had just rolled through, scattering the reporters on the front lawn and cooling down the temperature—a degree or two anyway. Meg and I had planned to go to a nearby Tex-Mex restaurant to pick up takeout, but thought better of it when we saw the media still parked outside. Instead, we'd decided to cook a pot of pasta and put together an avocado and tomato salad. Meg made her much-celebrated fresh-lime-

and-garlic salad dressing and put it in the refrigerator to chill.

"If I'd known it was going to rain on those reporters, I would have waited, and gone to El Niño's," she said, filling a large pot with water, placing it on the stove, and adjusting the heat.

"This is nicer," said Jack, handing his wife a glass of white wine.

"If I didn't have this stupid thing on my ankle, I could have gone for you," Ty said, pouring himself an iced tea. "I don't like the idea of you going to a restaurant and having people stare at you."

"They wouldn't do that," Meg said.

Ty gave her a skeptical look and changed the topic. "Now, this is the *real* Arizona iced tea, not that bottled kind," he said, taking a big sip and putting his glass down. He stretched his arms over his head, dropped them, and rolled his shoulders.

We were all functioning on little sleep and lots of nervous energy. Ty hadn't slept very long, just an hour and a half, after spending half the night sitting up in jail. Jack, Meg, and I had all tried to nap in the afternoon, but it was difficult to rest with Ty's fate looming so large.

"I remember that guy, the fan club guy," said Jack. "I've seen him at the games. What's his name?"

"I'm not sure," said Ty. "But I don't think he was that much of a Rattlers fan as much as he was a Junior Bennett fan. He was always clapping for Junior."

"What about him?" Meg said.

"He was there. At the Coyote. I just remembered.

Junior was dissing him, running down the way he dressed, his looks. It's true, the guy's a dweeb, but still, Junior really ripped him. The guy was bummed. Junior was his hero."

"Some hero," Jack said. He looked at me. "Do you need a translation, Jessica? Junior was rude to the president of the fan club."

"I got the gist of it," I said.

"Yeah, but he should have been used to it by now," Ty said. "Junior was always putting him down."

Jack's cell phone rang and he pulled it from the pocket of his slacks. He looked at the screen and pushed TALK. "Yes?" he said. "No, I didn't. How do you know? You sure? Well I'll be damned. No. No. It's okay. Yes, come on over. Plan to eat. We've got plenty of pasta to go around. Okay. See you then." He slid the phone back in his pocket. "That was Cole. He's on his way over."

"Is that it?" asked Meg, disappointed. "Sounded like he had some good news."

"I'm not sure if it's good or bad," her husband said.

"What does that mean?"

"It seems . . ." Jack paused. "It seems that they've found the murder weapon."

"Oh," said Meg, her voice small. "And?"

"And, it was a baseball bat."

Ty put his head down on the table. "They're going to pin this on me, I know it."

I sensed Meg's eyes searching for mine. I looked at her and then at Ty. "Let's not jump to conclusions," I said. To Jack I said, "Where did they find it?"

"In an open Dumpster in back of the stadium, according to Cole," he replied. "He just heard it on the car radio. They found blood on the bat and they're sending it for testing. But Cole says they're confident it's the one that was used to kill Bennett. There is one funny thing about it though."

"What's that?" I asked.

Jack kept his gaze on Ty as he answered. "It's an aluminum bat."

Ty sat up straight in his chair.

"Why is that funny?" I asked.

"I haven't used an aluminum baseball bat since high school," Ty said, watching his foster father. "I didn't even bring an aluminum bat to Arizona."

"I know that," said Jack. "Sylvester does, too. That's why he wanted to be the first to tell you the news."

A weight seemed to have been lifted from Meg's shoulders. "Well," she said, "that young man had better like pasta." She took a fistful of spaghetti, broke it in half, and dumped it into the boiling water. "Dinner will be ready in fifteen minutes."

"Wooden bats were once used exclusively in all baseball leagues, from Little League through high school, college, and in professional ball," Sylvester said, taking a second helping of pasta and tomato sauce.

"But not anymore?" I asked.

He shook his head, his mouth full. After he swallowed, he continued. "They tend to break. Even a Little Leaguer can split the wood with a good hit. That's dangerous, not to mention expensive, especially when budget time comes around. The leagues have to figure out how many bats they need to make it through a season."

"But I would think an aluminum bat would cost more than a wooden one," I said.

"It does, Jessica," Jack put in. "They cost a bit more initially, but they last a whole lot longer."

"They last longer, but they're not necessarily safer, Mrs. Fletcher," Ty said, reaching across the table for the salad.

"Why not?"

Sylvester didn't wait for Ty to respond. "Because the ball tends to fly off an aluminum bat at a much faster rate, which could pose a risk to the pitcher," he said, giving a sharp nod when Jack offered to fill his wineglass. He appeared as tired as the rest of us, with dark circles under his eyes and a heavy shadow on his strong jaw. The weariness seemed to intensify his good looks. It made him less pretty, more striking. I noticed that his manner was straightforward. He wasn't as bent on plying us with his charm as he had been with me at the baseball dinner. I liked this Sylvester better.

"But in Little League and high school, they don't hit the ball that hard," Ty added. "So it's okay to use an aluminum bat."

It occurred to me that we'd gotten away from the fact that an aluminum bat had probably been used to bludgeon Junior Bennett. I weighed whether or not to bring the topic back to its source and decided against it. The general conversation was more suited to dinnertime anyway, I thought.

"I like it that the professional leagues use wooden bats," Meg said. "It's traditional and baseball is a traditional game. Some things should stay the same, and not change."

"It also separates the men from the boys," Sylvester said. "Players and officials associate aluminum bats with the amateurs. Once a kid gets drafted into the pros, he needs to adjust to hitting with a wooden bat. Some do, some don't. A player who was a power hitter, a star on his high school or college team, could hit miserably in pro tryouts."

There's a trade-off in everything in life, I thought.

"That's what made Ty so attractive to scouts," said Sylvester.

"And to agents," Jack put in archly.

"Touché," said Sylvester, raising his wineglass to Jack and draining it. He turned to me. "It's unusual for a player to adjust so quickly to hitting with a wooden bat, Mrs. Fletcher. That's the sign of a pure, natural talent."

Ty's mouth quirked up. It was the first time I'd seen a smile on his lips since he'd been home. But it faded quickly. "Yeah, but all the talent in the world won't mean diddly if I'm convicted of murder."

We were crowded around a small table in the kitchen. The patio table seated eight, but even though it was the end of summer, it was still too warm to eat outside. More important, we wanted to limit the chances that a reporter lurking behind a fence or in a tree could listen to our conversation. Convinced that every click we heard outside was the sound of a camera shutter, we found the safety of the kitchen's four walls comforting, if confining.

The phone rang constantly. Jack was in charge of answering it. He'd look to see who was calling and sometimes he'd pick up; other times he'd let the machine get it. He'd turned the volume down so that we weren't privy to the recorded messages. It was better that we didn't know—as much as I was curious about who was on the line. When he did take a call, Jack retreated to the patio, pacing back and forth, his hand over his mouth to muffle his speech. He'd come back in, beads of sweat dripping from his forehead, a combination of the stifling Arizona heat and stress.

Another call came in. Jack picked up. "Hello, Carter. Yes, okay, thanks for asking. Ty's right here. Hold on."

He handed Ty the phone.

"Hey," Ty said, and went to the sliding doors to go to the patio.

"Better not," Jack said. "Better stay inside."

Ty took the phone upstairs.

"Nice of Carter to call," Meg said to me. "He's Ty's best friend on the team."

"What position does he play?" I asked.

Sylvester answered. "He's an outfielder—and a good one. I'd say he has a fairly good chance of making it to the Show."

"They have a lot in common, Carter and Ty," Meg

said. "He had a tough upbringing, too. His family was poor, single mom, rough neighborhood."

"Tougher than Ty's in many ways," Jack said. "Carter's dad was murdered when the kid was six years old."

"Oh, how awful," I said.

"Even worse than you think. It was a drug-related killing, but it was a case of mistaken identity. Carter's father was just in the wrong place at the wrong time. He died, leaving Carter and his two sisters with a mother who suffered from bouts of depression."

"She had good reason to be depressed," Meg said.

"He's another one that baseball saved," Sylvester said, wiping his mouth with his napkin.

"What about his sisters?" I asked.

He shrugged. "I think they live with an aunt and uncle."

"Carter always feels guilty that he's not helping out with them," Meg said. "Poor dear."

Sylvester stood. "Thank you for dinner, Mrs. Duffy, Judge, Mrs. Fletcher." He looked at each of us in turn. "I'd better go. I've got to stop at the cleaners, and I've got a long day tomorrow. Tell Ty I'll call him."

Jack stayed in his seat and pinned him with a stare. "How long are you planning on sticking around Mesa?"

"What do you mean?"

"Didn't you have plans to go back to L.A. earlier today?"

Sylvester looked uncomfortable. "I was supposed

to hook up with a scout for the Yankees. They're playing in L.A. this weekend. I put it off, considering the circumstances."

"Sylvester, now what?" Jack asked candidly.

We all knew what he meant. Where was Ty's future headed? Were all trade talks off? Were scouts no longer interested?

"I don't know, quite frankly," he said. "Too early to tell. I'm going to head back to L.A. tomorrow, and I'll have a clearer picture for you as the days progress. But right now, I can tell you what you probably already know. Ty won't be called up by the September first deadline. It just ain't gonna happen with this hanging over him."

Ty came down a short while later and took a seat on the window bench. Meg, Jack, and I were still at the kitchen table lingering after dinner. Before Carter's call he had begun to relax, probably relieved by the news that the murder weapon had been found and that it didn't implicate him—at least not yet. But he was more tense now, fidgety, his foot bouncing up and down to a silent beat. "Cole leave?" he asked.

"Yes. He said he'd give you a call," Jack said. "What'd Carter have to say?"

"Not much."

"Just called to say hello?" asked Meg.

"Kinda, I guess. He's pissed off—uh, I mean, annoyed—that he doesn't have his car. The cops won't release it yet. That really sucks."

"Are you finished eating?" Meg asked. "Can I get you some dessert?"

"I'm not really hungry anymore. It was good, though."

Meg smiled.

Ty stared down at his shoes, his eyes unblinking.

When I'd first arrived at Jack and Meg's house, and we'd stood in the foyer, I'd asked Meg what had happened to Ty's feet. She looked at me, puzzled. "Nothing, Jess, why do you ask?"

"Those look like casts," I'd said, pointing to the footwear in the corner. They were calf-high white leather, tall and stiff, with a thick sole and toe.

"Oh, Jess, those aren't casts; those are Ty's sneakers. Size thirteen."

"What did Sylvester mean by the September first deadline?" I asked Jack.

Ty looked up sharply.

Jack studied Ty as he replied to me. "The first of September is the last day that a team can file their postseason roster. So, for instance, if the Cubs were to make it to the play-offs—which they didn't—they can't call anyone up after September one. The roster has to be set by then. They can call up a player in September, but he can't play in the play-offs."

Ty blew out a stream of air, frustrated. "Yeah, now just watch. Junior'll be called up instead of me."

Jack and Meg looked at their foster son curiously.

It took a moment before Ty realized what he'd said. "Oh, God," he said, covering his mouth with his hand, his eyes distraught. "I forgot. It's like a bad dream. Like it's not real. That it isn't happening. It never happened."

But it had.

"You know you didn't have to have Sheriff Metzger call me. You could have called me yourself," Sheriff Hualga said, pulling his patrol car off the dusty road.

"I didn't want to tread on so short an acquaintance," I said. "I wasn't sure how my request would be received."

We were on our way to the crime scene. I had wanted to visit the place where Junior Bennett was murdered, but concern for the Duffys' feelings, as well as Ty's, of course, had kept me from asking them to drive me to a place that could only create painful memories. A call to Mort had resulted in a call from Sheriff Hualga, who had elected to take me there himself.

In the light of day, the Crazy Coyote was a rundown roadhouse sitting in the center of an unpaved parking lot located on a two-lane road, midway between Mesa and Apache Junction. To its left was a pizza parlor, taking advantage of the meager menu offered at the Coyote. Off to the right was a second-hand car dealership fenced in with chain link topped by razor wire. Across the road, scrub grass and scraggly bushes stunted by the sun were the only vegetation in an empty lot.

"Hard to see what the attraction is, isn't it?" Sheriff Hualga said as I climbed out of his car.

"When young people gather for drinks, the atmosphere is secondary," I said. "Evidently, the management doesn't pay close attention to the IDs of their clientele, and that's very attractive indeed."

Hualga huffed. "I gave my staff a thorough dressing-down about this," he said, taking off his cowboy hat and swatting it against his thigh. "The officer who was supposed to be patrolling this place on a regular basis came up with a million excuses why he didn't know the patrons were underage." He donned his hat again and adjusted the fit.

"I really appreciate your accompanying me to the crime scene," I said.

"Your reputation precedes you, Mrs. Fletcher. Mort was full of praise for your investigating abilities."

"He's a dear, but he does tend to exaggerate at times."

"Be that as it may, my guys combed this place pretty well. But if you're going to find anything, I want to be here to see it."

"I can't imagine any clues will jump out at me. I just wanted to get a feel for the scene, and perhaps talk to someone inside."

We tried the front door, found it locked, and walked around to the back. Yellow police tape fluttered in the light breeze caused by air currents rising from the scorched ground.

"The cars have already been impounded," the sheriff said, pawing through a line of tape, winding it around his hand, and tossing the wad into a Dumpster. "Here's where Junior was parked."

"Isn't that a handicapped spot?" I asked.

"Supposed to be, but this kid was not known to follow the rules."

I glanced up at his face. Was he telling me he was sympathetic to Ty?

"Don't think just because Junior wasn't one of Mesa, Arizona's finest gifts to the world that he deserved to die," he said.

"I would never think that," I said. "But I do wonder whether he'd been in any fights before."

"Meaning a personality like Junior's was bound to irritate other people, and that there might be a record of that?"

"It's possible," I said.

"It seems that Junior always managed to evade the law in any other dustups he participated in. Whether it's his father's influence, or less than vigilance on the part of my predecessors or myself, he has no record, not like the long list of violations Judge Duffy's foster son has to his credit."

"That was many years ago, Sheriff. He's been a model citizen since the Duffys took him in."

"So they say. But to a jury, all those petty crimes, gang-related associations, and Mafia ties don't match the image of the nonviolent, law-abiding, hardworking, ideal young man that your friends say he is today. And Martone, the district attorney, is eager to lay them out before the court and let the jurors judge the kid's worth."

"A suspect's past is not proof of a present crime," I said.

"Some people don't see it that way. And you

should know that Harrison Bennett, Sr., is very active in politics in this town and was a big contributor to the DA's last campaign."

That's not good news, I thought, but said, "I would hope that a political contribution would not sway the district attorney into pursuing a case where the evidence is scanty at best."

Hualga cocked his head at me and smiled. "I'm just trying to give you a picture of what you're up against. The DA is not a happy camper about Ramos getting bail. And he sees it as a case of political influence on the part of Judge Duffy. Martone's the kind of guy to look under every rock, if necessary. Look, if Ramos is innocent, I'm the first in line to help him. But if he did this, even if it was accidental, I'm going to come down on him in spades. And he'll go away for a long time."

The affable dinner companion whose company I had so enjoyed was not in evidence today. Instead, a stern lawman had taken his place, one who nevertheless had accommodated the request of an outsider to intrude on his territory.

We stood next to where the body had been discovered. An outline in white paint marked the spot. Dark splotches at the head indicated where Junior had bled into the porous earth. Homicide detectives had taken samples of the blood, leaving spoon-size scoops in the dirt.

"Where did you find Ty?" I asked.

"In Menzies's car over there." He pointed to the side of the bar.

"Was he asleep when you found him?"

"Oh, yeah. Out like a light, and reeking to high heaven. I wouldn't have lit a match near him."

"Had he gotten sick?"

"Not in the car anyway. We took his shirt. There were bloodstains on it. It's over at the crime lab."

"You took his shoes, too. Why?"

"Footprints. There were lots of footprints around the body and over there around the back door. And we also took them to check for any blood spatter."

"Did you compare the footprints around the body with Ty's sneakers?"

"Not my job. Forensics is looking at the crime scene photos and shoes."

"Did you take tire impressions as well?"

He shook his head. "There were way too many cars. I'm not even sure the footprints will yield any information, but since there were some around the body, I figured we should have a record of them."

I stared down at the outline of Junior's body and tried to visualize what happened that night. Did Junior get into a fight with someone else after Carter put Ty in his car? Were there other people in the bar who had a bone to pick with him? Had he fought with someone in the past, someone who waited until he was drunk to take revenge? Or could it have been a case not of murder but of self-defense? If only Ty could remember.

"If you're finished here, let's go see if anyone is inside," Hualga said.

I looked at my watch. "There should be someone,"

I said. "The sign on their front door says they're scheduled to open soon."

Hualga harumphed but didn't say anything.

The interior of the Coyote was as dim as I had expected it to be, but not as shabby as the exterior. It took a few moments for my eyes to adjust to the lack of light. When they did, I saw that someone had made an effort to make the bar look like a classic Western saloon. Cowboy memorabilia was everywhere, including several dozen boots set up one behind the other on a long shelf, as if they were dancing the two-step all by themselves. Dark wooden benches lined the walls with tables in front of them, topped by bentwood chairs resting upside down on their surfaces. A woman was mopping the floor under the tables, but the aroma of beer so permeated the wood that her efforts were ineffective—at least in eliminating the smell.

"Hello, Sheriff," she said.

"Ms. Wellwyn. This is Mrs. Fletcher, a colleague of mine."

"How do you do," she said.

"Very well, thank you. The sheriff has kindly allowed me to see the site of the murder, and I hope you won't mind if I look around and ask you a few questions."

"You can ask away, but I wasn't on the night Junior was killed. Kathy was bartending, but Ogden—that's the owner—he let her go after the sheriff gave him a citation for serving underage customers. I don't know that she could tell you anything anyway. She told me the bar was so busy she never saw a thing. Besides, the Diamondbacks game was on TV and she's a rabid fan."

"What's the occupancy permitted here?" I asked.

"Sign says seventy-five, but we average about forty or fifty most nights."

"It was crowded the night of the murder?"

"Kathy said it was the usual group. It's been up a bit since then, people wanting to see inside the police tape where the murder took place. A bit ghoulish for my taste, but if we sell a few extra beers, they can come and gawk all they want."

I wandered around the bar, imagining the tables filled with baseball players and their girlfriends, members of the fan club. I examined the back door and the short hallway that led to it, calculating that between the televised game and the voices of thirty or forty patrons, the noise level inside would have been sufficient to muffle any arguments in the parking lot, no matter how heated. I told the sheriff I was ready to leave and thanked Ms. Wellwyn.

"Sure. No problem," she said as she took down the chairs and pushed them under the tables. "Come back anytime. Too bad about Junior. I heard he was a great shortstop."

Chapter Nine

"**A** little to the left. Yes, that's it. Oops, no. A little farther down. Yes, there. Now a teeny bit to the right. Perfect."

I'd been looking forward to having a massage from the moment I'd booked my flight to Arizona. Meg had raved to me about the fabulous health clubs in Phoenix and Scottsdale. They were a big part of the area's appeal for her. Jack could keep those champion golf courses that he bragged about. Meg loved the rubs and wraps offered in the resorts' award-winning spas.

I had planned to explore some of those offerings when I arrived in Arizona. To my surprise—and sheer delight—sitting atop my pillow in the guest room at the Duffys' was a gift certificate for a "Day of Beauty" at the Arizona Biltmore in Phoenix. The Biltmore sits on thirty-nine acres, a grande dame of a resort with architecture inspired by Frank Lloyd Wright. The hotel has played host to many presidents and celebrities throughout the years. Guidebooks call it "the Jewel of the Desert," and it was only a forty-five-minute cab ride from Meg and Jack's home in Mesa.

While waiting for my massage appointment, I sipped a cup of soothing ginger tea in the spa lounge, a tranquil room complete with a tumbling waterfall and the silkiest chairs I've ever sat in. I skimmed through the pages of the latest *Vanity Fair* magazine and concluded that my wardrobe was completely out-dated. There wasn't a single peasant skirt or fringed shawl hanging in my closet at home. My boots were practical for rain or snow, and I didn't even own a piece of black clothing, with the exception of a belt. Perhaps that's an exaggeration, but the fashions in the magazine's editorial pages and advertisements bore no relationship to my life at all. *Just as well,* I thought.

Setting the magazine aside, I studied the ambitious guide to massages and treatments at the spa, many of which incorporated ingredients indigenous to the Southwest and inspired by Native American rituals, like Raindrop Therapy. I'd chosen the Cactus Flower Massage, which, true to its name, had massage oils in-fused with flowers from various cacti, as I discovered when I was brought down the hall into a small, dark room with aromatherapy votive candles flickering. New Age music played in the background, comple-menting the serene, relaxing mood.

The masseuse, Lily, was a young woman, no more than twenty-five. I've had massages in which the masseuse engaged me in a dialogue for the duration of the treatment, defeating the effect I sought—to get away from it all and relax. Lily was well schooled; she spoke only if I initiated the conversation.

I was dozing when she shook my shoulder and gently broke the bad news. "Mrs. Fletcher," she said, in a singsong, spa-y voice, "your session has come to an end." *One of life's biggest disappointments,* I thought to myself. But fifty minutes of bliss had melted away the stress of the last few days. I felt marvelously rejuvenated.

"Don't worry though," said Lily. "You don't have to jump right up off the table just yet. Lie there for a few more minutes and take your time getting up."

While she began to put away some of the oils and other massage paraphernalia she shyly asked, "I heard that you're a famous writer. Are you here on vacation?"

"Yes . . . well, yes, I am," I said, practically forgetting that this trip was originally planned as a vacation; with Ty's arrest it had become anything but.

"I'd love to be a writer," Lily said. "I take classes at Arizona Community College. I get A's and B's on all my papers. My professors always compliment my writing. I love to write."

"That's terrific, Lily. It's wonderful to have a creative passion."

"Yes." She laughed. "Writing and baseball are my two passions."

She didn't say baseball, did she? I thought. I had been wondering how to broach the topic with her.

After all, it had been one of the reasons I'd chosen to take advantage of my gift certificate at this time. Ty had said some of the girls with the ballplayers the night Junior was killed worked at the Biltmore spa. Could Lily have been one of them?

She'd taken me aback when she raised the subject herself. I couldn't hold out. "Did you say baseball?" I asked, struggling to sit up. My muscles were so relaxed, they objected to moving. Lily rushed to my side and assisted me to a sitting position. She wrapped a towel around my shoulders to keep me warm.

"Ah, that's better," I said, running a hand through my tousled hair. "You said baseball is one of your passions?"

"In a way," said Lily. "My boyfriend plays on a professional team, so I kinda had to learn to love it."

"Which team is that?"

"You wouldn't know them, I'm sure. He plays in the minor leagues, for the Rattlers. They're a Double-A team. They play in Mesa, less than an hour from here."

"I see," I said. Trying hard not to negate the serenity I'd just experienced, I took a deep breath and exhaled slowly.

"Actually, you could have heard about them, or you will, anyway," Lily continued. "One of the team members murdered another one. It's been all over the news, but since you're on vacation you're probably staying far away from the news." She laughed.

If she only knew, I thought. I didn't say anything,

but her description of what she'd heard on the news disturbed me. Interesting how people accept an arrest as proof of guilt. Yet there isn't a conviction in at least a third of all arrests for felony murder. Those cases may have resulted in an acquittal or dropped charges.

"Innocent until proven guilty." It's such an important plank in our judicial structure. But people tend to forget that in the swell of media coverage following an arrest. Perhaps it can be credited to the public's trust in their police departments. But any officer worth his salt would admit that mistakes get made, even in the most meticulous of investigations. And when the police are sure they have the right person, they're still required to present evidence at a trial, and convince a jury that the accused is guilty *beyond a reasonable doubt*. I had many reasonable doubts about Ty's guilt. Overcoming a difficult childhood, he had become a sensitive, nonviolent, law-abiding, generous, caring young man. The police evidence against him was skimpy and circumstantial from what I knew. Ty and Meg and Jack were going to have to struggle to counter the headlines, but I would be there to help them. I only hoped I could.

"Okay, Mrs. Fletcher, I'm going to leave the room now," Lily informed me. "Take your time getting up from the table, and slip your robe on. I'll come back to take you to the lounge, where you can wait for your next treatment."

"Before you go, Lily," I called. "Who's your boyfriend? Would I know him?"

She turned to me, her hand on the door. "His name is Steven Long," she said.

The name didn't ring a bell. It wasn't one of the names that Ty had mentioned when telling us what had happened at the Crazy Coyote.

"Long. What position does he play?"

"He's a pitcher. But he's been on the DL for about two weeks."

"DL?"

She laughed. "Oh, sorry. Disabled list. Believe me, I didn't know all this jargon either before I got involved with Steven."

"Why is he on the DL?" I asked.

"Tendonitis in his elbow. It flares up every once in awhile."

"Was he friends with the player who was killed or the player who is accused of killing him?" I asked, trying to come across as merely curious rather than as having an ulterior motive.

"Not really. I mean, all the guys know each other, but the pitchers kinda stick together, and neither of those guys was a pitcher. They were both shortstops, and there was a lot of jealous rivalry between them. The boy who was murdered was also the owner's son. I met him once—the owner, that is. He comes in here for massages." She lowered her voice. "No one here likes him, though. He's very demanding and doesn't tip." She slapped a hand over her mouth. "Sorry, I shouldn't say that," she whispered. "We're not supposed to mention tipping."

"Don't worry," I whispered back. "I won't say a

word. But tell me about the other shortstop. Do you know him?"

"That's Ty Ramos. Supposedly killed the owner's son. That's what they say on the news. But my boyfriend doesn't think he's the one who did it."

"You don't say?" I tried for a casual tone. "And why not."

"Because Steve says he's a nice kid and wasn't jealous of Junior at all. But Junior was really jealous of Ty because he was a better shortstop and had a hot agent after him, and all that. But these guys were all drinking, so I say to him, 'Who knows? It could have happened the way they say.' But Steve says that Ty was an easygoing kid. He said no one on the team, except for a friend of Junior's, thinks that Ty killed him."

"Hmm. So who do they think killed Junior, Lily?"

"Sheesh. I don't know. I don't think they know, except that I did hear Steve say something about his crazy girlfriend."

"Junior had a girlfriend?"

"Sure. They all do. We saw her on the news."

"Were the reporters interviewing her?"

Lily laughed. "No. She *is* the reporter. And Steve said he heard they'd had a big fight the night of the murder. Anyway, Mrs. Fletcher, you're all set now to put your robe on, and I've got to get to my next massage appointment. I'll give you a few minutes and then I'll be back."

"Oh, yes. Okay, thanks, Lily."

I put on my robe. As promised, Lily reappeared shortly to escort me down the hall.

As we walked, I commented, "Lily, I'm surprised that a young professional up-and-coming ballplayer has time for a girlfriend." I'd remembered a comment that the team players were not encouraged to have them.

Lily became flushed. "Well, yes, actually, Steve isn't *supposed* to have a girlfriend. The coach told them they aren't allowed to. But, well, no one really knows."

I thought she looked at me a little nervously, suddenly aware of how much she'd been chattering away. I put a finger over my lips. "I'll never tell," I said, smiling.

She seemed to relax. "Actually, everyone on the team has a girlfriend except for maybe a couple of them. Junior, the guy who was murdered, he always had a girlfriend, practically a different one every month. One of them was supposedly a drug dealer. Steve thought she also might be involved in his murder. She was always trying to sell stuff to the players. Steroids and other drugs."

"My goodness. Do the police know this?"

"I don't know, but she hasn't been around for a couple of months."

When we reached the lounge, Lily poured me a glass of icy water with several lemon wedges in it.

"Thank you, Lily." I handed her a generous tip. "And good luck with your writing." I sank into what was fast becoming my favorite chair.

"Gee. Thanks," she said, pocketing the bill and disappearing behind a patterned magenta curtain that hung in a doorway in place of a door.

* * *

"Yes, very comfortable, thank you."

The woman performing my facial introduced herself as Toni. She was perfect for a cosmetician. She had a peaches-and-cream complexion and not a visible permanent wrinkle on her oval face. Lines appeared when she laughed or frowned, but then seemed instantly erased. Of course, the fact that she was no more than thirty years old had something to do with it.

The same New Age music was piped into this room, which was a bit smaller and had a more clinical feel to it than the room in which I was given my massage, thanks to the bright light that shone on my face to expose my pores. Toni gently stroked the skin on my face, scrutinizing it with a "hmm," and "uh-huh."

"That bad?" I said and laughed.

"Oh, no, not at all. You have a lovely complexion, Mrs. Fletcher. I just needed to assess your skin to determine which facial would benefit you best. Now, I see here you signed up for our Turquoise Facial, but honestly, based on my examination, that might be too drying, thanks to the cornmeal we use in it. I recommend we do the facial to repair dry skin, with some jojoba, lavender, and aloe gel—all native Arizona plants, by the way."

"Sounds good to me," I said.

"I can also recommend some follow-up treatments you might want to consider, Mrs. Fletcher. There are some excellent Botox and laser treatments."

"Thank you, but not for this Maine lady," I said

with a chuckle. "Nature as Nature intended, I'm afraid. That kind of thing isn't for me."

I could see now why Toni didn't have any wrinkles. Her face didn't express any emotion when she replied very seriously, "Okay, then, let's get started."

Thankfully, the bright light that had magnified every line in my face was turned off and several votive candles and a small lamp in the corner set a less sterile mood.

Toni's hands were strong, and she rubbed my face and scalp assertively—but not too hard. I could practically feel the blood circulating in my face, guaranteeing a healthy glow. Like Lily, Toni didn't pepper me with small-talk questions, and I surrendered to a relaxed state, visualizing myself on a small island in the Caribbean, with George Sutherland, a bottle of wine, two lobster dinners, and the lapping of the cerulean surf at our feet. But the vision was short-lived; as if I had a TV remote, that channel was changed to a channel in which my conversation with Lily was playing. She said that Junior had a drug-dealing ex-girlfriend. Had she come back? I wondered. I took heart from her comment that none of the other players thought Ty had murdered Junior. Should I tell Meg and Jack this? Should I tell Ty? Surely that would cheer him, at least for a while. I wondered if Ty had a girlfriend whom Jack and Meg didn't know about. According to Lily, most of the players on the team did. I should have asked her. Maybe I could make a point of doing so before I left.

"I'm going to apply this gentle masque to your face and then leave you for about ten minutes to let the masque do its job. It's *very* hydrating and soothing. Then we'll just massage it into your skin. Don't wash it off tonight. You'll see a big difference tomorrow."

"Okay," I said sleepily.

Toni left the room. A minute or two later the door reopened. I was disappointed. Why had she returned so soon? I had looked forward to a ten-minute escape.

Thanks to the lavender-hued eye mask that blanketed my eyes, I couldn't see who it was. Maybe it wasn't Toni. About a minute passed and no one said a word, but I could sense someone in the room, although there was no discernible noise.

"Hello?" I finally said.

"Hi, Jess, it's me," Meg whispered.

"Meg?"

"Jess, I'm so sorry to barge in like this. They were kind enough to tell me which room you were in. But when I got in here I thought you were sleeping. You looked so relaxed, I didn't want to say anything."

I removed the eye mask, sat up, and looked at Meg, who hovered at the edge of the massage table. She was usually so well put together, but now her face was bare of makeup, and she was wearing clothing more suitable to gardening—a pair of navy cotton shorts and a white T-shirt that read, DON'T JUDGE ME, probably a souvenir Jack had brought back from one of his legal conferences. It wasn't the kind of outfit Meg would ordinarily let anyone see her in.

"Meg, is everything okay?"

She slumped into a chair near the door and raked her fingers through her hair. Her hands were trembling. Tears rolled down her cheeks. She dropped her hands to her lap. "Oh, Jessica. It's just awful. The preliminary DNA report came back. The blood on Ty's shirt. It belongs to Junior."

"But Meg, Ty already told us that he punched Junior in the nose. That would certainly explain why his blood was on Ty's shirt," I said, hoping to reassure her.

"But the police said they haven't been able to find anyone who witnessed that punch. And one of the television reports said that it was unlikely that story would hold up because Ty's Breathalyzer test indicated he was so out of it he never would have been able to land a punch hard enough to make Junior bleed."

"That's pure speculation on the part of the reporter," I said. "I wouldn't give it any credence."

There was a knock on the door. "Mrs. Fletcher, is it okay to come in now?" It was Toni's voice.

Meg nodded.

"Yes," I said, hopping down from the table and tightening the belt of my robe.

"Are we stopping the facial?" Toni asked when she saw Meg.

"I think it's enough," I said.

"We were close to the end, anyway," she said. "Don't forget. Don't wash your face tonight."

"I won't forget."

Toni escorted us down a narrow hallway, with soft

lighting that came from strategically placed sconces, and into the equally muted lighting of the lounge. I tipped her and expressed my thanks, and she left.

I poured Meg a cup of ginger tea. "Try this. It will help you to relax. I think you could use some of the services of this spa."

"I wish! I've been such a wreck since Ty was arrested. I can't seem to find a comfortable place for myself."

"Wait here," I said. I approached the pretty young woman who stood behind a blond wooden desk just off the lounge.

"Hello, Mrs. Fletcher," she said. "Did your friend find you? I hope it was all right to tell her where you were. We usually don't do that, but she seemed so upset."

"You did exactly the right thing," I said. "Thank you. Now, I have a favor to ask. Is it possible to transfer my next treatment to my friend? I'd like her to get the treatment instead of me."

"Sure, Mrs. Fletcher. No problem at all. Let's see," she said, scanning the appointment book. "Your next treatment is the Sonora Stone massage at noon. It's wonderful." She looked at her watch. "That's in fifteen minutes."

"Terrific," I said.

"I'll let Lily know."

I began to walk back to the lounge and then remembered that Lily's boyfriend was on the Rattlers. I hastily returned to the counter. "Lily is the woman who gave me my first massage?"

"Yes, that's right."

"Lovely girl," I said with a smile. "But do you suppose another masseuse would be available?"

"Was there a problem with Lily, Mrs. Fletcher? She's one of our most popular and most requested staff members."

"Not at all. She's a sweet girl and very good at what she does. I'll tell you what. How about I keep that massage with Lily, and my friend over there in the lounge can have another massage."

She scanned the appointment book once again, shaking her head. "We are so booked, I'm afraid that won't be possible." She ran her perfectly manicured fingers down the page and stopped. "Wait a minute. Hmm, I think it's your lucky day, Mrs. Fletcher. About ten minutes ago we got a cancellation for a Swedish Massage with Bethanne. Shall I schedule that for your friend?"

"That would be wonderful."

"May I have her name?"

I was loath to give Meg's real name, in the event someone would recognize it and make a comment that would make her uncomfortable. She was tense enough as it was.

"Your friend's name, Mrs. Fletcher?"

"Of course. It's, uh, Malorie."

"And her last name?"

"Muffet."

"Malorie Muffet?" the woman repeated, incredulous.

"Yes, Malorie Muffet," I said stiffly, and escaped back to the lounge.

"Jessica, you didn't," Meg said, totally surprised and, I could tell, equally pleased when I told her about the appointment.

"Meg, you're a poster child for a massage candidate. Think of it as a medical necessity. If Seth were here," I said, raising the image of my good friend and Cabot Cove's favorite doctor, "he would prescribe it for you."

"If Dr. Hazlitt prescribes it, then I guess I'd better take my medicine."

"That's being a good patient."

"But if the press gets wind of this—that I was out getting a massage while my foster son stays home waiting to be indicted—they'll have a field day."

"Precisely why I made your appointment under a fictitious name," I said, revealing her *nom de massage*.

"You told them I was Malorie Muffet?" Meg said, and started to giggle. I was glad to see her mood lighten.

"It was the best I could do under pressure," I said, chagrined.

A cell phone rang, and it took us a moment to realize the sound was coming from Meg's purse. The looks of disdain from several of the women seated in the lounge told us that a ringing cell phone was a big faux pas in a spa. Meg hurried to dig it out, pushing aside packets of tissues, an address book, a makeup bag, and a paperback novel, but by the fourth ring, it stopped.

"I can never find that darned thing in here. Jack always says I carry too much in this bag, but I can never decide what I don't need. When I leave something out, that's inevitably what I end up looking for the next time."

Whoever had called either had hung up or was leaving a message. A socialite-type middle-aged woman seated next to Meg reached over and handed her a laminated sign that read, PLEASE, NO CELL PHONES IN THE SPA. THANK YOU.

Meg handed it back to her and apologized. The woman accepted her apology with a nod of her head and placed the small sign back on the end table. I put my arm around Meg and squeezed her shoulder.

Lily entered the lounge with another woman, about the same age, but much taller and a bit overweight. Her name tag read BETHANNE.

"Mrs. Fletcher," Lily said.

"I could get used to this," I said, getting up and going over to Lily. It was time for my next treatment.

"See you later," I said to Meg. "I'll meet you back here after our massages."

"Ms. Muffet," said Bethanne.

No one moved.

"Ms. Muffet," she said again. "Is there a Ms. Muffet here?"

"Oh! That would be me," Meg said, blushing a bright red.

"She's a little distracted today," I said.

"Yes, I am," Meg said, giving me a wink as she followed Bethanne from the lounge. "Sorry. I was in another world," she said to her escort, and to all the other women in the room whose eyes were now focused on her.

Lily placed hot stones on my back as part of the Sonora Stone Massage I was about to enjoy. She explained that the combination of the penetrating warmth of the smooth basalt stones and gentle pressure of the massage was especially therapeutic, and beneficial to the circulatory system.

The heat from the stones felt surprisingly good, and I succumbed to the moody music and gentle kneading, hoping that Meg was getting the same enjoyment from her Swedish Massage. Lily, who was a font of information and gossip once the treatment was over, was a model of silence while she worked. For the next forty-five minutes not a word was spoken. I hadn't relaxed this much since arriving in Arizona—or during the many weeks and months before my arrival. I had traveled a lot this summer to promote my latest book and then returned home to find the edited pages of my newest manuscript, which had required my immediate attention.

I knew my time was up when Lily started speaking again.

"How did you like this one?" she asked.

"Oh, that was incredibly relaxing," I said groggily. My stomach growled.

Lily must have heard, because she immediately suggested lunch at the resort's restaurant. "We have a very healthy menu, and the food is delicious. You have plenty of time. Your next treatment isn't until two thirty."

The healthy spa lunch was included in my Day of Beauty package. I don't usually order from a diet menu. My philosophy is "Everything in moderation," and it's worked for me. That, and a morning run when I'm home, a good walk when I'm not. I asked her if there was a "regular" menu available in addition to the spa choices and she laughed and said, "Yes."

"I'm signed up to give you your next treatment," said Lily, "but I've asked my boss if one of the other girls can do it. I have to leave early today. I hope you don't mind."

"Not at all. You take off and enjoy yourself."

"It's not exactly something enjoyable. Remember I told you about the baseball player who was killed? They're having a memorial service for Junior Bennett tonight."

"Tonight?"

"Around five or five thirty, I think. But my boyfriend is meeting me here at three. He has an interview with my boss about a job. He worked here as a personal trainer in the off-season last year. That's how we met. I hope they take him on again. A lot of the players get jobs here and at the other resorts around town."

"You said he's coming at three?"

"Yes. Three. That's why I can't make your two thirty." She looked at me quizzically. "Your treatment lasts longer than a half hour."

"I understand," I said, thinking that Meg shouldn't be anywhere near here if one of the Rattlers was going to be at the resort at the same time. Surely Lily's boyfriend would recognize her.

"We're leaving right after the interview," Lily said while tidying up the room for the next customer. "If there's traffic, it could take more time to get to Mesa, and we have to stop along the way to pick up some of the other guys. We don't want to be late for the service. They're expecting lots of people. Hundreds, maybe thousands."

"That many?" I said. "Where is the service?"

"At Thompson Stadium in Mesa. That's where the Rattlers play. Then the guys on the team are all going out for dinner to Junior's favorite restaurant. He loved Italian food, I guess. They're going to Patsy's in Phoenix. His father is a very rich man and he's paying for everyone."

"Are you invited as well?"

"No. Just the guys. My boyfriend said there's a bet going around whether or not Ty, the kid accused of killing him, will show up at the service. He's out of jail because his dad is some big shot in the courts. He better not show his face. Even though a lot of the guys don't think he did it, my boyfriend said that Junior's father hates him. Of course, he hated him before the murder. That's because he was jealous because Ty's better than his son. It's so dysfunctional."

"It certainly sounds that way," I said.

"Okay, Mrs. Fletcher, you're all set. Put on your robe and I'll escort you back to the lounge. You know the drill by now," she said with a giggle.

"I need to cancel my afternoon treatments," I said. "I'm terribly sorry, but something has come up."

The woman at the desk smiled and said, "That's all right, Mrs. Fletcher. Would you like to reschedule? I can see if we have availability on another day and we can make up what you're missing. You had two more treatments scheduled for today, the Raindrop Therapy and the Reflexology Pedicure."

I was especially intrigued by the idea of Raindrop Therapy, whatever that was, and was disappointed to have to miss it. "I really appreciate that, but I don't know what my schedule will be for the next few days. May I call you?"

"Absolutely. Just give us as much notice as you can," she said. "As I'm sure you can see, we're very busy."

It would have been pleasant to have lunch with Meg at the Biltmore, but now that one of the Rattlers was due to arrive, I felt it was more important to usher her out of sight as quickly as possible. I walked back to the lounge to see if Meg was there. It was unoccupied. *All of the treatment rooms must be full,* I thought. While I waited, I picked up a book titled *The Zen of Massage.* Someone entered the room and I looked up to see if it was Meg. Instead, it was a petite woman in dark-rimmed glasses, her hair wrapped in a turban. She was draped in the same white robe as everyone else and carried a plate of crackers. She sat on a chair, her back to me, but her body language conveyed exhaustion. I resumed turning the pages in the book I was reading and wondered how much longer Meg would be.

"Hi. I'm ready for you," said Lily.

The woman put down the plate and stood. "Thanks for fitting me in. This is therapy for me and I really need it."

The voice was familiar and I froze, raising only my eyes to peek at Lily's customer.

"How are you doing?" Lily asked her, taking her arm. "I'm so sorry about what you're going through. I'm sorry about Junior." She spoke quietly, but in the empty lounge her words were audible.

The woman glanced toward me and said to Lily, "Shhh. We don't talk about that in public."

It was Karen Locke. Without cosmetics and contact lenses, she was a plain Jane with unremarkable features and acne scars. In front of the camera in full makeup, she was transformed into a very attractive woman.

"Let's go," said Karen. "I'm totally bushed." The two exited the lounge and rounded the corner.

I prayed that Meg wouldn't burst onto the scene just yet. Timing is everything in life, and in this case, my prayer was too late.

"Mrs. Duffy?" I heard Karen say. "What are you doing here?"

I hurried into the hall and grabbed Meg's arm, practically dragging her toward the women's changing room. "We're just on our way out," I said.

Locke abandoned Lily and followed us.

"Well, well, well," she said, her voice steeped in irony. "Your son has been arrested for murder and you're out getting a massage." She pulled a cell phone from her pocket. "I can't believe my luck." She stalked toward the lockers where Meg and I stood, all traces of her fatigue vanished.

"Ms. Locke, please," I said. "This is neither the place nor the time."

Ignoring me, Locke addressed Meg. "You've been avoiding the press all week, Mrs. Duffy," she said, punching a number into her phone. "Some people might think you're feeling guilty. Do you believe your son is a murderer?" she said.

"Of course not," Meg said.

"Here's your opportunity to set the record straight. Tell the public what you think. Inquiring minds want to know." She thrust the phone toward Meg. "My editor will record whatever you say."

"This is completely inappropriate, Ms. Locke," I said. "Being a reporter doesn't give you the right to intrude on someone's personal tragedy."

"It's okay, Jess," said Meg, defeated and visibly trembling.

"I don't agree, Meg. It's not okay," I said.

"No one's private life is sacred in a murder investigation," Locke said to me. "The public has a right to know what the mother of a suspected murderer is thinking." She held the phone out to Meg. "They want to hear your side, Mrs. Duffy. They want to know what a mother feels when her only son is arrested for a brutal murder. They want to hear from you how hurt and worried you are."

"If the public is so hungry for news," I said, "why don't you tell them if the baby you're carrying is Junior's?"

Karen snapped the phone shut and glared at me. "How dare you. That's no one's business. Who told you I'm pregnant?"

Lily joined us in the locker room. "Karen, let me take you to the massage room. Come on."

"Didn't I just hear you say no one's private life is sacred in a murder investigation?" I said. "In that case, why haven't you reported that you were dating Junior Bennett? Could it be because it's a conflict of interest to cover a baseball team when you're dating one of the players? Rumor has it you two had a big fight the night he died. Where were you when Junior was killed?"

"Of all the nerve," Karen huffed. She turned on her heel and walked swiftly out of the locker room, Lily right behind her.

"Inquiring minds want to know," I said as the door closed softly behind them.

Meg sank onto a bench.

"I'm sorry, Meg," I said. "I just couldn't stand by and let her exploit you."

Chapter Ten

It took quite a while for Meg to calm down after we returned to the house. The confrontation with Karen Locke had shaken her to the core. She spat out condemnation after condemnation of the press in a constant, staccato monologue. I occasionally tried to intervene, but my efforts were minimally effective, at best.

Finally, after a large glass of wine, her emotional energy waned and she slumped on the couch, her face an ashen mask of anger.

"I know how you feel," I said as I sat next to her, "but the reality is that Ty's arrest and Junior's murder are big news here, maybe the biggest news story they've ever had. I've had my run-ins with the press, and there have been times when I was angry, too. Today, for instance. But I also realize they have their job to do, as unsavory as that may be at times."

"I know, I know," she said. "You're right, Jess. Jack always says that no matter how the media abuses its power, it is the best hope we have for a true checks-and-balances system in government." She managed her first smile since leaving the spa. "How did you know that she was pregnant, Jess?"

"There have been a number of clues, nothing definitive, but it turned out that my putting two and two together was correct. Sometimes it isn't. Look, Meg, I have a feeling that things might begin to fall into place shortly. At least, I hope they will. The answer lies with the team and—"

"The team? Do you think one of the other players killed Junior?"

"I don't know," I replied. "I just have this feeling that the answer could come out of the team, maybe the Bennett organization, maybe not. But I'm determined to start aggressively pushing now. The team is gathering after tonight's memorial service for Junior at the stadium."

"That's right," Meg said. "At Patsy's in Phoenix. They always go there."

"I wish I could go, too," I said, "to pick up on the interaction between players and management."

A small smile played on her lips. "Knowing you, you could probably wangle an invitation."

"I doubt that very much," I said, laughing. "But I may be able to get close enough to see something that would add another piece to this puzzle. I have an idea."

"You never seem to be without one," she said.

"I don't know whether that's a compliment or not," I said. "Tell me about Patsy's. Is it a big restaurant?"

"Not very big, but with a nice dining room. Jack and I have been there several times. The food is hearty Italian, the atmosphere very lively. The bar is lovely, too."

"Good," I said, going to a window and looking out to the street, where a TV remote truck had just parked across from the house. "They're back," I said.

"Who?"

"The press."

"The ghouls, you mean."

I turned to face her. "Meg," I said, "I noticed that you have a collection of wigs upstairs."

"Oh, those," she responded. "I saved them from the time I went through that bout of cancer and chemo a few years back. I figured if I was going to lose my own hair, I had a right to see how I'd look with different colors and styles."

"I'll bet you looked beautiful."

"That's kind of you to say. Funny, our first year coming to Mesa was the year after I'd stopped chemo and was pronounced in remission." She knocked on a wooden table. "Jack and I came here on vacation before Ty ever ended up playing ball here. We vacationed here when Ty was younger, and even went to a few Rattlers games. Ironic, isn't it, that he now plays for them?"

"The wigs," I reminded her.

"Oh, yes. I wore them for a long time after the treatments and carried them everywhere with me. We fell in love with Arizona and Mesa and decided to make our stay here a yearly ritual. By that time, my hair had grown back pretty well, although I was still more comfortable wearing a wig. I almost think I'm a little afraid to be far away from them. Silly, I know."

"Can I borrow one?" I asked.

"You, Jess? You have beautiful, natural hair."

"Thank you, but I'd prefer it to be black tonight."

"What?"

"I'll explain."

I found a seat at the far end of the long bar in Patsy's. A huge mirror behind the bar allowed me to take stock of how effectively I'd disguised myself for the evening. The black wig from Meg's collection was long and curly and fell perfectly to cover the sides of my face. Although I'd brought sunglasses with me to Arizona, I chose an oversized pair of Meg's to wear. I realized I'd been a little heavy-handed in applying makeup, but it served to further conceal my features.

"Drink, ma'am?" the young bartender asked pleasantly, placing a napkin in front of me.

"Just a club soda if you don't mind," I said, "with a wedge of lime. I have quite a bit of time to kill before meeting someone. I hope you don't mind my lingering here."

"Not at all," he said. "This is usually a quiet night at the bar. Stay as long as you like."

"Thank you. That's quite a crowd in the next room," I said, indicating an adjacent dining room that was visible through a wide arch separating the bar from the rest of the establishment.

"The Rattlers," he said.

"Oh," I said. "Why would they be called Rattlers?"

"I guess you don't follow baseball," he said. "And you're not from around here."

"No, I'm not, and you're right. I don't follow baseball, or any sports for that matter."

"The Rattlers are our local minor-league team," he explained. "We had a tragedy recently. One of the players, the owner's son, was murdered, and a teammate has been accused of killing him. Maybe you've read about it in the papers, or seen TV coverage."

"I seem to remember seeing something about that. How terrible, a young man struck down in his prime."

Another customer took a stool at the opposite end of the bar, diverting the bartender's attention from me. But before he left to serve the other customer and to make my drink, he laid a copy of the *East Valley Tribune* in front of me. The Junior Bennett murder was the lead story on the front page.

The headline read, SHORTSTOP DOUBLE PLAY. I began to read.

Evidence is now starting to indicate that Ty Ramos, the talented and handsome young shortstop on the Mesa Rattlers, didn't act alone in the murder of lesser-talented Junior Bennett. According to a detective involved in the case, the police are looking for a man who was spotted at the team's dinner at the Mesa Hilton earlier that night. Ramos reportedly spent some time with this mystery man before leaving the hotel for the Crazy Coyote, the scene of the bloody murder.

Ramos has been in trouble with the law before, mostly drug-related robberies and one assault when he was a teenager growing up in New Jersey. He was reportedly part of a gang in Jersey City.

According to Sheriff Hualga, a phone call came in to Ramos's cell phone about eleven that night from a number that the police have traced to this second suspect, whose name the police are not releasing at this time.

Meanwhile, a memorial service is scheduled for tonight at five thirty at Thompson Stadium, where hundreds are expected to attend. Ramos is out on $250,000 bail, in part because of his foster father's, Judge Jack Duffy, connections on the bench. Duffy, a judge in New Jersey, is said to be working a plea deal for Ramos, who has lived with Duffy and his wife, Meg, since he was twelve.

Harrison Bennett, Sr., father of the murdered shortstop, has not spoken to the press. Nor have the Duffys. The family has been in seclusion since Junior Bennett's body was discovered and their foster son was arrested and charged.

In an interesting twist, police in connection with the case have reportedly questioned WXYK reporter Karen Locke. A reliable source, speaking off the record, said that Locke was Junior Bennett's girlfriend and that, in fact, it was she who called 911 to report the murder. WXYK spokeswoman Donna Smallin would neither

confirm nor deny the allegation, nor did the sta-
tion include this information in any of its on-air
reports, many of which, interestingly enough,
have been reported by Karen Locke herself.

My timing was good. The memorial service at the
stadium had evidently ended, and players, some of
whom I recognized, and people who I assumed were
invited guests, started filing into the dining room. I
wondered if H.B. would be with them. No matter. I
was confident that no one would recognize me in my
black wig, large sunglasses, and heavy makeup. I
checked myself in the bar mirror again. I looked a little too sexy, I decided, and hoped no one would mistake me for "a professional woman."

I was contemplating that when my cell phone rang.
I glanced at caller ID. It was Meg.

"Hello," I said in a low voice.

"Hi, Jessica," she said in a somewhat upbeat tone,
everything being relative. "I wanted to fill you in on
some news we just got. Turns out you were right
about Locke and Junior. There's a story in today's
paper that suggests the same thing."

"I just read that," I said.

"But there's a twist that Jack told me about. It
seems that Locke has been involved in an ongoing investigative report about sports gambling in the
Phoenix region. The station was waiting to run her
story during sweeps in September, but they've put it
on hold indefinitely. There's also growing speculation
that she's being forced to resign from the station be-

cause of conflict of interest. I guess her involvement with Junior is common knowledge now."

"Interesting," I said. "Who gave Jack that information?"

"I don't know. He's staying mum about that. Are you at the restaurant, Jess?"

"Yes."

"I wish I could join you," she said. "I haven't worn one of my wigs in a very long time."

"Better you don't," I said. "It might bring back unpleasant memories. I take it Jack is there. Ty, too?"

"They're both here. We're going to have a family dinner together, and we've rented a movie—one of Ty's favorites, *The Natural*. Jess, I'll save some dinner for you. Pork chops. Is that all right?"

"One of my favorites," I said, "but you don't have to do that. I'm at a restaurant. I may as well have something to eat here."

I was glad to be out of the house for the evening so the Duffys could enjoy a family meal together. As much as I hoped I was a comfort to Meg and Jack during this difficult period, I was also certain that my presence had to have been intrusive at times, especially for Ty.

"You enjoy your evening, Meg," I said.

"We will," she said, "and don't you dare call a cab to come home. It'll cost you a fortune. Call Jack. He'll be more than happy to pick you up."

"I appreciate the offer," I said. "I think I'll just settle in and see what unfolds."

"You take care," she said.

"Don't worry about me," I said. "I'll be in touch later."

My vantage point from the bar gave me a view of not only the dining room, but a portion of the parking lot as well, which I could see through a large plate-glass window. I'd just concluded my conversation with Meg when a black Subaru pulled into the parking lot with four young men in it, two in the front and two in back. I lifted my sunglasses to see better and saw Carter seated in the passenger seat. I returned the glasses to the bridge of my nose and turned away slightly. As Ty's best friend, Carter was the one player I feared might recognize me. Two more cars with team members entered the parking lot and their occupants got out. Moments later, a silver Jaguar pulled up to two of the boys. The driver's-side window went down and there was an exchange of words. It was H.B. I assumed the older woman in the passenger seat was his wife. He said something to Carter, and I had the feeling it wasn't pleasant. The conversation was brief. The window was rolled back up, and the car circled the lot and ended up pulling into a handicapped spot directly in front of the front door. It didn't seem to me that H.B. was handicapped, but he was certainly arrogant. He strode into the restaurant a few paces in front of his wife, and they were followed by the team's manager, Buddy Washington. His wife wasn't with him, and I assumed she was too ill to attend.

Outside, one of the players who'd been in the car with Carter put his arm over Carter's shoulder and walked him into the restaurant's foyer. But instead of both of them entering the dining room, Carter separated from his teammate and, to my chagrin, came into the bar, where he slumped at a seat several tables from one that two young women had taken a few minutes earlier, directly to my left.

I kept my back to him but watched his actions in the mirror. A waitress took his order for coffee and left him alone, brooding it seemed, an unhappy young man. At the same time, the two young women recognized him and started talking just loud enough for me to hear.

"He's so cute," I heard one say.

"I know who he is," said the other. "He was on the cover of *Mesa Magazine* last month, the issue that featured the Rattlers players."

"He reminds me of Derek Jeter," her friend said.

"He's such a hunk. The article said that his best friend on the team is Ty Ramos, who killed Junior Bennett."

That Carter was a handsome young man was beyond debate. His dark complexion, sandy-colored hair on the longish side—for a baseball player anyway—and piercing blue eyes turned plenty of female heads, I was sure. He was dressed this night in a gray pin-striped suit that seemed molded to his sculptured body, and a mauve tie. He looked like an ad straight out of a men's fashion magazine.

The two young women finished their drinks and left, making eye contact with Carter on their way out.

I hoped he would leave, too, and join his teammates in the next room. Why wasn't he doing that? I wondered. Then, to my disbelief, he got up from the table, came to the bar, and took a stool one away from mine. I barely breathed. I thought about leaving, but was afraid any movement would draw attention to myself. As it was, he seemed totally disinterested.

"Hey man, it's Carter. How you doing?"

Should I turn? Was he talking to me?

"Get this. I was just at Junior's service. Not as many people showed up as I thought."

He'd dialed someone on his cell phone. It was one of those rare times when I didn't mind listening to someone's cell phone conversation in a public space.

"Anyway," he continued, "we all came over to Patsy's for dinner on H.B. Old Moneybags was actually going to spring for the meal. I bummed a ride off of Wilson because the cops still have my car. That's another story. So, we get here to the parking lot and we're all walking toward the restaurant when H.B. pulls up in his big fat Jaguar, stops the car, rolls down the window, and while puffing on one of his stogies calls Wilson and me over. So we go to the window and H.B. starts yakking at us, you know, like he always does when he's mad. Then he rolls up his window, drives off, and parks in a handicapped spot. Just like him, right? You know what he said to me?"

He paused to allow whoever was on the other end to guess.

"He tells me that he doesn't want me at the dinner because his son didn't like me."

He waited for this to sink in.

"Hey, Ty, of course it's because you're my closest friend on the team. Can you believe that? He actually told me that I couldn't go into the restaurant to have a dinner that he was paying for."

Now I knew who he was talking to.

"No, Ty, I'm not kidding. I wouldn't make this stuff up." He laughed. "H.B.'s always gotta run the show, even after his kid is killed."

Ty evidently said something, because Carter stopped talking for a moment.

"Yeah," Carter said, "Buddy's here. But he's in your corner, Ty. I know he is. And most of the guys are, too. Believe me, it's just a matter of time before the truth comes out. Where am I? I'm in the bar at Patsy's. I'm stuck here because Wilson's my ride, and I'm not about to spring for one of those expensive cabs. You can't come out, right? It would be great if just the two of us could sit here and pop a few and have H.B. see us together."

Another pause.

"Man, that's not fair. How long you gotta be under house arrest? Can I visit you? Okay, good. To-morrow afternoon. Yeah, lunchtime is good. Your mom's a good cook. I was looking forward to a big plate of Patsy's veal parm and pasta tonight, but I'm not picking up the tab myself. All right, man. Yeah, I'll let you know what I find out. Yeah, all right, buddy. You take care. Call me if you need me. I'm sticking with you through this. Remember that."

I imagined that Carter's phone call made Ty's

night. Carter was a very likable and mature young man for his age. He seemed to know when to do the right thing, and I liked to think of Ty that way, too. No wonder they were close friends.

"Excuse me, ma'am," Carter asked.

This can't be happening.

"Yes," I said, not turning. He must have thought I was being rude.

"Ma'am, are you done reading that paper?" I'd placed the paper on the bar in front of me.

"Why, yes," I said, in a disguised voice, one or two octaves lower than my usual one.

And then I decided to surrender. I handed him the paper, turned to face him, removed the sunglasses, and said, "Hi, Carter. Jessica Fletcher."

"Mrs. Fletcher? I didn't recognize you with—" Surprise was written all over his face.

"It's the wig," I said. "I decided to—I decided to change my hair color for the evening, but I'm sure I'll go back to the old one tomorrow."

"Will you be staying in Mesa long?" he asked.

"Good question, Carter. I'm not really sure."

"Not much of a vacation for you, I guess."

"No, not really, but I'm glad I'm here to help Ty and the Duffys. How are you holding up, Carter?"

"Okay, I guess. It's hard. You know, Ty's my best friend. The team is in there eating. The memorial service was earlier. It was sad about Junior, but I also hated listening to the things people were saying about Ty. Especially H.B. He even said something when he spoke to the crowd. Kind of a eulogy, I guess."

"What did he say?"

"Don't tell Ty, 'cause it'd kill him," Carter said. "H.B. said that the motive for his son's murder was jealous rage. He didn't mention Ty by name, but we all knew who he meant. Most of us know the real story, that it was Junior who was the jealous one, and so was H.B. Ty wasn't jealous of Junior. Yeah, he wanted more playing time, but he was the one with the big-time agent chasing him and with the best chance of getting called up to the Big Show. Of course, I'll be next," he said with a rueful laugh.

"Why aren't you inside eating with the team?" I asked, although I knew the answer from having eavesdropped on the call he'd made to Ty.

"H.B. didn't want me there. I came in Wilson's car, so now I'm stuck until they're done eating. Oh, well."

"You must be hungry, Carter," I said.

"A little," he admitted politely.

"Carter," I said, "I haven't eaten and don't have any plans. Would you be my guest for dinner?"

He smiled and said, "Really? Yes, that'd be great, Mrs. Fletcher."

"Terrific," I said, meaning it. Carter needed a mother figure at that moment, and I enjoy a surrogate son every once in a while.

Chapter Eleven

A gentle breeze shifted the tepid desert air, aided by a pair of portable air coolers, which blew out steady streams of mist, not quite enough to simulate an air conditioner but sufficient to move the thermometer down a notch and dull the heat. It was not the best weather for eating al fresco, but since the dining room inside was closed to us, Carter and I had agreed to take a table in the restaurant's patio and garden. Our hostess had apologized for the inconvenience. A private party, she said, had taken over the inside of the restaurant for the evening. We were lucky there was any table available. As it turned out, we were the only ones seated outside.

Carter took off his jacket and hung it from the back of the chair. He loosened his tie and rolled up his sleeves.

The waitress arrived and handed each of us a leather-bound menu. "Good evening, folks. I'm Florence," she said. "Can I get you something to drink?"

Carter wasted no time ordering an iced tea.

"Make that two." I put down the menu. "Isn't this a pretty place," I said when the waitress had gone.

The patio, paved with yellow and rust-colored Saltillo tiles, was bordered by several saguaro cacti, the waxy white bloom of which is the Arizona state flower. We were also shielded from the parking lot by rows of tall bushes. Red-and-white-checkered tablecloths draped the wire tables, and the seat cushions were covered in matching material. A vase with a single rose was placed on each table, as well as a votive candle that hadn't been lit yet.

The real beauty of the patio, though, wasn't its decor, but its location. It sat well off the main dining room of the restaurant, and we had been directed to a separate side entrance to reach it.

I was surprised to see how relaxed Carter was—or at least how calm he appeared to be. He smiled easily and his eyes didn't dart about but stayed focused on the table and immediate surroundings. Conscious of my scrutiny, he said, "You probably think I'd rather be inside at the team dinner, but I'm way happier sitting out here with you."

My expression must have indicated skepticism, because he continued, "I tried to offer my sympathies to H.B. the other day, and he turned away from me. If I was in there, he'd just make my life miserable. Ty and I were both hoping to be traded. But Mr. Bennett, he likes to keep around the people he doesn't like—just to torture them."

"Isn't that a little harsh?" I asked.

"It sounds that way now, being that he just lost his son and all. And I feel bad for him about that. But I've seen him do it and have been the victim of it, too. So had Junior, for that matter."

Our waitress didn't waste any time bringing our iced teas, along with a basket of warm garlic bread.

"Nice out here. And you got the whole patio to yourselves. Still too hot for most folks, but that'll change soon. We hope, anyway," she said, laughing. "But it's peaceful out here, isn't it?"

"Lovely," I said.

"Actually, tonight it's just as quiet inside," she continued. "That baseball team, the Rattlers, is in there with the father of the kid who was killed. He owns the team. The mood is very somber. Very sad, really. Anyway, ready to place your orders?"

Carter and I stole a glance. Florence nodded at me, poised to take my order. "Carter, you go first," I said. "I need another moment." I still hadn't made my way through the lengthy menu, which read like a book. But I could tell that Carter was famished, and I didn't want to send the waitress away to have to come back later.

"Okay, Mrs. Fletcher, if you insist." He smiled. "I'll have the veal parmigiana with pasta on the side, please."

The waitress then turned to me and said, "If you're not sure what to order, I can recommend the pasta primavera. It's light with just the right amount of garlic to give it a nice kick."

"Sold," I said, closing the menu. "Actually that was one of the dishes I was contemplating."

"Let's order a couple of appetizers," I said to Carter. I handed Florence my menu. "Maybe you can recommend one of the house specialties," I said.

"Sure," she said. "I highly recommend the antipasto for two: hot peppers, pepperoni, marinated artichokes and mushrooms, and Patsy's famous homemade mozzarella. Never had an order sent back. Not once and I've been here twenty-five years."

Carter smiled and gave a thumbs-up to her recommendation. "I love antipasto," he said.

Our waitress had a laissez-faire manner about her, yet she was extremely efficient. Even if she hadn't told us she'd been working there twenty-five years, it was obvious that she was nearing fifty. She struck me as the kind of woman who had a few good stories in her, and for a minute I indulged my habit of imagining the life of a stranger. So often, I used these chance encounters in a book if I needed to create a special character. Our waitress, Florence, would make a good one. Her face had a hard expression thanks to a ruddy complexion and extremely parched skin. Probably a smoker, I thought. Then again, the dry desert air will do that, too. Her auburn hair was brassy and didn't have any sheen, which spoke volumes about the do-it-yourself hair dye kits she'd undoubtedly used over the decades.

My friend Loretta Spiegel, who owns the beauty shop in Cabot Cove that I patronize, used to point out "bad dye jobs" of women who walked past the large picture window in the front of her shop, sometimes in a voice loud enough to be heard outside.

Last year, she brought in a top-notch hairdresser, Christina Estler, a specialist in color, and allowed her to set up in a section of the shop. Christina had owned a salon in New York's SoHo district, only to give up the fast track to retreat to Cabot Cove, to the benefit of the local ladies like myself. She's become a regular fixture at Mara's Luncheonette. We kid her that she isn't in New York anymore, but her fees give the impression that she is. She just laughs and doesn't budge her price list by a cent.

I wasn't quite as relaxed as Carter, and for a moment second-guessed my decision to come to Patsy's for dinner. Not only were the team and H.B. inside, but I'd come with a player who was asked not to participate. I rationalized that it wasn't fair of H.B. to do that and I felt bad for Carter. Then, *if you need excuses,* I told myself, *you've had your fill of Southwestern cuisine; some good Italian food sounded like a treat.*

"Too bad Ty couldn't have come with us," said Carter. "He loves this place."

Another reason we shouldn't have come here to eat, I thought, reminding myself not to tell Ty and thinking about asking Carter to do the same. Then again, if we were to be spotted by one of the players, or H.B. himself, Ty would very likely find out. Given the intrusiveness of the press, it could even end up front-page news.

The antipasto arrived at the table and looked to be as good as promised. The waitress set it in the middle of the table, but I pushed it toward Carter and encouraged him to dig in first.

He took a generous helping, but there was plenty to go around. I filled my plate, took a bite of the warm, buttery mozzarella, and savored it.

"Carter, do you have any hunches about who might have killed Junior?"

Carter had his fork halfway to his mouth, but he put it down before he spoke. "Boy, Mrs. Fletcher, you sure know how to start a conversation."

"I could apologize," I said, "but I must admit it was on my mind when I invited you to dinner. And since I have you as a captive audience, so to speak, I thought I'd take advantage of your insider's perspective."

"Since you're buying, I can't complain too much," he said, taking a quick bite. He waited until he finished chewing before saying, "I've given it a lot of thought, too. I don't know for certain who killed Junior, but I do know that it wasn't Ty. First, he isn't the type. He used to take Junior's crap all the time, and almost never responded."

"All that abuse could have built up quite a bit of resentment," I said. "Sometimes, it takes just a small trigger to make people explode."

"It's just not like Ramos."

"Remember, he wasn't his usual self. He was drunk. People often behave in a way they never would if they were sober."

"Listen, Mrs. Fletcher, if you say I said it, I'll deny it to the sky. But this wasn't the first time Ty got drunk. It doesn't happen often, but I'll just say it's not the first time. I've seen him drunk and I've seen him sober. He's the same guy. He might scuffle with you, but he'd never kill someone."

"It could have been an accident."

"I don't see how it was an accident when Ty told me that Junior was killed with an aluminum bat. Ty hasn't had an aluminum bat since I've known him here. Second, there are other guys on the team, Muscarel and Oliveri, for two, who would have more motives than Ty to do it. Muscarel's father is crazy, and while Musky isn't as bad as his dad, he's got a temper. And, between you and me, Mrs. Fletcher, Oliveri's a bit of a psycho, so he's unpredictable."

"Really?" I asked, with an inflection in my voice that indicated I wasn't averse to learning more about it.

"Yeah, but he has an alibi."

"Carter, I know the minor leagues monitor players through drug testing like the majors do," I said.

"Probably worse," he laughed. "But there's always someone who knows how to hide it."

"Is it prevalent?" I asked.

He shrugged. "Not street drugs, like cocaine or marijuana—they'll show up in your pee and you're out—but steroids are always a factor in ball. Some of these guys—they want to get called up so badly, they might risk it. That's one of the reasons I like Ty," he continued. "Ty and I have both already seen firsthand what drugs do to a person, a family. There's no way either one of us would mess around with anything like that."

"Carter, the police said they found Ty in your car, intoxicated."

"Yeah, I know. They questioned me for a long

time. And they probably will again. My lawyer told me that."

"They said by the time they got there, you were gone."

"Of course I was gone. When I left, Ty was in my car, out cold—with a newspaper on the floor so if he threw up, he wouldn't ruin the carpet—and Junior was staggering around cursing. I didn't need to stick around for either scene. Besides, I wasn't too sober myself. I got a ride home. My lawyer says my time is accounted for."

"Do you like your lawyer?" I asked.

"He's okay. Very *lawyery*," he said with a smile. "He's a friend of Ty's lawyer. Pierce hooked us up. The cops didn't take blood samples from me, but probably will, my lawyer said. In the meantime, he told me to just keep a low profile and go through with my day as I normally would."

"So, I'm assuming the police asked how it was possible that Ty was in your car if he doesn't remember you putting him there?"

"Yes, they did. And they didn't like my answer. I said I had no idea why Ty doesn't remember. They told me to think about it and let them know when I came up with a *better* answer. That really bugged my lawyer." He shook his head. "You know, the whole thing is a mess. I haven't been sleeping well," he said. "I don't know how we got into this predicament. I replay that night over and over in my head."

"When you got to the Crazy Coyote, was Ty already there?"

"I was there first," said Carter. "Ty stopped for some pizza. I went to get the guys some drinks. We were sitting with some babes at a couple of tables in the back. Ty and me, we weren't at the same table, so we didn't really talk. Then he bought a round. I was chatting up a girl at the bar when the whole thing with Junior blew up."

"Carter, I have a question, and I'm not asking you to betray the friendship the two of you have. Close friendships like yours are built on trust. But I'm asking you to try to find a way to help exonerate Ty."

Carter had stuffed an ambitious forkful of antipasto into his mouth and chewed and grinned and held up a finger to tell me he would answer as soon as he was done.

"Delicious, isn't it?" I asked. He nodded vigorously, still chewing. We both chuckled.

"Okay, shoot, Mrs. Fletcher."

"Well, it's common knowledge, at least to family and close friends, that Ty was involved with a gang when he was younger. And drugs are a part of the gang culture. I'm also aware that that's all behind Ty and he is lawabiding and lives a responsible life. But my question is this: Is there anyone from his past, from the gang or the old neighborhood, anyone still in his life in some capacity—whether it's to call and say 'hi' or to come to see him play, or, worse, to try to get him involved in the gang again? I don't have experience with the world of gangs, but I know how insidious it can be and I thought perhaps—"

"Mrs. Fletcher, with all due respect, I want Ty exonerated just as badly as you do—all of us who care for him and *believe* him do—but I think that is a question only Ty can answer, and that he would have no problem answering. I just don't feel it's my place."

"Of course. I respect that," I said. "I just didn't want to burden Ty with these kinds of questions." What I didn't say was that I also thought Ty's lawyer would prefer that I not get too involved, given the investigative nature of the case. I also wanted Ty to think of me as a shoulder to cry on, rather than another person peppering him with questions.

"You're an honorable young man," I said, sliding a piece of prosciutto over onto my plate. "Ty is very lucky to have a friend like you."

"He's a good guy. I don't think you have to worry about asking him questions, because he thinks of you as a friend," Carter said. "Ask him that question. I really think you should. You might be surprised at the answer."

"Thanks, Carter. I think I will."

"Mrs. Fletcher, there is one thing that I can tell you that Ty won't, something you should know."

"What's that?"

"Well, I don't think he'd be upset if I told you this. In fact, I think he'd appreciate it. But, still, he shouldn't know that I told you."

"All right," I said.

"Ty's not sure Judge Duffy believes him. He thinks that even though he didn't do the murder, he's letting the judge down just by getting arrested again. He hasn't gotten into any trouble since the judge and

Mrs. Duffy took him in. Till now. And he's really upset about that, and worried they'll give up on him."

"I imagine that would be very upsetting for him," I said. "However, I've known Jack Duffy a long time, and I do think that he believes that Ty is innocent. He's upset himself, and perhaps disappointed that Ty was breaking the law by buying drinks when he knew he shouldn't. But more important, I know he loves Ty and will stand behind him through whatever happens. I'm glad you told me this though, Carter. I'll try to help them past this hump. I'll let Jack know he needs to reassure Ty that he still believes in him."

"Thanks, Mrs. Fletcher."

We'd finished the appetizer and our waitress expeditiously took away our plates to deliver our steaming hot entrées. I laughed when I saw the size of the portions. "This is enormous," I said. "It's lucky that I'm hungry tonight." It smelled wonderful.

Carter grinned from ear to ear.

"*Bon áppetit*, Mrs. Fletcher," he said, devoid of even a hint of a French accent.

"We're eating Italian food, Carter. *Buon appetito*," I said.

"Whatever."

The pasta primavera was as good as its aroma. We both concentrated on our food, speaking little, and not about the murder.

"This is delicious," I said to Carter. "Are you enjoying your dish?" I glanced up at him. "What's the matter?"

Carter had slumped down in his seat, ducking his head and pretending to cover his face with a napkin. "Oh no," he groaned.

"What is it?" I heard people speaking, then saw a group of young people being shown to a table on the patio.

"Who is it, Carter?" I asked under my breath.

"Carter!" a high-pitched voice said. "Carter, why aren't you inside with the rest of the team?"

"This guy has no couth," said Carter as one of the guys walked toward us. He was wearing a rumpled denim jacket over a Hawaiian shirt.

"Hey, Lou," replied Carter unenthusiastically.

"They wouldn't let us inside, but why are you out here?" he asked.

"They wouldn't let you inside?" Carter said, chuckling. "Wonder why," he said sarcastically.

"Very funny, Carter," said Lou. "They said it was a private dinner just for the team and managers and coaches. But heck, you're one of the players. Or were you traded or something?"

"Nope. I'm still a Rattler," said Carter.

There was a long pause. Then Carter realized Lou was waiting for something. He waved toward me. "Lou, this is Ms., um, Ms. Flocker," he said, stumbling over "Flocker." He'd obviously felt it necessary to introduce me out of politeness but realized in midsentence that I was wearing a disguise. "She's my aunt," he said, smiling, almost giving way to a laugh.

Lou was about five feet, five inches tall, maybe a bit taller if he'd had better posture. His shoulder-length black hair badly needed to be shampooed, and he wore a pair of the thickest glasses I'd ever seen. Ty had described Lou as a "dweeb." He wasn't being kind, but I understood the reference.

"You didn't tell her who I am, Carter." Lou smiled at me. "I'm the president of the Rattlers Fan Club," he said, wearing pride on his sleeve.

"Yup. That's who he is."

"To tell you the truth, I was a little disappointed not being able to sit with the team," Lou continued. "I mean, after all, I am the *president* of the fan club and responsible in part for their success. A team without fans will never win. We have the best fan club in the minor leagues—anywhere in the country." He was on a roll. "Look at the thousands who showed up tonight for Junior's service."

"No way," said Carter. "I don't know where you were, but I was there and the stadium was practically empty, a couple of hundred people at most."

"Yeah, but fans came from all over Arizona—and even farther. One guy told me he drove from L.A. to pay his respects. Another fan came from San Diego. Hard to believe, I know. Junior had a lot of fans. Way more than Ramos. I should know, I'm the president."

"Yes, you are," Carter said.

"Have you spoken to Ty?" Lou asked.

Carter paused. "Look, Lou, my aunt and I are having dinner and . . ."

"All right, all right. Just a question. Weird you're out here and not in with the team. Guess it's because you and Ty are tight. And they found Ty in your car and of course they think you're involved. That's just what I heard. As the president of your fan club, I feel I have a responsibility to tell you that I think they're watching your every move. That's probably what those guys in the parking lot were doing. They must know you're in here, Carter. There are about four guys, big guys, in a sedan out there."

"Lou, if you'll excuse us while we finish eating, perhaps you can talk to Carter later," I said.

"Okay, sure," said Lou. "We're sitting over there. Me and a couple of the fans."

"Great. Thanks," Carter said, barely civil.

Lou left our table, but instead of going to his table, he went to a door between the main dining room and patio and opened it and then, much to my relief, closed it. I was afraid he was going to go in and report to the team that Carter was here.

"Lou," Carter said loudly, too loud for the setting we were in. Lou was only too happy to come back to our table.

"Lou, man, look, do me a favor, okay?"

"You got it, Carter."

"Don't tell the team I'm here. Okay, dude?"

"You got it, Carter," he repeated. "I was just looking to see if they were still there."

Lou was an eager-to-please fellow, but I didn't trust him. He'd be just as eager to "yes" the next guy.

"Are they still there?" I asked.

"Yes, ma'am," said Lou.

He crossed his arms and stood at our table's edge.

"Okay, Lou, go order your food," said Carter. "Talk to you later."

"Okay," said Lou. "I'll be right over there if you need me."

"Right." Carter smirked and shook his head. "Can you believe this guy?" he asked me. "If you created a character like him in one of your books, your publisher would probably send it back with a note telling you this guy wasn't believable."

We both laughed.

"Uh-oh," said Carter. He was looking beyond me and toward the fence that surrounded the patio. "H.B.'s out there smoking a cigar."

"Did he see you?" I asked.

"I don't think so. I hope not."

"Switch seats with me," I said.

We hurriedly exchanged places as if we were playing musical chairs and the song was about to stop. Now Carter's back was toward the fence and H.B. couldn't see his face if he turned our way. I didn't think the team owner would recognize me in my wig, even if he happened to notice the tables on the patio. I had a good view of his profile. He dragged slowly on his cigar and spoke into his cell phone. Just then, another man appeared and went up to him.

"Carter, turn around quickly and tell me who that gentleman is with H.B." I said.

Carter took a swift glance over his shoulder. "I don't know. I don't think I've ever seen him before."

I heard the strains of "Stompin' at the Savoy," and

realized my cell phone was ringing. The sound caused Lou and those seated with him to look our way. I grabbed my bag and scrambled to retrieve the call, hoping the ringing didn't attract the attention of H.B.

"Hello," I said practically from beneath the table. I hadn't taken the time to glance at caller ID before answering the phone.

"Mrs. Fletcher, hello. This is Sheriff Hualga. Sorry to be calling you on your cell phone. Mort gave me your number."

"I don't mind at all. What can I do for you?"

"Well, I'd like to talk to you. In private. Without the Duffys, if you're willing."

"Certainly," I said. "May I assume this is in reference to the case?"

"Yes, ma'am, it is." The sheriff's tone was businesslike. "I know you don't have a car," he said. "I'll pick you up. Where are you now?"

"Now is not a good time, I'm afraid. Can it wait until tomorrow?"

"It'll have to, I guess," he said. "How about I send someone for you around nine tomorrow morning?"

"The time is fine, but you know I'm staying with the Duffys. You mentioned you want my visit with you to be confidential. Surely they'd know if you picked me up at their house."

"Do you have another suggestion?"

"Actually, I do. I take an early-morning walk around the neighborhood. It's lovely. There is a lake. Are you familiar with it? It's on Hedgehog Court, down at the end."

"Hedgehog Lake. Around nine fifteen then."

"I'll make sure to be there," I said. I hoped Meg or Jack wouldn't ask to accompany me on my walk. They hadn't so far. But if they did, I'd have to make up some excuse, or insist that I needed to be alone.

"Where will we be going?"

"To headquarters," he said.

"Are you bringing me in for questioning?" I asked, only half kidding.

"I'll see you tomorrow."

That won't give me a good night's sleep, I thought.

Chapter Twelve

It was a beautiful, sun-kissed morning in Arizona, with temperatures in the eighties, not too hot yet for the bicyclists and joggers I passed while walking from the Duffy home to Hedgehog Lake. The properties in this upscale Mesa neighborhood were, for the most part, meticulously cared for, with manicured lawns and neatly designed desert rock gardens, so different from the homes back in Maine with their scrubby pines and leafy landscapes. I honestly preferred the more unkempt look of New England, and I especially loved the change of seasons we experience there. Of course, dealing with the bitterly cold and snowy Maine winters was another matter. But I don't think I could ever be satisfied living in what was basically a constant climate without the pleasure of anticipating changes to come.

I would have enjoyed a leisurely stroll around the lake that morning, but there wasn't time for it. Sheriff Hualga was scheduled to meet me in fifteen minutes to take me to his office at Mesa's police head-quarters. I'd intended to leave the house earlier to get in at least one lap around the lake before rendezvousing with the sheriff, but Meg and Jack were late departing for an appointment they'd scheduled with their lawyer, David Pierce, in Phoenix. Ty was still asleep when I left.

As pleasant as Sheriff Hualga was, I was well aware of my place in his investigation. I'd been in this situation too many times before, and an outsider injected into a local police matter didn't always sit well with the authorities. Law enforcement professionals are usually extremely protective of their turf, and battles are frequent and sometimes ugly. Having someone like me, a writer of murder mysteries, sticking her nose into official police matters was dicey at best. So far Hualga seemed receptive. But I kept reminding myself to toe the line and not overreach. "Jessica," I whispered to myself under my breath, "you are not the investigator in this case. Know who your audience is." I smiled and shook my head. I'd been giving myself more frequent pep talks of late and wondered if that was a sign of senility or of mature wisdom.

As I continued walking toward the lake, I heard a car approach from behind and slow down. I turned as it came to a stop beside me.

"Hello, Mrs. Fletcher."

It was Sylvester Cole, driving a maroon convertible, so new I could practically smell the leather seats from where I was standing. The car's top was down and Cole looked every bit the movie star from a Hollywood publicity poster. That he was a handsome man was beyond debate, and I was sure his good looks had charmed him into—and out of—many a situation.

"Good morning, Sylvester," I said, my smile reserved. I was not pleased to see him, since the sheriff was due to pick me up in a matter of minutes and we'd deliberately chosen this spot to avoid speculation.

"Beautiful day, isn't it?" he said, flashing his million-dollar smile.

"Absolutely," I said. "It's lovely." I stole a look at my watch, not so much to check the time as to drop a subtle hint to Cole that I had other things to do than engage in a pleasant chat.

He took the hint. "Well, I won't hold you up," he said. "Better get your walk in before it gets too warm. And believe me, things heat up fast around here."

"They certainly seem to," I said with a laugh. I looked back up the road. No sign of the sheriff.

I assumed that was the end of our conversation. But he didn't drive away, and I felt obligated to say something.

"What brings you here this morning?" I asked. "Visiting the Duffys?"

"I'm dropping off some papers for the judge," he answered. "Didn't see Jack's car in the driveway, so thought I'd take a little ride down by the lake and shoot back there later."

I almost told him why Jack and Meg had left, but

thought better of it. Their meeting with the attorney was their private business, and it wasn't my place to explain where they'd gone. "Maybe I'll see you later at the house," I offered.

"Yeah, maybe," he said. "Enjoy your walk, Mrs. Fletcher."

He pulled into a driveway ahead of me, backed out, and headed up the street toward the Duffys'. He waved as he passed, and I returned it as I resumed walking at a good clip. My watch indicated it was almost nine and I didn't want to be late.

The lake shimmered in the early-morning sun ahead of me. So did the reflection off the windshield of a dark-colored car. Could that be Sheriff Hualga driving an unmarked police vehicle? I wondered. I'd been looking for an official police car, which represented sheer assumption on my part. Considering that our meeting was somewhat clandestine, it only made sense for him to drive a vehicle without markings. It was also possible that he'd dispatched someone from his department to pick me up.

As I neared the car I saw that the driver was a female. She rolled down the window and motioned for me to come to her. As I approached, I saw that there was a second person with her in the passenger's seat. I'd almost reached the car when something quickly darted in front of me, causing me to stop short and gasp in surprise. It was a small animal with a back full of what looked like quills, and its face was not unlike those of the raccoons that occasionally attack my garbage pails back home. "What in heaven's name—?"

The woman in the driver's seat and the man on the passenger side laughed loudly. I recognized one of the laughs, and a moment later saw that the man was Sheriff Hualga. He leaned toward the driver's window and said, "Don't worry, Mrs. Fletcher. That's only someone's pet hedgehog. He won't hurt you."

I smiled nervously.

Hualga got out and came around to my side of the car.

"Well, I do know I'm on Hedgehog Court," I said, "but I thought it was just a name." I'd never seen a live hedgehog before, but had always enjoyed a wonderful book by the British author and illustrator Beatrix Potter, *The Tale of Mrs. Tiggy-Winkle*, in which the main character, a hedgehog, was a matronly washerwoman.

"Actually, an Arizona hedgehog is a cactus," the sheriff said, opening the car door for me. "That's probably what the street is named for. That little guy must have escaped his cage. We'll call the animal-control people to take care of him."

I got into the car and Hualga introduced me to the woman. "This is Detective Raff, Mrs. Fletcher. She's working undercover on the Junior Bennett case, along with almost everyone else on the force."

Detective Raff turned and extended her hand.

"Pleased to meet you," I said, shaking it.

Detective Raff appeared to be about forty years old. She wore minimal makeup, just a bit of lipstick, and her brown hair was wrapped tight in a bun. She wasn't in uniform and certainly didn't look the part

of a police detective, which, of course, is the idea behind undercover police work.

The sheriff was also not in uniform this morning,
but the car was "in uniform"; unmarked police cars
used by undercover cops always seem to be midnight
blue sedans. At least that's been my experience.

We pulled away and headed back toward Jack and
Meg's home. As we approached it, I saw that Cole's
car sat in the driveway.

"Do you know whose car that is?" Hualga asked.

"Yes," I said. "It's Sylvester Cole's."

"Cole, huh?" the sheriff responded. He turned to
Detective Raff and said, "Ramos's agent."

The drive to the sheriff's office was quiet for the
most part, with the exception of the police radio,
which chimed in from time to time. I took out a pad
of paper and a pen and scribbled notes, hoping that
my visit this day would shed light on: "autopsy report," "fingerprints," "aluminum bat."

As we approached the driveway leading to police
headquarters, two satellite TV trucks came into view.
I didn't need my face plastered all over the five
o'clock news, and was thankful when Raff steered
away from them and pulled up behind the building
into a private area, where we entered through a back
door.

The mood inside the busy station house was pleasantly positive and upbeat, almost festive, a far cry
from most police headquarters I've experienced.
Sheriff Hualga was certainly an affable leader. As we
snaked through winding corridors toward his office,

he high-fived clerks and other officers, asking, "How's it going today?" and saying, "You're looking good this morning."

We arrived at his office, at the end of a narrow hallway. He pulled up a chair for me and offered to get tea or coffee.

"Tea would be lovely, thank you."

"Tea it is," he said. "I'll be right back. I could use a cup of coffee myself. Make yourself at home."

Hualga's office reminded me of a quintessential bachelor's pad. Pictures hung crooked on the walls. A couple of crates overflowed with papers. On his desk was a picture of a teenage girl who I presumed was his daughter. There were several plaques on a chair that he evidently hadn't gotten around to hanging yet. Two Styrofoam cups, one lying on its side, sat atop his brown wooden desk. A plastic tray that resembled an in-box had a sign taped to it on which was written in black capital letters, EX TEMPORE. "Without preparation." Maybe he approached the business of policing with that philosophy, I thought. Next to his desk was a table with a computer and speakers on it, and next to that were several formidable metal file cabinets. Taped to the side of one of them was a photocopy of an eight-by-ten black-and-white photo. I got up to take a closer look.

"Hello, Mrs. Fletcher."

I turned to face Detective Raff in the doorway with her arms crossed. Did she think I was about to riffle through the files?

"Oh, hello, Detective," I said, startled. "I was getting a closer peek at this picture. I know his face, but I can't—"

"That's Jon Stewart," she said, "from Comedy Central's *Daily Show*. The sheriff is a huge fan."

"Of course," I said. "Yes, it's a funny show. Our sheriff back in Cabot Cove, Maine—that's where I live—is a big fan as well. I see it's made out to the sheriff."

"Yes," she said, entering the room and joining me by the file cabinets. "Mr. Stewart was here recently for some sort of promotional appearance, and the sheriff got to meet him. He's a sweetheart. The sheriff asked for a signed photograph and Mr. Stewart didn't hesitate to give him one."

"I'm glad to hear that," I said. "It's always heartening when a celebrity takes the time to accommodate his or her fans."

"You certainly fall into the category of celebrity," she said, taking a chair in a corner of the office as I returned to my seat.

"Oh, I hardly think so," I said, "but I do have some very loyal readers. Whenever I get to meet them in person—which I love to do—I try to go out of my way to show my appreciation. After all, without readers an author has nothing."

The sheriff interrupted our conversation as he returned carrying the tea and coffee. I was glad that Hualga wasn't one of those bosses who considered such chores beneath him.

I took a sip of my tea while Hualga searched through a pile of papers and folders on his desk.

There was a knock at the door.

"Come on in," Hualga said.

A clerk handed him an envelope. "This was just delivered," she said.

He opened the envelope and pulled out its contents. "Good," he said. "Junior Bennett's autopsy report." He scanned the first couple pages of the report. "Hey, Raff, look at this." She walked to his desk and read over his shoulder. He looked up at her and raised his eyebrows.

"Sorry to hold you up, Mrs. Fletcher," he said. "I've been anxious to get this."

"Please," I said. "I don't mind at all. I've spent enough time with Sheriff Metzger to know that when a much-anticipated autopsy report comes in, it takes precedence over anything else that may be going on."

"Appreciate your understanding," he said.

I waited silently until he'd concluded his reading of the report.

"Anything unexpected in it?" I asked, deliberately curbing my enthusiasm so as not to appear eager to read it.

"Nothing glaring," he said, picking it up to read it again.

"I assume the report indicates that Junior was indeed hit with a blunt instrument, consistent with the preliminary report?" I said.

"That's right," he replied. "The autopsy shows that Mr. Bennett's nose was broken and that his two front teeth and left incisor tooth were chipped. There was also a split lip. And a blow to the left side of his head."

I quickly considered what he'd just said. "Sheriff, the split lip, cracked teeth, and broken nose are consistent with being struck in the face by a fist. But it wouldn't be consistent with a blow to the left side of the head with a baseball bat, would it?"

"Hard to say," he responded. "It is interesting, though."

He carefully placed the autopsy report back into the envelope and was equally careful to place it out of my reach on his desk. He clasped his hands together, sat erect in his chair, and said, smiling, "Okay, Mrs. Fletcher. I'm really sorry to have kept you here so long. I want to ask you just a few questions. As you can imagine, this is a big case, with some important people involved. I'll be honest with you. While I need to question you as part of the investigation, I'm also hoping to tap some of your experience with murder. We have more than our share of auto theft here, but not many murders."

"I'm happy to help," I said, "although I must warn you that my 'experience,' as you term it, has usually been purely accidental, classic examples of being at the wrong place at the wrong time."

"Or at the right time," he said. "Your reputation precedes you, not only as a best-selling author but as a pretty successful amateur sleuth, too."

"I'll take your word for it," I said. "I'll do anything I can to help clear Ty."

"You're that certain he's innocent?" he asked.

"Yes."

"You can't be plainer than that. Okay, Mrs.

Fletcher, I have a problem. I know of Ty's troubled past, and unfortunately the rest of the nation now does, too. This is a sexy story that's all over the news. Problem is, Ty's past paints a picture of a troubled ballplayer who might have been experimenting with drugs, who was definitely associated with a gang in his younger years, and who maybe killed his teammate for money, drugs—"

"No," I said firmly. "I can't speak as to whether or not Ty ever used drugs when he was younger. I rather doubt it. But I definitely do not believe that he is involved with drugs now."

"How can you be so sure, Mrs. Fletcher?"

"If Ty were doing drugs, he wouldn't be the wonderful player that he is," I answered.

"I can name plenty of major-league players—good ones, too—who've been involved with drugs," he said.

"Are you a baseball fan, Sheriff?" I asked gently.

"Nope. Not my sport. Never got into it. Too slow."

"It's true, Sheriff, that a number of recently celebrated stories about major-league ballplayers and drugs have made the news. However, you should also know that the minor leagues have a very strict drug-monitoring policy. A player would have a very tough time surviving in the minor leagues if he was doing drugs—any sort of banned substances."

The sheriff sat back in his chair and crossed his legs. "Sounds like you're a big baseball fan, Mrs. Fletcher."

"Since coming to Mesa, I've been reminded of

how much I always enjoyed watching a baseball game. Ty and his promising career added an extra fillip to that. It's been a number of years since I attended a game as exciting as that championship the other night."

"Always exciting when a game, any game, is won in the final minutes. Tell me something. How do you come to know so much about the minor-league drug-monitoring policy?"

"There's no mystery to it," I said. "Earlier this summer I attended the wedding of a friend's daughter at the Otesaga Hotel in Cooperstown. I spent a long weekend there and took a tour of the Baseball Hall of Fame. During the tour, our guide spoke at length about the minor-league drug policy. Ironically, when I got back home, the local newspapers were filled with stories about a player on the Portland Sea Dogs, a Boston Red Sox farm team, who was suspended because he'd failed the drug test. It was a big deal because the boy was from the next town over from Cabot Cove, where I live."

"So you're a Red Sox fan, Mrs. Fletcher?"

"Perhaps if I followed baseball more closely, I would style myself a fan. But the Rattlers' game the other night was one of the few games I've attended in person, although I do recall seeing a local Little League game about fifteen or twenty years ago because the ten-year-old son of a friend was playing. I remember that I didn't enjoy it because the parents were more fiercely competitive than the youngsters."

"What a shame."

Do it now, Jessica, I thought to myself. *He's in your corner.*

"Sheriff, do you suppose I could take a peek at the police report? Perhaps there's something in it that I could—"

"I'm afraid not, Mrs. Fletcher. That's official police business, part of an ongoing investigation."

"I understand," I said.

"Look, Mrs. Fletcher, I can appreciate the predicament you're in. It's my understanding that you came to Mesa for a little R and R with your friends the Duffys. Right?"

"Right."

"And you're still here in Mesa, days after their son has been arrested for murder, not to vacation but to give the family support."

"It's true. My visit to your lovely state and city is no longer a vacation. I am now a friend to friends in need."

"I understand you were at the Biltmore Spa the other day with Meg Duffy."

His question took me by surprise, and I hesitated before answering. *How did he know that?*

"Yes, we were," I said.

"Was that the vacation part of your stay here, or the friend helping a friend in need?"

"Actually, a bit of both. When I arrived, the Duffys gave me a gift certificate for a day at the spa. A few days after Ty's arrest—when things had calmed down somewhat—and at the insistence of Meg and Jack, I went to the Biltmore to use the gift certificate for a little of that R and R you alluded to."

"And Meg Duffy also had a certificate?"

"No. That was my doing. I felt that Meg could use a massage, too, and offered to buy her a treatment."

"And that would be the friend helping a friend in need part, right?"

"I suppose so."

"Mrs. Fletcher, are you aware that several of the players work at the spa as personal trainers, and that H.B., Junior Bennett's father, is a frequent, almost daily, client?"

"I didn't know that before I arrived for my treatments, but I learned it when I was there."

"How did you learn it?"

"My masseuse told me," I answered.

"I ask this," he said, "because someone brought it to my attention and I found it curious that Mrs. Duffy was at the spa at a time like this."

I looked at him and waited for him to continue.

"A word to the wise, Mrs. Fletcher. There are lots of rumors flying around, lots of gossip if you will, lots of nasty accusations. How the family comports itself at this time is under scrutiny, maybe unfairly, but that's what happens."

He was right. Despite my good intentions, my efforts to help Meg through this difficult time may have backfired.

Hualga continued. "What little evidence we have points to Ty as not only having a motive for this murder but having opportunity. He's my prime suspect. There are no witnesses other than Ty's best friend to say Junior was still alive when Ty was sleeping off a bender in the car. That means his alibi is weak; it still places him on the scene at the Crazy Coyote that night, and that makes it difficult." He looked at me, took a deep breath, leaned over his desk, and said, "Between you and me, the police report isn't conclusive. The evidence is circumstantial. Also off the record, I'm not convinced the right man is under house arrest. I think our killer may still be out there."

"Excuse me?" I said.

"Here," he said, handing me a file folder. "Changed my mind. You take a look. But if anybody asks, I didn't give it to you."

He winked and leaned back in his chair.

I skimmed the report. Nothing jumped out as being strange. But then I got to item number five on page seven: "Footprints found at scene adjacent to the body (inconsistent with forensics)."

I continued to read, going as fast as I could for fear Hualga would change his mind and take it away from me. According to the report, the murder weapon, the aluminum bat, was found in "Dumpster number 7345, on the northwest corner of Thompson Stadium." No other details were given.

I handed him the police report and asked, "May I see the forensic report?"

The sheriff smiled. "I'm embarrassed to say that I've never read any of your novels. I intend to rectify that. I'll bet you're a real good mystery writer."

"I try to be. The problem is that while I'm supposed to be writing fiction, reality too often rears its ugly head."

He gingerly opened another folder and handed me a document stamped FORENSICS. "I can let you take a quick look," he said, "but I have to get going in a minute. Detective Raff will give you a lift home."

"I appreciate that," I said, knowing that meant I wouldn't have the report in my hands for very long. I wasn't sure why I was suddenly privy to all of his files and reports, but I was glad nonetheless.

"The only fingerprints found on the bat were Junior's?" I said.

"That's what it says."

I turned a page, looking for the details. There had been a single thumbprint on top, and some latent prints, inconclusive, beneath a blood smear on the head of the bat. The neck of the bat, where a batter would grip it, had been wiped down with a cloth; the forensics team had recovered white cotton fibers that had clung to the metal.

"We never found whatever the killer used to wipe off the prints," Hualga said.

"White cotton," I said. "That could be a T-shirt, and almost impossible to trace, unless you found the garment itself."

"We didn't, and we checked every Dumpster in the vicinity of the Coyote as well as Thompson Stadium. It wasn't Ramos's shirt. He was wearing blue."

I sat up pencil-straight in my chair, repositioned

my glasses, and scanned the paper à la Evelyn Wood searching for the word "footprint."

> *Myriad footprints found at scene. Appear to be made by sneaker-type shoes, sizes varying between 9 and 13. One set of prints found, not consistent with sneaker sole print.*

Behind the report was a set of police photographs of the crime scene, including close-ups of the footprints. I studied them carefully before returning the folder to Sheriff Hualga.

Chapter Thirteen

"Thank you for meeting with me like this," I said. "I really appreciate being able to talk with you about what happened that terrible night at the Crazy Coyote."

"Sure, Mrs. Fletcher," Ty's friend and teammate, Carter, said in his usual friendly tone. "Anything we can do to help Ty."

"The very best thing you can do is just tell me the truth. In other words, don't embellish the story because you feel it might make Ty look better."

"Just the facts, ma'am," said Carter in an attempt to emulate Jack Webb from *Dragnet*, the popular TV series of yesteryear.

Another of the players, Sam Bobley, slapped him on the arm and said, "You're too much, man."

I'd asked some of the players to meet me, with the promise of lunch. Actually, I'd asked Carter to arrange it. He'd called the Duffys to speak with Ty and I had answered the phone. Ty was in the shower and the Duffys weren't home. It was a spur-of-the-moment act on my part, asking Carter if he'd be willing to get some of the players together to meet with me. He readily agreed, and suggested we all meet at Burrito Heaven, an upscale fast-food eatery in Mesa.

It turned out to be not exactly heaven, but it was a good place for us to gather. A busy restaurant with a tin roof, the place had a noise level loud enough to buffer our conversations so that others wouldn't overhear. At the same time, we managed to secure a large booth in a corner of the spacious room that separated us somewhat from other diners. Carter ordered a burrito practically the size of the hedgehog that had dashed in front of me near Hedgehog Lake; I ordered a taco salad with spicy chicken.

Three players besides Carter had agreed to join me for lunch. There was "Speedster," or Sam Bobley, the smallest kid on the team (everything being relative, that made him about five-eleven). He was also the fastest, hence his nickname. Another kid, who was called "Murph," had come. His real name was Billy Murphy, and he was a catcher on the team, the huskiest of the players and the most reserved, at least at this juncture. Billy Nassani, the first baseman, was already familiar to me. He was one of the team's leading home-run hitters, and he had hit a beauty during the game I'd attended on that fateful day. Home-run hitters have a way of being remembered. Carter assured me that these were the smartest kids on the team and would be the most articulate about what had happened.

"Any other players joining us?" I asked Carter.

"Long said he might try to make it," Carter answered. "He had to work. Got one of those cushy personal trainer jobs at the Biltmore."

Steven Long. Lily's boyfriend, I thought. Interesting. I hoped he'd show up.

"Sam, why don't you begin by telling me your best recollection of what happened that night," I asked slowly and deliberately, not wanting anyone to feel rushed. I wanted them to process things fully and to think clearly.

"Where do I start?" he said. "Okay." He wiped his mouth, eliminating a small glob of sour cream and salsa. He inhaled deeply and then exhaled. "We were all hanging out at tables in the back, having a beer and tequila Jell-O shots. I went up to the bar. Well— I mean . . ." He looked quizzically at Carter.

"It's all right, man," Carter said. "The truth." He winked at me. Sam was obviously reticent about divulging that they'd been drinking, and I wondered if he, too, was underage.

"Anyway, next thing I know, there's all this commotion and everyone's running out the back door. There's Junior on the ground with blood pouring out of his nose and all over his face. I saw Ty there, too. He had some blood on his hands and was wiping them on his shirt. I remember that because I thought it was crazy. I mean, he had a nice shirt on." The boys laughed. Sam continued, "And then he tried to help Junior up off the ground, but Junior was shouting for him to get away, calling him dirty names and stuff.

Next thing I know, there's Carter helping Junior off the ground. I didn't see where Ty went. I went back inside. Most of us did. It was starting to rain. Besides, I didn't want to be involved if the cops came." Another furtive glance at Carter. "Half of us would have been nailed for underage drinking, so we wanted to keep a low profile. I mean, the cops come in there sometimes, but they know we're Rattlers and most of the time they let us off the hook. It's like we're famous or something." Sam looked at the others for approval. Carter nodded in agreement while the others looked ready to plead the Fifth against self-incrimination.

Among my many thoughts at the moment was the conviction that Sheriff Hualga wouldn't be too happy to hear about some of his officers turning a blind eye to underage drinking.

"So, you went inside," I said. "Did you see Junior come back in, or Ty?"

"Gee, no," Sam said. "I can't say that I did. I saw Carter come back in, though. I asked him what happened and where Ty and Junior went—" He looked at Carter.

"It's all right, man," Carter said encouragingly. "I have nothing to hide. Go ahead."

"And Carter told me that Ty punched Junior and that he was afraid Junior was going to get up and kill him, so Carter said he dragged Ty away and put him in his car. Carter said Ty wasn't feeling so great. Ty doesn't drink a lot. Maybe a beer or two, but we were doing shots that night, too."

"Ty said he was nauseous and felt groggy," Carter chimed in. "And I was really afraid that things between Junior and Ty would get worse, so I put Ty in my car. He sprawled on the backseat and was out, like he'd passed out or something. He was gone really fast."

"Carter, how do you think Junior's blood got on Ty's shirt?" I asked.

"He wiped his hands on his shirt to get the blood off his hands after he punched Junior," said Carter. "Just like Sam said."

"Yeah," interjected Sam. "I saw him do it."

"Sam, who do you think killed Junior?" I asked.

"I really don't know. I mean, I guess it's possible that Ty maybe woke up and saw Junior near the car or something and killed him then. I don't know. I know they hated each other, or at least Junior hated Ty. Maybe Ty didn't know what he was doing because he was, like, drugged or something."

"No way," said Murph. "There's no way Ty did this."

"Yeah, no way," said Carter. "Believe me. Ty was in no shape to kill anybody. He was out of it."

"The thing that struck me as weird that night," said Nassani, "was Junior's car."

"Huh?" asked Carter.

"He had his old man's brand-new car. Big bad green Mercedes convertible."

"Why was that weird?" I asked.

" 'Cause Junior was always complaining how selfish and cheap his dad was, how he never let Junior drive his cars or boats."

"That's right," Murph said. "And H.B. had just gotten that car, like, that morning because at dinner at Patsy's after Junior's service, I overheard him tell Buddy that he had picked it up from the dealer the morning of the championship game and never even had a chance to drive it."

"And I heard he's going to sell it now," Nassani continued, "because he just can't keep the car knowing that Junior had been the last one to drive it."

"You don't think maybe H.B. gave Junior the car as a gift to celebrate the team's victory?" I said.

"No way, Mrs. Fletcher," Murph said. "Junior would've been bragging if the car was his. He'd never let us forget it if he got a new car. I bet he just found it in the garage and took it. I can't imagine that H.B. let Junior take his Mercedes to the Coyote."

"He probably didn't even know," Carter suggested. "He would've have killed Junior if he did."

"Except he'd be a little late," said Murph with an inappropriate snicker.

My disapproving expression prompted him to say, "Sorry, Mrs. Fletcher."

"It's all right," I said. "Everyone is under a lot of strain over what happened."

There were nods all around the table.

"Ever see Junior use an aluminum bat?" I asked no one in particular.

"No, but that doesn't mean he didn't have one," said Nassani. "I have one. It's my lucky bat."

"But you can't use it in the games, right?" I said.

"Right," he said. "It's just, like, it's my rabbit's foot sort of."

"I don't have an aluminum bat," said Sam.

"Me neither," said Carter. "I left my aluminum bats from high school and Little League back home. I hope they're still there. My mom has a habit of holding yard sales and selling anything that isn't tied down." He chuckled.

"Has anyone seen Ty with an aluminum bat?" I asked.

"Nope," said Carter. The others shook their heads in agreement.

"Hey, wait a minute," Sam said. "Aluminum bat. I remember someone—who was it?—someone telling me that after the last game, some guy wanted the players to sign his aluminum bat."

"Yeah, I remember that," Murph said.

"He was a fan, right?"

"Uh-huh. It was that dweeb. The fan club dweeb."

The "dweeb" description seemed to be the general consensus.

"You met him, Mrs. Fletcher. Remember?" Carter said. "At Patsy's after Junior's service."

"You weren't at Patsy's, dude," said Sam.

"Oh, right. Not Patsy's," Carter said, shooting me a glance.

"Let's get back on track," I said. "Did anyone sign the aluminum bat?"

"No, and the guy was ticked off about it," Nassani recalled. "We were too busy celebrating. We told him—hey, I think I told him I'd sign it later, another time. I wonder if he was at the Crazy Coyote."

"Did any of you see him?" I asked. Ty had said he was there.

"Yeah, I did," Murph said.

"Me, too," said Sam.

"He always wants to hang out with the team," Carter added.

"Was he carrying the bat?"

"I didn't see it, but that doesn't mean it wasn't there."

"Did any of you see the bat at the bar?"

Denials all around.

"Anybody ever see H.B. with an aluminum bat? Do any of you suppose that he might have had an aluminum bat in his car?" I asked.

"Maybe he kept one in the trunk for protection or something," Carter said. "But nobody ever saw him swinging one or anything."

"Did they find fingerprints on the bat?" Murph asked, somewhat nervously.

"Yes, they did," I said. "They found Junior's fingerprints."

Nobody said a word. Finally Nassani said, "Not Ty's?"

"No, not Ty's," I answered.

"So how can they say Ty did it?" Sam asked.

"That's a good question, Sam," I answered.

"Those are the only fingerprints they found?" Carter asked.

"I believe so."

"Well, just 'cause there aren't any other fingerprints on it doesn't mean no one else touched the bat," said Sam.

The other players looked at him.

"I mean, someone could have wiped the fingerprints off the bat," he said. "Right?" he asked, looking my way.

"Right," I said.

"Then, anybody could have done this," Carter said. "Even H.B."

"Yeah, he's a weird dude," Nassani said. "He and Junior never got along."

"I saw him hit Junior once," said Sam. "After a game. Junior was a good player, but I think he was nervous all the time because he knew he'd hear it from his ol' man if he struck out or made an error."

"I think Junior hated his father," said Nassani.

"I don't know about hate," Murph said. "But it wasn't a good relationship, that's for sure."

That H.B. had hit Junior was news to me. Neither Ty nor the Duffys had ever mentioned a physically abusive relationship between Junior and H.B. Still, the idea that a father would kill his own son was too grim for me to deal with at the moment. Evidently, the young men at the table had the same feeling. It got very quiet.

"As long as we're talking about Junior's family," I said, breaking the silence, "what about Mrs. Bennett, Junior's mother?"

Carter shrugged. "She was never around, but Mrs. Washington was. Buddy's wife was always there for us. Wonder how she's doing."

"Not too good, I think," said Sam. "I hear she's gone from bad to worse."

"I'm sorry to hear that," I said. "She sounds like a wonderful woman. And Buddy, at least from what I could determine from his speech at the celebration dinner, seems like a rare find, a dedicated and decent man."

"If it wasn't for Buddy, I wouldn't still be on the team," said Murph. "He really helped me adjust. Man, I owe him big time."

"Buddy's the best," said Nassani, and the others agreed.

"H.B. always fights with him, though, mostly about Ty," said Carter.

"That's because Buddy knows that Ty's more talented, and that frosts H.B."

"They used to argue a lot because H.B. is so cheap," said Bobley. "Mr. Washington was always fighting with him over money."

"Yeah," Murph said. "I remember the day we all got the memo saying we had to use the water fountains, that the franchise would no longer provide Gatorade or bottled water for the players."

The boys laughed. "That lasted for a day," Carter said. "I think Buddy said he'd walk if H.B. didn't provide drinks for the team members and managers."

"As flashy as H.B. is, he's a real cheapskate," said Murph. "And I think he bets on the games, too."

"No doubt about it," said Carter.

"I've even seen his bookie," said Sam. "I saw him at the dinner the other night."

"No way," said Nassani. "I don't think he bets. He'd have to be an idiot to. Well, maybe he does. Who knows?"

"Is betting prevalent in the minor leagues?" I asked.

"There's betting on everything, Mrs. Fletcher," Carter offered. "From high school to college games, the minor leagues *and* the majors."

"It actually starts in Little League," said Sam, laughing.

"Even in T-ball," said Nassani, his comment causing the players to crack up.

"T-ball?" I asked.

"Kindergarten ball, Mrs. Fletcher. T-ball is for little kids. They put a ball on a tee and the kids swing at it."

"I quit T-ball," said Murph. "I hated it. I wanted live pitching."

"Any of you fellows bet on the games?" I asked.

"Not us, Mrs. Fletcher," Carter replied. He looked at the others at the table, who seemed happy that their unofficial spokesperson had spoken on their behalf.

"Somehow," I said, "I'm not quite convinced." I smiled to lessen the cynicism in my comment.

There was silence.

I realized I would never get a straight answer, and had probably been naïve for posing the question. The last thing I wanted was to alienate these young men and lose their willing input.

"Dessert anyone?" I asked.

"No thanks," Carter said, patting his toned stomach. The others also declined.

"Hey guys, sorry I'm late."

"Nice of you to show up, Long," Carter said.

The other players adjusted to make room for the latecomer. "I'm Steven Long, Mrs. Fletcher," he said. "I apologize for being late. I'm really pleased to meet you. I just got off work and—"

"Please, no apologies necessary," I said. "I'm just glad you could make it at all."

Long was an especially lanky fellow, with a toothy smile and glowing black skin. He sported cornrows and a beard.

"Have you ordered at the counter?" I asked him.

"No, not yet, ma'am."

"Lunch is on me. Please go ahead and get something to eat. Sure I don't have any takers for dessert?" I asked.

"Well, okay," said Carter. "I might as well. I'd hate to see Steve have to eat alone."

Not surprisingly, the others agreed to dessert, as well. I was glad they had. I was afraid I'd scared them off by asking questions about betting, and I didn't want the session to end on a sour note.

"Hey, Mrs. Fletcher, we can buy our own desserts," Carter said. "We'll treat you."

"I won't hear of it," I said. "You're my guests. I insist." They didn't know how much I was enjoying buying them lunch. Being in their company was a delight for me.

Carter, who'd become our unofficial waiter, took

orders for deep-fried ice cream tacos from the others. Long started to get up, but Carter placed his hand on his shoulder. "Chill, man," he said. "I'll get it for you. What do you want?"

Long told Carter his preference.

"And a cup of tea for me, please," I said.

"I understand you met my girlfriend, Lily," Long said once the business of food was resolved.

He seemed to be mature beyond his years. While he didn't appear much older than the others, he acted it.

"Yes," I said. "A lovely girl."

"I got a job at the same resort," he said, "as a personal trainer. Today was only my second day on the job."

"Congratulations," I said.

"Thanks."

"How did it go?" I asked.

"Okay," he said. "A little stressful. Some of the clients are . . ." He shrugged.

I didn't press him to finish what he was about to say. Instead, I said, "The resort is lovely, Steven. And very busy, I imagine."

"It sure is. Seems like people with money can't get enough pampering. Maybe I shouldn't say that. If they're willing to spend their money on massages and saunas and facials and personal trainers, who am I to judge? If they didn't come, I wouldn't have a job."

"That's the way I feel about writing books," I said. "If people didn't buy and read them, I wouldn't be writing for a living. You, ah—you started to mention your clients."

He nodded. "I like them for the most part," he said. "But there's always one who—"

"H.B., right?" Nassani said.

"You said it, not me."

Both Lily and Sheriff Hualga had said that H.B. was a regular client at the spa.

"Come on," Nassani said. "Tell us more."

"I don't think I should."

"If you're uncomfortable discussing your clients," I said, "I can certainly understand that."

Long looked around as though to ensure that no one was eavesdropping. He leaned closer to me and said, "I know that you're trying to clear Ty and find out who really did kill Junior."

"That's right," I said. "I believe Ty is innocent, and I'm determined to get to the truth. As I said, I understand your not wanting to tell tales out of school from your job, but if there's anything you can offer that might help in what I'm doing, I would really appreciate hearing it."

Long thought for a moment before saying, "H.B. came in today and insisted that I be his trainer. But all he did for the entire session was question me. He wasn't interested in working out. He kept suggesting that I might know something bad about Ty that he could use against him. It got really uncomfortable. Here he is, owning the team I play on, which put me in a tough spot. I don't want to cross the owner, but I also don't want to see Ty go down for something he didn't do."

"I hope you set him straight," said Murph.

"I tried to, but the guy is so intimidating. After all, he's my boss. I had to tread carefully."

"He's still convinced Ty did it?" Murph asked.

"Absolutely. It's like a real witch hunt. And get this. He even hinted that he'd buy me a car like that convertible Junior drove to the Coyote that night."

"You've got to be kidding," Bobley said. "Buy you a car? For what?"

"He wants me to tell the press about the time Ty and I had that argument."

"Argument?" I said.

Long replied, "It was nothing. No big deal. It blew over fast. I was on the mound and was pitching a complete game. It was the ninth inning and we were on top by two, but I walked two guys and the next batter hit it hard, really hard, to shortstop. Ty should have made the play and thrown the guy out, but he missed it. Went right between his legs. Ty's a hell of a shortstop. I think he only had two errors all season, and this was one of them.

"I shook my head at him, not in disgust or anything. I don't know why. I mean, I wasn't mad at Ty. He's awesome, the guy I want behind me when I'm out on the mound, not Junior. But the truth is he blew that game. Anyway, when the inning was over—we were tied and had to go extra innings— Junior told Ty in the dugout that I'd bad-mouthed him. I didn't, I swear. All I did was shake my head. Anyway, Ty confronted me about it. I told him that Junior lied and that I wasn't angry at him. Everything was cool.

"Anyway, H.B. comes into the spa and tells me that Junior told him—man, Junior is such a liar—he told his old man that Ty threatened me, said he wanted to kill me. He wants me to talk it up, tell the cops, go to the press. But it didn't happen like that!"

"And he offered you a car if you passed along that lie?" I asked, incredulous.

"It sounded that way." He shook his head sadly. "You know what? I think I should quit the spa. I can't handle H.B. If he's there every day—and I'm told that he is—I don't need this. He's scaring me, man. It's illegal what he's doing."

"What did you tell him?" Bobley asked. "Did you tell him you'd do it?"

"Of course not, but I didn't actually say no, either. I kind of fudged it. But he'll ask again."

"You're right," I said. "Asking someone to lie to the police is a crime all by itself. Maybe you're right. Maybe working at the spa puts you in too tenuous a position, considering who he is."

"I have to think about it," Long said. "Oh, by the way, Mrs. Fletcher, I almost forgot. Sylvester Cole said to say hello and he'll see you later. He stopped in at the spa. He said you were going to have dinner with him tonight at the Duffys'."

"I wasn't aware he would be joining us for dinner, but thanks for the message."

We spent the rest of the lunch chatting about many things, few of which had anything to do with Junior Bennett's murder or Ty's arrest. When we parted ways in front of the restaurant, they all shook my hand and thanked me for lunch. I watched them walk away, impressive young men with dreams of taking the field at a major-league stadium and winning the hearts of millions of baseball fans, and perhaps becoming rich in the bargain.

I could only wish them well, and hope that one day Ty Ramos could realize that dream, too.

Chapter Fourteen

"Yes, Seth, I'll remember. Don't worry. An Arizona Diamondbacks hat or T-shirt, a Mesa Rattlers bumper sticker, and a string of red chile peppers. Yes, the hottest I can find. A tall order, but I'm up for it. It'll be my pleasure. Enjoy yourself at the Red Sox game. Drive carefully."

I was about to hang up but thought I'd have some fun. "Seth? Seth? Oh, good, you haven't hung up. Would you be a dear and bring me back a Red Sox key chain and a can of Boston baked beans?"

We shared a laugh and I ended the call. I occasionally become a personal shopper for my friends back home when I travel. Not that I mind being asked. There were times when the orders became unwieldy and my baggage threatened to exceed the airlines' weight limits, but I always enjoyed arriving in Cabot Cove and distributing the goodies I had carried back with me.

It was a rainy evening in Mesa, a rare event in this

part of the country. It wasn't a downpour but a gentle, steady drizzle, a refreshing cooling off of what had been another Arizona scorcher.

After returning from lunch with the team, I took the walk around the lake that I'd missed that morning. It felt good to get in some exercise, as mild as it might have been, and to burn off the calorie count from lunch and clear my head. The rain started on my way back to the Duffys' house; it felt good and I didn't try to rush to avoid getting wet.

Meg was out when I arrived. Jack was still huddling with Ty's lawyer, David Pierce, but expected to be home for dinner, according to a note Meg left on the kitchen table. Cole would be joining us as well. Ty had become increasingly quiet and introspective since being arrested and charged with Junior Bennett's murder, which I knew concerned Meg. I'm sure she thought a nice dinner with Cole would liven things up and hopefully help Ty snap out of his funk, at least temporarily.

I'd noticed that Ty hadn't shaved in the past couple of days and that he'd worn the same shorts and T-shirt two days in a row. He was obviously depressed, and for good reason. I'd suggested to Jack and Meg that Ty speak to a psychiatrist, but Jack nixed that idea, insisting that it could conceivably be used against him in the press and if the case went to trial. One reporter had actually speculated that Ty was mentally unbalanced and that his defense would probably be insanity. Seeing a psychiatrist would only fuel that sort of irresponsible journalism and taint his already shaky image. "Besides," Jack said, "I'm not of a mind these days to trust anyone, even a shrink who's supposed to honor doctor-patient confidentiality. Some tabloid reporter, or even someone from the DA's office, might buy off a psychiatrist with money or God knows what else, and get him to leak damaging information about Ty. No, there'll be no shrinks if I have anything to say about it. End of story."

He was probably right, although I silently wondered whether he might be demonstrating a little too much paranoia. I just hated to see Ty suffer in silence.

I was sitting on the window bench in the kitchen enjoying a tall glass of Meg's iced tea when Ty came in. The bench, my favorite perch in the house, was usually drenched in sunshine, although at this moment I was enjoying watching the quiet raindrops hit the windowpane and make interesting patterns as they slid down the glass.

"Hello, Ty," I said. "How are you feeling?"

"Okay, Mrs. Fletcher," he said weakly, a trace of a smile on his handsome face.

"Can I get you some iced tea?" I asked.

"No, thanks. I can get it."

He poured himself a glass and sat at the kitchen table.

"Cole's coming for dinner tonight, right?" he asked.

"I believe so. Are you hungry? I can fix you a snack."

"I don't have much of an appetite," he said. He looked down at the table and shuffled through some papers that had been lying there.

The lull in conversation was uncomfortable. "Ty, I want you to know that I'm here to talk if you want."

He continued to fix his eyes on the table, saying nothing. "Thanks," he managed, obviously beginning to choke up. "Excuse me." He left the kitchen and went upstairs.

I had just started to take another sip of tea when the doorbell rang. I went to put my glass on the windowsill, but some of the tea spilled onto the yellow-and-white gingham seat cushion. I jumped up, grabbed a couple of sheets of paper towel, and tried to soak it up.

"Cleaning up the evidence, are you?" Sylvester Cole said, laughing and standing at the entrance to the kitchen. "I let myself in. The door was ajar. Hope I didn't startle you."

"Oh, no, not at all," I said, chuckling. "You caught me in the act. I spilled my iced tea on Meg's lovely cushions. Have a seat. I'll just be a minute."

"No bother," said Cole. "Ty home? Meg and Jack here?"

"Yes, Ty is home. Meg had a quick errand to run and Jack should be here soon."

"In town with his lawyer, David Pierce, I heard," he said.

"You know him?

"Sort of."

Cole's appearance struck me as being uncharacteristically disheveled this evening. He had a five-o'clock shadow—more like a four-o'clock shadow, I suppose—and he wore a pair of gym shorts, a nonde-script orange T-shirt, and sneakers.

He must have read my mind. "Sorry for the way I look tonight, Ms. Fletcher. I was going to work out, then hit the showers and shave at the gym, but I ran out of time—not to mention steam. Never made it to the gym. Busy day."

"You look just fine," I said. "In fact, you're one of the few people I know who seem to be able to look good no matter what they're wearing."

He smiled. "Thanks for the compliment," he said. "Let me return it. You look lovely this afternoon."

"Thank you, but I certainly don't feel very lovely at the moment. The stress of the week is beginning to catch up with me."

When I'd put on my makeup that morning, I'd no-ticed that my skin was paler than usual, and that the circles beneath my eyes were absolutely huge. I looked like I usually do at midwinter in Maine, I thought, not at the end of summer in Arizona.

"How about going out to the patio?" I said. "It's covered, so we won't get wet. I'm feeling sleepy. I think the air will perk me up a bit."

"Sure thing."

He picked up my glass of iced tea, opened the slid-ing door with his elbow, and led us out to the patio. I considered asking Ty if he'd like to join us but de-cided to let him set his own schedule.

"Ty sleeping?" Cole asked, sitting in one of the wooden chairs. I sat in a matching chair; a wooden table separated us.

"I don't think so," I said. "He was downstairs a short while ago."

"My heart aches every time I think of that kid," said Cole. "He's the kind of person you gravitate to. I wasn't drawn to Ty only because of his baseball talent. The kid's got so much charisma and a lot of smarts. Those are the kinds of things that make a superstar, and even more important, a great person." He shook his head. "It's such a shame he's got to go through all of this. Who knows how it'll end up?"

"You don't think he'll be exonerated?" I asked. "I assume you feel as I do, that he had nothing to do with Junior Bennett's death."

"Sure, I feel that way, but I'm enough of a realist about the legal system to know that being innocent doesn't always translate into being acquitted. You read about all these cases where someone spends years behind bars, only to have new DNA evidence prove he or she couldn't possibly have done the crime. Of course, it depends a lot on this Pierce guy. If he's as good a lawyer as Jack thinks he is, then the kid has a chance. But the DA has an agenda, and this is one DA who's out for blood and to make a name for himself."

"What *is* his name?" I asked.

"Larry Martone. Young guy, mid-thirties, a real hotshot."

"Martone. I noticed a Martone Plaza somewhere in Mesa. Is that—?"

"Yep, same family. Lots of Martones in Mesa. They own a ton of real estate. Good reputation. Martone

Plaza is going to be a new strip mall with a Starbucks, gourmet food store, places like that. I'm sure you've seen those big billboards announcing the new mall."

"I can't say that I have," I replied. "So you're convinced that Ty didn't do this but that the legal system might fail him?"

He looked at me, paused, and said, "Ty is a class act. The Ty Ramos I know would never have done this. He's learned the lesson of life at the School of Hard Knocks. He came up the tough way, which is what makes this all so sad. This is a kid who has worked so hard to become what he is, and he ends up accused of murder. The irony in this isn't lost on me, nor on you either, I'm sure. That's what makes it so crazy and so hard to swallow. I want to work with this kid, be his agent. We have all the details of a contract hammered out—Jack and I did that the other night— and I've already started promoting him. Then this had to happen. He's got the potential to be a star, and I know I can help him achieve it. At least that's my prayer, my plan. At least it was my plan until this happened. Ty's going to be acquitted—he didn't do it, right? Then, we can forge ahead."

"Sylvester, what do you know of Junior's relationship with his father?"

"Whoa. That was one dysfunctional relationship. That was textbook. Overbearing father—always-looking-to-please son—son never good enough in father's eyes—son constantly trying to impress dad. Lots of anger issues because of it. Very unhealthy."

I appreciated Sylvester's use of psychobabble,

but I was looking for more specifics. "Have you ever witnessed an incident between the two of them? A physical confrontation?"

He took a long look at me before replying, "Of course. We all have."

"An example?"

"Like the time he hit Junior for no reason. Why? Because he found out I was at the stadium to scout Ty. I was in the men's room and heard H.B. tell Junior that if he didn't make it to the big leagues, he'd be a disgrace to the family, 'family' meaning, of course, H.B. I hear this whacking sound, and when I come out of the stall, Junior is washing his face and there's a big red mark on his cheek."

"Oh, how awful," I said. "That poor boy. What he must have gone through growing up."

"You want to know the saddest part, Mrs. Fletcher? Junior was a good kid with God-given talent. But his dad ruined him. H.B. is ambitious and greedy. He's all about showing off. Fancy restaurants, state-of-the-art electronics in his home, private planes, cigarette boats. That guy's got at least half a dozen cars, including a brand-new Mercedes. If I were going to buy a new car, I sure as heck wouldn't get a green one. Kind of have a superstition about the color green—unless it's money."

"I remember reading that Duke Ellington felt the same way," I said. "He refused to ride in a green car."

"See? I'm not the only one. Nice to know I'm not crazy," Cole said. "Of course, to H.B. the money he spends on such stuff is just chump change. He must have been furious with Junior for taking the car to the Crazy Coyote that night. What could Junior have been thinking? That's what happens when you have an overbearing, super-strict parent. Kids rebel, one way or the other."

"Sylvester, when was the last time you spoke to H.B.?"

"Not for a couple of days at least. Not since the murder, actually. Let's see, it must've been at the victory dinner, when he came to our table. H.B.'s in mourning, you know. I don't want to disturb him. Besides, I'm the last guy he wants to hear from. I'm public enemy number one in his book because I wasn't interested in signing his son."

We were interrupted when Meg opened the sliding door and joined us. "Hi, Sylvester, Jess," she said. "Sorry it took me so long." We followed her into the kitchen, where two overflowing grocery bags sat on the table.

"I think I got everything," Meg said. "I thought it would be nice if we made tacos. I got all the trimmings. Ty loves making tacos; it's kind of festive and casual. Hope everyone's up for it. I got some fish for those who want fish tacos, and ground beef for the carnivores among us." She laughed. Her mood seemed lighter, probably because she had people to entertain at dinner.

"You sure you want me in my ruffian clothes?" Cole said.

"You're welcome anytime, Sylvester. You know that. Besides, I love to entertain. There's nothing as satisfying as sharing time with people you enjoy being around. If I had my way, I'd throw a dinner party every night of the week. Of course, Jack doesn't necessarily share that view. He likes his quiet nights with just the two of us, or three of us if Ty is home. But we compromise pretty well." She started emptying the bags. "Did you notice that the press has abandoned us?" she asked, glee in her voice.

"They'll be back," Cole said.

"I suppose you're right," she said, "but even a brief respite is welcome."

"The menu sounds delicious," he said.

I agreed with him, even though I had to admit that I was somewhat "tacoed" out. But as long as it lifted Ty's spirits, I was up for anything.

I've always loved a kitchen gathering where everyone chips in to make a meal that will eventually be enjoyed by all. Ty arrived in the kitchen, and while Meg and I took care of prepping and cooking the fish and ground meat, he and Sylvester handled the chopping of onions, peppers, and tomatoes. Jack had called and told Meg that he wouldn't make it home for dinner after all. He and Pierce needed more time together because Ty was due back in court the next day for a hearing with the judge, something to do with motions by the DA and Pierce that were, according to Jack, vitally important. Meg seemed almost relieved that Jack wouldn't be joining us. I hated to admit it, but I shared her feeling to an extent. Jack was tightly wound of late and snapped easily. He would always apologize afterward, and I couldn't blame him for being uptight. Still, it became uncomfortable at times, and I knew Meg suffered through those moments.

Ty shared some laughs with Sylvester during their kitchen prep duties. It was nice to see Ty enjoying himself, and Sylvester seemed up to the task of keeping things light without forcing the issue.

"Hey, Ty," said Sylvester, "you cut up the green peppers, I'll cut up the red. I hate green." Sylvester looked at me and winked. "Did you hear that H.B. bought a flashy green Mercedes convertible?"

"No," said Ty.

"Yeah, that was the car Junior drove to the Crazy Coyote," Sylvester added.

"Oh," Ty said quietly, almost a mumble. It was obvious he didn't want to speak about that night.

"Anyway, I hate green, Ty, so you cut up the green peppers."

"Okay," Ty said, shaking his head and laughing. "But will you *eat* the green peppers?"

"Oh, yeah, I'll eat anything," said Cole. "I don't care what color it is as long as it tastes good. But don't ask me to look at it if it's green. I close my eyes when I eat green things."

"Okay," said Meg cheerily. "Meat and fish are ready. You guys set to go?"

"Ready to rock 'n' roll," Cole said. "Time to chow down."

Meg and I knew and appreciated that Cole was making an effort to relate to Ty and to speak on his level. Although he was older than Ty, he came off as a cool sort of guy, comfortable and conversant with the younger man's world. Like his teammates, Ty used what sometimes seemed a different, almost foreign language. But Cole was able to fit in, a chameleon of sorts.

We all took a plate, created our individual tacos, and sat down to enjoy them. I had a fish taco and a beef taco, both of which were delicious. Meg had made a batch of margaritas for herself, Sylvester, and me, and a virgin margarita for Ty.

When dinner was over, Ty excused himself, saying he was tired and didn't feel well. He left us and went upstairs. Cole said he had to leave because he had an early-morning appointment and wanted to hit the gym before it.

"I think it's still raining out," I said as Meg and I walked Sylvester to the front door.

"I heard it's going to rain tomorrow, too," said Cole. "Arizona in the summer loves rain. Bring it on!"

Cole thanked Meg for dinner and left. Meg went back into the kitchen, but I lingered at the glass front door for a minute, watching Cole walk down to the driveway. As he navigated the path, he stumbled on an uneven stone and inadvertently stepped in a small puddle, leaving muddy footprints behind, illuminated by a row of solar lights that flanked the walkway. *Footprints,* I thought. *Whose footprints were at the murder scene?* When I glanced back up, Cole had stopped and was watching me curiously from outside his car. I waved and he responded in kind before getting in the car and driving away.

* * * *

"I just don't understand who's leaking all this erroneous stuff to the press," Jack growled as he paced back and forth, a crushed newspaper in his hand. "Are they making it up? It's like they're dressing him up to be a giant monster, and dancing around their own creation."

Meg and I were seated on the buttery leather sofa in the den, sipping from dainty glasses filled with Sambuca, while Jack nursed his second martini since getting home.

"Jack, you're going to have a heart attack if you don't stop," Meg said. "You've got to calm down. There is nothing you can do, absolutely nothing, to prevent the stories in the press. I suggest you forget about reading the papers. In fact, I'm going to cancel the subscriptions in the morning."

"You're right," he said. "I'm going nuts." He came behind the sofa and rubbed her neck. "It's just that the DA is getting a rise out of all this and it really burns me. Meg, they're saying the most awful things, digging up Ty's past and embellishing it with stories about how he has a child with a drug-addict girlfriend who gave birth when she was fourteen, how he went from bad to worse, from bad parents to worse parents. Listen to this quote: 'Jack Duffy is a poor excuse for a father, a hapless, desperate man who took in an antisocial felon when his marriage was falling apart because he and his wife, Meg, couldn't have children of their—' "

"Enough, Jack! That's enough," said Meg.

"Please." She turned to me. "They are just awful, Jessica. And there's nothing we can do."

I touched her arm. "It's okay, Meg," I said. "It's going to be okay."

My voice conveyed more conviction than I felt inside.

Chapter Fifteen

The mood in the Duffy house the following morning was understandably glum. The prospect of having to appear in court is unpleasant even for minor legal matters. But today's hearing was about murder and the fate of a young man who, I was convinced, was unjustly accused.

I was up and dressed early and assumed that I'd beaten everyone downstairs. I was wrong. Jack and Meg were already having coffee on the patio when I arrived. Their greetings were strained, at best, and I wondered whether they preferred to be left alone with their thoughts. I started back inside, but Jack said, "Please, Jess, sit down. There's something we'd like to discuss with you."

I joined them at the table, and Jack poured me coffee from a carafe. Meg said, "I'll get breakfast going in a minute."

"Don't worry about breakfast for me," I said. "I've been eating far more than I'm used to and—"

"Jess," Jack interrupted, "I hope you plan on being with us today for the court hearing."

"Of course—if you think it's appropriate."

"It's more than appropriate, Jess," he said. "Ty needs to be surrounded by positive people. Judge McQuaid is the sort of man who puts a lot of stock in the caliber of people a defendant associates with. It also turns out that he's a big fan of yours and of your books."

"That's very flattering," I said, "but I don't see why it's relevant."

"I know Mike McQuaid from back East. He's always been a judge who wears his heart on his sleeve. Some claim he's too easy on defendants, too quick to latch on to their positive attributes and forget the crimes they've committed. That should be good for us."

"You saw how he congratulated Ty on getting the winning hit," Meg said. "That's typical of him, according to Jack."

"It strikes me," I said, "that such behavior could get a judge in trouble, and create the basis for a mistrial."

Jack was thoughtful. "I'm not worried about that, Jess. He knows when to put on the brakes and get tough. Besides, once a defendant is found not guilty in a trial, the prosecution can't claim a mistrial and call for a new one. That would be double jeopardy. Only the defense can do that if they lose a case and the judge has misbehaved or made legally questionable decisions. At any rate, David Pierce told me that

Judge McQuaid is aware that you're staying with us, and presumably in Ty's corner. He said he'd enjoy meeting you following the hearing this morning. He's bringing a couple of your books for you to sign."

"I'll be happy to sign his books," I said, "as long as you think it's not a legal misstep to do so."

"It might be if you bought the books for him, but the ones he's bringing already belong to him and his wife. She claims to be your number one fan."

"Fair enough," I said. "What's today's hearing about?"

"Larry Martone, the DA, has filed a motion asking that Ty's bail be rescinded."

"Oh? On what basis?" I asked.

"Martone claims that Ty's been having too much contact with his teammates, which he claims is a breach of house arrest rules."

"Is it?"

"Not as far as I'm concerned, but that doesn't mean he won't prevail. He's also asking that the court subpoena Meg and me and take our depositions."

"Whatever for?" I asked.

"Martone says that since Ty lives with us, there must have been numerous conversations with him about the murder. Pierce has countered with a claim that anything we might have heard from Ty would violate the hearsay rule if we were forced to testify. He's not technically right. What a defendant in a felony case says to others can be used against him. Pierce is also claiming lawyer-client privilege because I'm a lawyer and a judge."

"It sounds outlandish to me that the district attorney could expect to have the judge rule favorably about something like that. Isn't there such a thing as a parent-son privilege in the law?"

"Afraid not," Jack said. "Keep in mind that Martone is a very ambitious young man—and that he has the backing of important men in this town, including one Harrison Bennett, Sr."

"And the district attorney's office is an elected one," I offered.

"Right. And those campaigns rely on contributions. Judge McQuaid is also elected, but he's not the sort of man to make rulings based upon his political future. Then again, I may be wrong. I've been wrong plenty of times when it comes to reading people. It can't hurt having you there—you're obviously part of Ty's life—and it may, I believe, help sway McQuaid in a positive direction."

"This sounds more like a public-relations hearing than a legal one," I said.

"Unfortunately, the law and PR often intertwine. That's why judges impose gag orders on attorneys in high-profile cases, to keep them from launching their own PR campaigns out of court. I've done it many times. All I'm saying, Jess, is that not only will your presence be a boost to Ty's morale, it could have a good impact on the outcome of the hearing."

"I'll do whatever you ask me to do," I said. "Speaking of Ty, where is he?"

"Still sleeping," Meg said. "I figured he could use all the rest he can get. Besides, the less time he has to think about what's coming up this morning, the better it will be." She stood. "Eggs over easy for everyone? I'm up for some crisp bacon. Are you?"

"Not only are you a wonderful cook," I said, getting out of my chair, "you're a mindreader. Let me help you. I'll get out the eggs."

Ty looked good for his court appearance. Meg had picked out a fresh white shirt, dark blue tie, and chino pants with razor-sharp creases for him. One of the legs bulged at the bottom where it covered his ankle bracelet. I'd heard Jack tell him to shave, and Ty had balked, but not for long. "Don't argue with me," Jack said. "When I say you shave, you shave."

Ty shaved.

Meg tried to inject happy chatter during the ride to the court, but much of it fell flat. This was serious business, and no one in the car could forget that for more than a second or two.

The Mesa courthouse was a busy place when we arrived. Jack used the rear entrance we'd taken advantage of when leaving the court the last time, which spared us the media extravaganza that had gathered at the front of the low, Southwestern-style building.

I always find courthouses as fascinating as they are sad. The entire human dilemma is on display, with people trapped in the legal system by their own doing, or because they were dealt the wrong cards at birth. It was especially tragic to see young mothers conferring with their lawyers, many of them presumably court-appointed public defenders, while the mothers tried to manage a couple of naturally lively toddlers. Hopefully, many of those who crowded the halls and benches that morning would find a satisfactory resolution to their legal travails.

Judge McQuaid was holding court in a relatively small room at the very back of the building. A sign outside it read, MOTIONS—PEOPLE VS. RAMOS. The door was open. Inside, court employees scurried about preparing the room for the day's proceedings. I spotted the district attorney near the bench, conferring with two other people. One of them, to my surprise, was Harrison Bennett. I pointed him out to Meg, who sat with Ty on a bench across the hall.

"He's so powerful," Meg said, shaking her head. "I sometimes think he controls everything that happens here in Mesa."

"I'm sure he doesn't control the legal system," I said, hoping that was true.

Ty's attorney, David Pierce, arrived just minutes before we were due in the courtroom. "Sorry I'm late," he said. "Some mornings I just can't escape from the infernal phone. Everyone here?" He did a head count and went to where Ty sat with Meg. "How's my favorite shortstop?" he asked, slapping Ty on the shoulder.

"I'm okay," Ty said without looking up.

"Hey, my young friend," Pierce said, "lighten up and get a smile on that handsome face. Judges don't take kindly to sullen, surly young guys in their courtrooms."

"Listen to Mr. Pierce," Meg said. "It's important

that you present a pleasant, cooperative image for the judge."

"Let's go," Jack said.

There was a section of spectator seats to the left and right of the door that we hadn't been able to see from outside the room. The moment we walked in, it was obvious who was filling those seats. The press!

"Damn," Jack muttered under his breath as we went to the front row, where one side of the aisle was reserved for the defense team. "Don't look back," he said. "It'll just give some damn photographer a shot of us."

Ty took the chair next to David Pierce at the defendant's table. Meg, Jack, and I sat behind them in the first row of seats.

"All stand!"

Judge Michael McQuaid entered the courtroom and took his seat behind the bench. He looked down and nodded at Jack, and then he grinned at me. It made me uncomfortable, and I averted my eyes from his gaze after returning a small smile.

"All right," McQuaid said, "let's begin this hearing. Before we do, I remind our friends from the media that no cameras are allowed in the courtroom. I will not tolerate any pictures being taken during the proceedings, still or video, nor will I allow the use of any recording device. Do I make myself clear?"

There were murmurs of assent.

"Good," he said. "Don't force me to have you removed. Let's proceed."

I glanced across the aisle to where Martone, the

DA, sat with a female assistant. Harrison Bennett sat in the first row, directly behind them.

"The first order of business is a motion filed by Mr. Martone on behalf of the People. You've read it, Mr. Pierce?"

"Yes, sir, I have," Pierce said, standing.

"Let's hear it."

Pierce gave what seemed to me to be a cogent and easily understood defense of Ty's bail. When he was finished, the judge invited Martone to rebut. The district attorney was a smug man whose condescending expression underscored his belief that everything he said was imbued with wisdom and truth. He postured in front of the judge like an actor on stage, gesturing for dramatic effect. Pierce, in contrast, had been straightforward and sounded considerably more sincere than his adversary.

". . . and so in conclusion," the DA intoned, looking intently at Ty, "the defendant poses a distinct threat to the community at large. His previous record of having broken the law in another state is well documented. This is a young man who, in a fit of anger and jealous rage, bludgeoned to death a teammate, a decent young man whose future was bright. To allow this misfit and threat to the safety of our fellow citizens to be free on bail would be, in my judgment, a drastic mistake with potentially lethal consequences. Thank you."

I was seated next to Jack Duffy, and even though we weren't touching, I could feel his rage at the DA's mischaracterization of Ty. His face was beet red, and veins in his neck pulsated. *Please,* I silently thought, *don't give vent to your feelings and lash out at Martone.* It was unlikely that he would, I knew. He was a judge himself, and I was certain he wouldn't stand for outbursts in his own court. Still, his anger was palpable, but he remained in his chair, his jaw working furiously.

Martone took his seat in front of H.B.

"Anything further, Mr. Pierce?"

"No, Your Honor."

Judge McQuaid consulted some papers before looking up and intoning, "Motion denied. Bail shall remain in effect. Next motion, Mr. Martone?"

The district attorney was barely out of his seat and starting to speak when Bennett jumped to his feet and said in a booming voice, "This is a travesty of justice. I have lost a son at the hands of this, this monster and—"

McQuaid pounded his gavel. "You're out of order, Mr. Bennett."

"This entire proceeding is out of order," Bennett barked back.

"Sit down, Mr. Bennett, or I'll find you in contempt."

Martone grabbed Bennett by the shoulder of his suit jacket and pushed him back into his seat. I glanced at Jack and Meg. She was pale, her eyes wide and frightened at Bennett's outburst. Jack took her hand, a small smile on his face.

Martone presented his next motion, asking for depositions to be taken of Jack and Meg Duffy.

"Mr. Pierce. Your objection, please."

Pierce kept it short and concise.

"Motion denied. Anything else, gentlemen?"

Both attorneys stood and said, "No, Your Honor." Ty scrambled to his feet next to Pierce.

"This hearing is adjourned. My clerk will inform the parties of a trial date."

We all stood as McQuaid left the bench. We waited until the press had departed before preparing to leave the courtroom. Martone, his assistant, and H.B. walked past us without saying a word, although Bennett couldn't resist looking back, his face a mask of fury. As the three of them pushed through the doors into the hallway, a cry arose from reporters waiting for them, and we saw the flash of cameras.

"Round one went well," Jack commented. "But there's still a long hill to climb."

We'd packed up and were about to follow Pierce from the room when a court clerk came to us. "Judge Duffy, Mrs. Fletcher? Judge McQuaid would like to see you for a few minutes in his chambers."

"All right," Jack said. "You and Ty stay here," he told Meg. "I don't want you going outside with that swarm waiting for us."

"I'll wait with them," Pierce said.

Judge McQuaid's chambers consisted of two rooms. A secretary and a law clerk occupied desks in the outer one. The judge, who'd taken off his black robe, sat behind his desk in the inner space. He wore bright red-and-yellow suspenders over a blue-and-white-striped button-down shirt with the sleeves rolled up.

"Hello, Jack," he said, getting up and shaking hands with us. "It's a real pleasure to meet you, Mrs. Fletcher."

"The feeling is entirely mutual," I said.

"Not concerned at having us back here without the other side present?" Jack asked.

McQuaid's laugh was hearty. "Hell, no. Your lawyer's not here. We're not discussing the case, are we? I just wanted the privilege of meeting Mrs. Fletcher and imposing upon her to sign a few books for me and my wife."

He'd brought six of my most recent novels to sign, and I dutifully wrote a personal message in each before signing my name.

"Much obliged, Mrs. Fletcher," he said. "Plan to be in Mesa long?"

"As long as it takes for—" I stopped and smiled. "We're not discussing the case," I said.

He laughed. "That's right. Maybe one of these nights, before you leave town, you'd be our guest for dinner at the house. My wife makes a hell of a chicken pot pie."

"One of my favorites," I said. "I'll look forward to it."

We left the judge's chambers and joined Meg and Ty in the hallway, where Pierce had brought them.

"What a lovely man," I commented as we headed for the car.

"He certainly comes off that way," Meg said. "Let's get home."

"Do you mind if I don't join you?" I asked.

"No, of course not, but if there's anything you need, we can get it for you."

"What I need is an hour or so just to walk around town, and do a little shopping for souvenirs to take back with me. I can get a cab and catch up with you around lunchtime."

"Suit yourself," Jack said.

"Mrs. Fletcher, I really appreciate your being here for me this morning," Ty said. "I can't thank you enough."

"This morning went extremely well," I said, kissing him on the cheek. "Keep your spirits up. I'm sure things will work out for you just fine."

I took care to leave the courthouse via a back route to avoid any lingering press, and spent the next hour doing what I'd set out to do, window-shopping and browsing the myriad stores in the center of town, many of which featured arts and crafts created by local artisans. I made a few small purchases, including a jar of chipotle sauce for Maureen and Mort.

Mesa had a lovely downtown, and I thought of Cabot Cove and its central area, not as large as Mesa's but with a similar feel (and decidedly different weather—it was brutally hot in Mesa).

I'd reached the end of the main street and looked beyond, where an expanse of dusty desert land stretched out before me. To my right was a three-story, concrete, open-air municipal parking garage. I'd been walking in the sun, and the oppressive heat was making me light-headed. *I should have bought that festive sombrero I admired in one of the shops,* I told myself.

The shade afforded by the concrete overhangs was inviting. I entered on the first level and breathed a sigh of relief at the damp, cooler atmosphere. I spotted a soft drink machine in the distance, next to an elevator. I went to it, plugged in money, and down dropped a can of diet lemonade. The cold metal of the can felt good in my hand, and on my brow and cheeks as I pressed it against them. I was about to open the drink when I heard loud voices from behind a concrete pillar a dozen feet from where I stood. One of the voices was strangely familiar. Where had I heard it before? Of course. In court just an hour ago. It was H.B., arguing with someone. I didn't recognize the other man's voice.

"Don't you dare threaten me, you little creep," Bennett said.

"You owe me the money. You place a bet and lose, you owe the money," said the second person. "My people are—"

"You tell your people who they're dealing with. I've got connections all over town. I can put you out of business in a second, and don't you forget it."

"I want my money now," the other man shouted, "or I will tell people that you bet against your own team. You know what people will say if I tell them that? Maybe I'll tell the reporters at the newspapers and the television stations. Yeah, pay me the money right now or I'll—"

"You open your mouth, and that's the last time you'll talk."

The thump of someone being struck was loud enough to reach me. So was the thud of someone hitting something hard. I heard loud footsteps coming in my direction, and quickly used the vending machine to duck out of sight. Bennett rushed past me and up a stairwell, never seeing my hiding place. I listened as the sound of his shoes on the concrete echoed off the hard walls.

Moans came from where the altercation had taken place. I circumvented the concrete pillar to find their source and saw a man sprawled on the floor, blood gushing from a gaping cut on his head.

"Oh, my," I said, going to him and dropping to my knees, ignoring the sting of the coarse concrete digging into my skin. "Sir, you're hurt."

His response was another pained exclamation.

I pulled a handkerchief from my shoulder bag and handed it to him. He tentatively sat up and pressed the cloth to his head wound. "Thank you," he said.

I looked into his face and was startled to realize I recognized it. He was the small man I'd seen, and heard, talking on a cell phone outside the hotel the night of the team celebratory dinner.

"I'll call for an ambulance," I said as he struggled to his feet with my help.

"No, no," he said. "I don't need a doctor."

The screeching of tires on the floor above alerted us that the danger to him wasn't completely gone. He hobbled to the soda machine and I followed, both of us seeking to use it as a shield from the careening car—a silver Jaguar with H.B. on the license plate—that raced by a moment later.

The man sank back against the wall.

"That was Harrison Bennett who hit you," I said.

My blunt statement had its intended effect. He looked at me with wide, frightened brown eyes, his lips quivering.

"I heard you say that he bets against his own team. Would that be the Rattlers?"

"Look, lady, here's your handkerchief back. I can't—"

"Please, listen to me," I said. "I don't wish you any harm, nor do I care what your role might be in any betting that goes on. But you've bloodied my handkerchief, which, I should tell you, has always been one of my favorites, and in addition, I scraped my knee badly in trying to help you. The least you can do is hear me out. Come along, I'll buy you a soda. There's something I must know."

Chapter Sixteen

My conversation with one of Mesa's resident bookies started out well. But as the pain in his head subsided, he seemed to realize suddenly that he was telling tales out of school to a perfect stranger, hardly prudent for someone engaged in illegal activities. I thanked him for his time and watched him walk away, my handkerchief pressed to his gash. He kept looking back as though to confirm he'd actually been revealing secrets about his clients to a woman who asked a lot of questions she had no business asking.

I walked through town again until I reached a pocket park I hadn't noticed before. I entered it and sat on a bench beneath a leafy tree that afforded protection from the blazing sun. I looked up and saw a cerulean sky dotted with enormous puffy white clouds that would eventually give way to a still Arizona night, with winking stars and a slice of a moon. Meg had expressed disappointment that my visit to Arizona hadn't coincided with a full moon. "The desert is especially beautiful when the moon is full," she'd said. She'd also hoped that I would get to experience a sunrise hot-air-balloon ride over the desert, something I'd wanted to do along with getting in an hour or two of flying time in a rented private plane. It didn't look like I'd get to enjoy either diversion. All our plans had been set aside because of Ty's arrest.

I stayed in the park for a half hour, not so much to rest as to try to clear my head and focus on what my timely conversation with the bookie—Harrison Bennett's bookie—meant to Ty's defense. I felt the pressure of time. I couldn't stay in Arizona forever. His trial, if there was one, would be months in the future. His teammates would begin scattering across the country. Recollections of what had happened that fateful night at the Crazy Coyote would fade. I needed to process what I'd learned, put it in some semblance of order, and force a resolution.

The sun's rays played off water bubbling up from a fountain a few feet away. The gentle sound added to the tranquility of the park, and threatened to lull me into a sleepy, hypnotic state. But I was snapped out of my trance by the ringing of my cell phone. It was Mort Metzger.

"Everything okay with you, Mrs. F?" he asked.

"Yes, Mort, everything is fine. At this moment, I'm sitting on a bench in a pretty little park with a fountain in the center of Mesa. You know how much I enjoy taking walks by the sea. In Arizona, you settle for water of any kind, wherever you can find it. How are things back home?"

"Not as exciting as they must be for you," he said. "I've been following what's happening with the Ramos case on ESPN and Court TV. Are you still in the middle of it?"

"Yes, I'm involved, Mort, but—"

"Last time we talked, you were asking about sports gambling."

"Yes, I remember that," I said. "As a matter of fact—"

I told him of my encounter with the bookie without mentioning names.

"Stay away from the gambling crowd, Mrs. F," he said, his voice firm and stern. "It's all mob related. You get yourself involved with somebody who owes a bookie money, you're liable to end up with a broken kneecap, or worse. You know, I was a cop in New York—" He went on to remind me of how naïve—and stubborn—I can sometimes be. And I was not thrilled to learn that he and Seth Hazlitt had been discussing my flaws and that Seth had wholeheartedly agreed with him.

"I'll be careful," I said. "I hear you loud and clear."

"Hearing's one thing, Mrs. F. Acting on what you hear is another. When are you coming home?"

"I have no idea," I responded. "But tell Maureen I found your chipotle sauce and bought you a jar."

"We're not concerned about that, Mrs. F. We're concerned about you."

"You tell Seth Hazlitt to mind his own patients or I won't give him the Diamondbacks cap I bought him today. Seriously, Mort, I can't leave just yet. I'm

needed here, not so much for Jack and Meg—they
have one another. And Jack has so much experience
with the legal end that he doesn't need any help
there—not that I would tread in that territory anyway. It's Ty who I feel needs me more than anyone.
He's such a nice, deserving kid, and his dream is
about to go down the drain. All that hard work, on
and off the field. It's heartbreaking to see him trying
to cope."

"That boy is lucky to have you on his team, Mrs. F."

The conversation with Mort had roused me from my
lethargy. I now knew things I hadn't known earlier
that day. The question was to what use to put my
newfound knowledge. I had walked out of the park
with the intention of heading back to the Duffys'
house when I happened to notice three medium-rise
office buildings lined up against the horizon. One had
large red letters at its top, but I was too far away to
read them clearly. It looked like it might say BENNETT
BUILDING. I walked toward the buildings to see if I
was right. My eyesight was still working. Sure
enough, BENNETT BUILDING was emblazoned across
the structure's upper span.

I crossed the street, leaving the leafy protection of
the park and wishing I'd bought that pretty sombrero. The sun was brutal, bringing to mind the
proverbial egg frying on the sidewalk. In this case, my
head was the egg. I reached the building's entrance
and gratefully stepped into the air-conditioned lobby.

The directory indicated that Bennett Enterprises was on the top floor.

The elevator opened into an expensively decorated and furnished reception area where an older woman with perfectly coiffed blond hair wearing a colorful cowboy shirt sat behind a very large desk.

"May I help you?" she asked pleasantly.

"I hope so," I said. "My name is Jessica Fletcher. I was wondering whether—"

She popped up and came around from behind the desk, her ankle-length blue denim skirt with patches of horses and cows sewn on it swirling around her. She extended her hand. "My, my," she said, "it really *is* Jessica Fletcher. I recognize you from your book covers. This is such a pleasure. I've read every one of your books, and so have my nieces and nephews. I tell them there isn't a lot of senseless gore and sex and bad language in them, and that they'll enjoy figuring out who dunnit."

"I'm pleased to hear that," I said.

"I can't believe you're really here," she said. "Come, sit down. Would you like a cold drink, some coffee perhaps?"

"Thank you, no," I said. "Actually, I was hoping to catch Mr. Bennett for a few minutes. I know I'm barging in but—"

She became conspiratorial. "Don't you worry about that," she said. "He's probably in his office trying to put his silly little golf ball into the cup he has on his carpet." She shook her head. "Boys and their toys. Do you find that men become more childlike as they get older?"

I couldn't help but laugh at the direction the conversation had taken. "I really hadn't thought much about that, but—"

A large set of wooden double doors behind her desk opened and Harrison Bennett stepped into the reception area. He spotted me and frowned as if trying to force recognition.

"H.B.," his receptionist said, "do you know who this is?"

His frown deepened. He wore lime green slacks, a bright yellow polo shirt, and white loafers, and carried a gold putter.

I took the initiative, walked up to him, and offered my hand. "Jessica Fletcher, Mr. Bennett. We met at the team dinner following the Rattlers' win."

"Yeah, right," he said, ignoring my hand.

He started back toward his office and I stayed at his side. He stopped and glared at me.

"I came to express my condolences, and—"

He cut me off. "Thank you. Now, if you don't mind—"

"I think we should have a talk," I said.

"About what?"

"Why don't we go into your office? This is really a private matter."

"I have no private business with you. Now, tell me what you want."

I lowered my voice so the receptionist couldn't hear. "Oh, I was wondering who'll place your bets against the Rattlers now that Junior is gone."

I'd certainly surprised him. He stood in the hall-way, his mouth open.

"I understand you lost a lot of money on that game," I said, meeting his angry eyes.

"You don't know what you're talking about," he said.

"I think I do," I said. "Would you like to discuss it out here, or do you think we can find somewhere less public?"

He answered by pushing through the double doors. I followed. He closed the doors behind us and said through clenched teeth, "I lost a son, that's what I lost."

"And I am terribly sorry about that," I said. "Truly I am. I'm not out to hurt you, Mr. Bennett, but Ty Ramos did not kill your son, and I am determined to clear him of the charge against him."

"What do you want from me?"

"I'm here to talk about integrity, about a minor-league baseball team owner who bets against his own team."

"What the hell does betting have to do with my son's murder?"

"I'm not sure yet, sir, but I'm becoming increasingly convinced that there could be a connection. I happened to be at the wrong place at the wrong time this morning—or the right place at the right time, depending upon your view—and I overheard you berating and physically attacking your bookie. I heard it all, Mr. Bennett." I decided not to mention my follow-up talk with the bookie, to spare him any retribution.

I paused, expecting some kind of reaction. He

didn't speak, but his rage was palpable. I was tempted to stop but felt compelled to continue. "If anyone asked, I'd have to say the most despicable part of your unscrupulous behavior is that you had your own son place your bets for you."

In all my years of stumbling into murders, I've only occasionally been afraid for my physical well-being. This was one of those rare times, and it immediately brought to mind the conversation I'd just had with Mort. H.B.'s face was a deep purple, as if his bruised ego had surfaced. His head visibly shook and his fists were clenched. He shifted from one foot to the next, rocking back and forth. His eyes bored into mine with laser intensity. If his receptionist had not been within screaming distance, I would have been in danger of his lashing out, just as he did with his bookie, or worse. I wondered if I should back off and soften my assault on his character. The cognitive part of my brain suggested I do that, but the emotional component told me to stick to my convictions.

"You've been following me," he said, pointing an accusatory index finger at my face. The glint from a large square diamond-and-ruby-encrusted ring flashed light in my eyes.

"No, I haven't followed you," I said.

"Who have you been speaking to?" he asked. "I'll find out. I have my ways."

"You will not threaten me, nor will you intimidate me," I said. "Your jealousy and anger at Ty Ramos is misplaced. Even you have to admit that sending an innocent young man to prison is wrong. Most important, it won't bring back your son. Nothing will. But I believe that you can help bring your son's real killer to justice."

His face didn't appear as swollen with anger as it had a few moments ago. His shoulders slumped, and he looked down at his feet.

"What do you want from me?" he asked, the fire in his voice extinguished.

"If you'll allow me to sit here with you for a few minutes," I said, "I'll tell you."

Chapter Seventeen

My unpleasant visit with H.B., if you could call it a "visit"—"visits" back home have a much more sanguine connotation—left me both somewhat shaken and more optimistic that I might finally get to the truth about Junior Bennett's murder and the accusation that Ty Ramos was responsible for it. I grabbed the first taxi I could find outside Bennett's office and went directly to the Duffy house. Both Jack and Meg were there.

"How was your shopping expedition?" Meg asked.

"Successful," I said, pointing to the small bag of things I had purchased. "But I found more than I'd bargained for."

"Happens to the best of us," Jack said. "Meg always ends up with more than she set out to buy."

"I'm not talking about purchases, Jack," I said. "Where's Ty?"

"Upstairs, trying to catch up on some of the sleep that he missed last night," Meg said. "He was just exhausted when we got home. I don't think he closed his eyes all night, worrying about whether his bail would be revoked."

"Good," I said. "I hope he gets some rest. In the meantime, I have something important to tell you."

I recounted for them the scene I'd overheard between H.B. and the man with the cell phone—who I now knew was named Jake Giacondi—and how it had ended with H.B. knocking Giacondi to the ground, opening his scalp, and threatening worse.

"This is remarkable news, Jess," Jack said. He got up from his chair and began to walk back and forth. "You say this Giacondi fellow is a bookie?"

"That's right," I replied.

"And Bennett has been betting against the Rattlers?"

"Right again, at least according to Giacondi. I believe him, and not just because he said so. I overheard the exchange between him and Bennett, when he threatened to go to the press. There's no doubt in my mind that the owner of the Rattlers has been betting against them. That would help explain his mood following their win in the final game."

"He *was* very sour for a man whose team had just won the championship," Meg said. "Remember, in the locker room?"

"Exactly," I said. "And at the dinner, too. We all thought that he was angry because the manager pulled his son from the lineup for Ty to pinch-hit. But I kept thinking there had to be more to it than that. He evidently lost a lot of money on that game and was furious, which would account for his unpleasant postgame behavior."

"Yes, but the question is, with whom is he furious?" Jack said.

"Sit down, Jack," Meg said. "You'll wear out the carpet."

He stopped pacing and turned to me. "What I'm trying to figure out, Jess, is how this information you've come up with ties in with Junior Bennett's murder."

"I don't have the answer for that just yet," I said. "I'm not a betting person, but if I were, I'd wager that it ties in directly."

"How can we find out?" Meg asked.

"The only way I can think of is to confront some of the people who might be involved in betting."

We were so engrossed in our conversation that we failed to see Ty, who stood in the doorway.

"What are you talking about?" he said, stifling a yawn.

"Good nap?" Meg asked.

He rolled his shoulders. "Yeah, um, I mean, yes. I feel a little better."

"Come in, son," said Jack, taking a seat on the sofa. "There's something I'd like to ask you."

Ty took the space next to his foster father.

"Mrs. Fletcher has come up with some interesting information," Jack said.

I hoped he wouldn't share with Ty what I'd learned about Harrison Bennett. It was better to keep it between us, at least for the time being.

"How much betting on baseball goes on with your teammates?" Jack asked.

"Betting?" Ty said, surprised by the question—and not pleasantly. Whereas he had been lethargic and still sleepy when he entered the room, he was now tense, his posture stiff.

"Yes, betting, particularly on your games."

Ty avoided looking at Jack. "Some, I guess," he said, rubbing his hands together.

"Some? Can you be a little more specific?" Jack's voice had an edge to it.

"What difference does it make?" Ty asked. "It won't help me."

"We'll be the judge of that," Jack said. "Who bets on the games?"

"Ah, sir, please, I—"

"Have you bet on them, son?"

Ty didn't respond. We all sat in silence.

"Once," he said. "Maybe a couple of times."

"Did you bet *against* the Rattlers?" his foster father asked.

"Never!" Ty said, completely out of his lethargy and animated now. "I would never do that. I never even bet on a Rattlers game. It was always one of the major-league teams."

"Always?" Jack said. "Sounds as though it was more than once or twice."

Ty said nothing.

"I'm glad to hear that you never bet on your own team," Jack said, "for *or* against."

"May I be excused?" Ty asked.

"No! I want your promise you'll never place another illegal bet."

"It's not like I was doing it all the time. And, anyway, I'm not the only one."

"Oh, Ty," Meg said, a world of disappointment in her voice.

"Who else on your team was placing bets?" Jack asked.

"You know I'm not going to tell you that. I'm not going to rat out my teammates. It was no big deal. If a guy needed a little money, sometimes he would bet if he thought it was a sure thing."

"How much did you lose?"

"Maybe ten bucks. I won a couple of times, too, but I didn't bet very much. I don't like to lose."

"Thank goodness for small favors," Jack said. "Don't you know every time you break the law, no matter how innocent you think it is, you're supporting the criminal population? They don't make it day to day without you and your small-time bets. You're supplying their everyday meat and potatoes so they can go on to gorge themselves on bigger feasts. Your little breach of the law keeps them going."

He looked at Ty, who was visibly upset. "All right. Get out of here."

Ty bolted from the room and took the stairs two at a time, returning to his room, and likely his bed.

"I'm shocked," Meg said after Ty was gone.

"At least he gave us an honest answer," Jack said. To me: "It doesn't help tie anything to the murder, Jess."

"I'm not so sure," I said. "Meg, you called me on my cell phone when I was in Patsy's restaurant wearing your wig. Remember?"

"Sure. I was envious. I wanted to be there, too."

"You said during that conversation that Jack had learned Karen Locke was involved in some sort of investigation of sports betting."

"Yes, I did. Jack, remember you told me that?"

He nodded.

"Who told *you*?" I asked him.

"A friend at the club. He runs a PR agency in Mesa. He pretty much has a finger on the media pulse."

"Do either of you know where Ms. Locke lives?"

Meg and Jack looked at each other and shrugged.

"We can look it up," Meg suggested.

"She'll have an unlisted number and address," Jack said. "Everybody in the media does."

Meg ignored his negative comment and pulled out a local phone directory from a cabinet. "Here it is," she said. "K. L. Locke. Must be her. The only other *K* here is Kenneth." She read off the address and phone number, which I noted on a slip of paper.

"Do you know where this is?" I asked.

"I think it's a condominium development on the southern edge of town," Jack said, "not far from where I play golf. But you'd better call first. K. Locke could be Kerry Locke, or Keith Locke, or—"

"I'd rather assume it's her," I said, "and show up unannounced. Will you drive me?"

"Sure," Jack said, picking up a Rattlers cap and

putting it on, "but I still think you're off on a wild-goose chase."

"That may be," I said, "but I learned long ago to never second-guess my gut instincts."

Jack was right. The address in the phone book for K. L. Locke was a new condominium development on a rise that afforded a limited view of mountains in the far distance. We pulled up in front of a town house with the number listed in the book.

"So, what do we do now?" Jack asked. "Are we on a stakeout?"

"Let's just give it a couple of minutes to see if anyone comes in or out," I said. "Then I'll ring the bell."

"Okay, but I think you're wasting your time." He slid down in his seat, pulled the bill of his cap down over his eyes, and pretended to snore.

"There she is," I said, watching the door on the attached garage go up.

Karen pulled her car in, got out, climbed the stairs, and disappeared inside the house.

"I'll wait for you," Jack said.

"Please don't," I said, opening the car door. "I have no idea how long I'll be."

"Not a problem," he said. "I'll go hang out at the clubhouse. It's only a few minutes from here." He wrote down his cell number and handed it to me. "Give a call when you're finished."

"I will. And thanks, Jack."

"Hey, you have a lot better instincts than mine at this point. Go for it, whatever it is."

He drove off, and I approached the front door,

which was up a set of three brick steps. I rang the bell. I heard movement inside, but no one answered. I was then aware of someone peeking through a curtain on a narrow window at the side of the door. I rang again. The door opened and I was face-to-face with Karen Locke.

"What do you want?" she asked.

"I was hoping to have a chance to speak with you," I said. "I apologize for just barging in like this, but it's terribly important."

"You're Jessica Fletcher, the mystery writer."

"That's right," I said.

"I didn't appreciate what you said to me at the spa," she said. "I didn't deserve it."

"You're right," I said. "I'm afraid I allowed my emotions to get the better of me. It was just that my friend Meg Duffy was in a difficult situation and I couldn't—"

To my surprise, Karen opened the door wider. "Yeah," she said, "I guess I was a little too aggressive, considering what she's going through. Why are you here?"

"To ask you some questions about the investigative report you've been working on."

Her eyebrows went up into question marks.

"About betting on sports," I added.

"How did you know about that?"

"A friend of a friend," I answered. "It's not idle curiosity on my part," I said. "I believe that the murder of Junior Bennett is linked, in some way, to gambling. I don't know what that link is yet, but I was hoping you might help me establish it." I paused. "A young man's life hangs in the balance."

"Ty Ramos," she said flatly.

"Yes."

"Who is it?" a male voice asked. He came to the door and stood behind Karen. He was a good-looking middle-aged man, slightly taller than she. His hair and eyes were brown, his expression pleasant.

"This is Jessica Fletcher," Karen said. "She's a mystery writer."

"Sure," he said. "I've heard of you."

"She wants to ask me a few questions," Karen told him.

"Oh? Are you going to be in one of her novels?"

"I don't think so," Karen said.

There was an awkward silence.

"Come on in," he said.

Karen shot him a hard look. "Yes, come in," she said. "I don't have a lot of time. I'm due at the station in a few hours."

"I promise not to take too long," I said, following them inside.

"I'll leave you two alone," he said. "I'm marinating a steak for the grill. There's plenty if you want to join us for dinner. My name's Jerry, by the way. Jerry Lansing." He extended his hand and smiled.

"Nice meeting you," I said, "and thank you for the invitation, but I'm expected for dinner elsewhere."

He left us alone in the somewhat disheveled living room. Clothing fresh from the dryer and in need of folding was piled on chairs. Stacks of cardboard boxes took up much of the floor space.

"Pardon the mess," she said. "I haven't been here very long and still have lots of unpacking to do."

"I know how difficult moving is," I said. "One of life's primary stresses. I promised I wouldn't take too much of your time, Ms. Locke, so let me be direct. I've learned that Harrison Bennett bets on Rattler games, often against his own team. Does that match up with what you've uncovered during your investigation?"

A delayed nod was her answer.

"What about Junior Bennett?"

"What about him?"

"Did he bet against his own team, too?"

"Since you seem to know a lot, Mrs. Fletcher, why not tell *me* the answer."

"I understand he did," I said.

"Your source?"

"A man named Giacondi."

"Jake Giacondi," she said.

"You obviously know him," I said.

"Sure. Everybody in Mesa knows Jake. He's kind of a sad case, a wise-guy wannabe who doesn't have what it takes to move up. He's been around as long as I've been here, running numbers, booking bets, handling errands for some of the real wise guys in Arizona. He told you about Junior?" She shook her head. "Wouldn't you know it?"

"Yes. He said Junior was the one who placed bets with him on behalf of his father. Is he correct?"

Another nod of her head.

"Were other members of the team betting?" I asked. I knew my time with her would be limited and wanted to make optimum use of every minute.

"Some of the players," she replied.

"Ty Ramos?"

"Not that I heard," she said. Her answer pleased me.

"Which players?"

She laughed. "You were critical of me, Mrs. Fletcher, for being aggressive in my questioning. I think *you* might be crossing the line."

"If I am, I apologize," I said, "but Ty Ramos's life has already been thrown into turmoil and his future compromised. I assure you, Ms. Locke, that I'm not out to hurt anyone over the gambling issue. But I am out to clear Ty."

She pondered my comment, chewing her cheek and allowing one foot to bounce up and down. "Some of the players are into gambling on the games more than others. Carter Menzies was heavy into Jake Giacondi."

"Carter?" I said, incredulous.

"Yeah, I know," she said, "it goes against type. Nice guy, good ballplayer, clean-cut, handsome, every mother's dream of a potential son-in-law. Look, Mrs. Fletcher, I'm not being critical of Carter and other players like him. He came out of a tough childhood. Players at this level don't get paid much and are always looking for some extra money. They get a few so-called insider tips, latch on to someone like Giacondi, and put down a few bucks. Innocent enough. The problem is that it becomes a habit. You lose a few bets and double up to recoup your losses, only the losses keep getting bigger. Don't get me wrong. I have no information that Carter ever bet against the Rattlers, and I'm not about to point to him by name in my report. But you wanted an example of a player who bets, and I gave you one."

"I understand," I said.

She pulled a stick of gum from a pocket in her blouse, unwrapped it, and began to chew.

"Does that help with the morning sickness?" I asked pleasantly.

She couldn't help but smile. "You're a very astute lady, Mrs. Fletcher. You picked up on my pregnancy before anyone else did."

"It just made sense to me, that's all."

"You know what?" she said.

"What?"

"I'm going to level with you, completely level with you. I'm really not sure why, but I sure don't want to see Ty take the rap for something if he didn't do it. Somehow, I trust you to do the right thing."

"Thank you," I said. "I know it's difficult for you because of your relationship with Junior Bennett and—"

"You were right about my being pregnant, Mrs. Fletcher, but wrong about the father. Junior wasn't the father."

"Oh?"

"My fiancé is," she said, indicating the kitchen with

a nod of her head. "Jerry and I are getting married. That's why we just moved in together."

"That's nice," I said.

"Yeah, I think so," she said, smiling. "You want to know about Junior? I went out with him to learn what I could about H.B.'s gambling. It was basically an undercover job, but nothing happened under the covers, so to speak. I couldn't stand Junior, although I'm not glad he's dead. He was a spoiled, selfish, nasty young guy. How I put up with him for as long as I did is beyond me."

"It must have been difficult, engaging in a relationship in order to get a story."

"I know what you're thinking," she said. "Not very nice of me to use someone like that. Well, the FBI does it all the time. So do the cops. My editor knew what I intended and had okayed the project ahead of time. And Jerry knew about it, too. So, it's not like I'm exactly a Jezebel."

"It's not my place to be judgmental, Ms. Locke. As I've said, my only interest is to clear Ty Ramos."

"I appreciate that," she said.

"You were with Junior at the bar the night he was killed."

"Is that a question?"

"No. I know you were the one who called nine-one-one."

"That's right."

"I also understand that you and Junior had a fight that night."

"Is there anything you don't know, Mrs. Fletcher?"

"Lots, I'm afraid. What did you fight about?"

"We fought about Ty."

"Ty? Why?"

"Junior was bad-mouthing Ty something fierce, calling him every name under the sun. I wouldn't want to repeat what he said."

"There's no need to. My only question is why you were compelled to come to Ty's defense."

"Because I'd had enough of Junior's nastiness. If he thought he could get away with bad-mouthing someone, he did. He just tortured that poor guy from the fan club. It made me sick. By that point, I had decided to break off the relationship, if you can even call it that. I had what I needed, anyway."

"So you were a witness to Junior's abusiveness to Ty?"

"It went beyond that. Believe me, Mrs. Fletcher, Junior Bennett's enmity against Ty was an obsession. I suppose he got a lot of his hatred from his father. God, how I detest that man. Anyway, Junior was determined to sink Ty's chances of making it to the major leagues. He lied about him constantly, made up stories about how Ty was dealing drugs and having sex with underage girls and placing bets against his own team. It was all a lie, and I'd reached a point where, story or no story, I wasn't about to be a party to it any longer. Ty Ramos is as nice a guy as you could ever meet, a straight shooter in every sense of the word."

I thought of Ty's admission that he, too, had placed some bets on sporting events, and was glad Karen Locke wasn't aware of it.

"Tell me about finding the body," I said.

She shrugged. "Junior had too much to drink, as usual, and went after his two favorite victims. He had already reduced the fan club president to tears. All the kid wanted was for him to sign his bat."

"An aluminum bat?" I asked.

She nodded. "Carter took it and said he'd get the guys to sign it."

"And did he?"

"I didn't see."

"And Junior's other favorite victim was Ty, I assume."

"Yes. Junior was at his bigoted best that night, calling Ty every name in the book, and then disparaging his mother. Anyway, the boys decided to take it outside. I went to get a ginger ale and talk to the bartender. She and I went to school together. The whole team went outside to watch the fight, but they came back right away. I didn't see Junior, but I didn't think anything of it. The guys on the team took off, and when Junior didn't come in after an hour, I went to find him."

Jerry poked his head into the living room. "Steak's ready to go," he announced. "Sure you can't stay for dinner, Mrs. Fletcher? We have lots."

"Again, thank you, no. I'd better be going."

He disappeared again into the kitchen, and I stood. "I can't tell you how much I appreciate your openness, Ms. Locke. And I apologize if what I said at the spa offended you."

"I deserved it, Mrs. Fletcher. Frankly, I'm seriously considering getting out of television reporting after the baby is born. You may not believe this, but I was ashamed of what I did to Mrs. Duffy. I don't enjoy sticking microphones in the faces of grieving people. Please pass along my apologies to the Duffys."

"I'm sure they'll be happy to hear that, Ms. Locke. I have to call Judge Duffy for a ride home. He's at a golf course near here."

"You can use the phone in the den."

I called Jack and he said he'd be by to pick me up in fifteen minutes. Karen invited me to join them on the patio, where her fiancé had set a table and served up sliced steak, a leafy green salad, French bread, and a bottle of Zinfandel, which he insisted I taste. "Karen can't have it," he said, "and I want someone to appreciate what a great vintage this is."

"It's delicious," I said, and turned to Karen. "Have you finished your report on gambling?"

"Just about," she said. "It's a sad story, far beyond the segment on sports betting here in Arizona. People use their mortgage money to buy lottery tickets. They place bets with money that should be used to put food on their tables. It's tragic, really. Gambling can be an insidious addiction, a disease. It's ruined so many people."

"A piece of bread?" Jerry asked me. "Goes nicely with the wine."

"No, thank you, I—"

"Sylvester Cole is a case in point," Karen said absently, sprinkling dressing on her salad.

I'd picked up my wine glass but stopped with it halfway to my lips. "What do you mean?" I asked.

"He's an example of gambling being capable of ruining someone," she said. "He was a successful sports agent a while back, but his gambling habit got the better of him. From what I've been able to dig up, he's on the brink of bankruptcy. That's why he's pursuing Ty so aggressively as a client. He needs a big score to pull himself out of debt, and Ty could be his savior."

"I see," I said, wondering whether the Duffys were aware of the agent's dire financial straits. If so, I was certain they wouldn't encourage Ty to sign with him under any circumstances.

A car horn sounded.

"That's my ride," I said, taking a last quick sip of wine. "I can't thank you enough for your hospitality— and your candor. Congratulations on your pending marriage and the birth of your baby."

She walked me to the door.

"Good luck with clearing Ty," she said. "I hope he didn't do it, and, if so, I hope you can help get him off."

"Thanks," I said, thinking that if Ty were to be cleared, it would take a lot more than luck.

I climbed into Jack's car, my mind racing with all I'd learned and put together.

"Any luck?" he asked.

"Maybe," I said. "I've got to make an important phone call."

Chapter Eighteen

Thompson Stadium was an eerie place without fans cheering for their favorite teams. There was a deathly stillness, interrupted only by loud claps of thunder, and streaks of vivid white lightning in the dark skies above. The weather forecast was for a violent cold front to move through, with thunderstorms producing heavy hail and downpours. A flash flood warning was in effect.

Meg Duffy had wanted to accompany Jack and me, but Jack persuaded her to stay home with Ty. "No telling what's going to happen," he told her. "I'd feel more comfortable with you here." She protested mildly but eventually agreed. Ty had wanted to come, too, but Jack reminded him that he was under house arrest and would be in violation of his bail if he left the house for anything other than court appearances and doctor visits. I knew how much he wanted to be with his teammates again, and felt bad for him. But the law is the law, and violating even a minor aspect of it would be foolhardy.

Jack peppered me with questions as we drove to the stadium. I answered as best I could without giving away too much information.

"You're convinced you've identified Junior Bennett's murderer?" he asked more than once.

"I believe I have," I replied each time.

"Well, who is it?" he responded, sounding as though he were demanding an answer from his customary perch behind a courtroom bench.

"I know it's difficult for you," I said, "but you'll just have to exercise some patience." I had to smile at the expression on his face. Patience was not Judge Jack Duffy's strong suit.

We pulled into the parking lot, unmanned now that the season was over, and crossed it to spots reserved for players, team managers, and stadium employees.

"That's H.B.'s car, isn't it?" Jack asked, pointing to a silver Jaguar with its owner's initials on the license plate, followed by a number indicating which car it was in his fleet of vehicles.

"Yes, I've seen him in it before," I said.

"What's he doing here?" Jack muttered as he pulled into a space a few removed from the Jaguar.

"We'll find out soon enough," I replied.

"You knew he'd be here," he said.

"Let's just say I'm glad he is." I turned and placed my hand on his arm. "Look, Jack, I know I'm keeping you in the dark about tonight, but I feel it's necessary if I'm to be successful."

"And I don't want to do anything to get in your way, Jess. All I want is for Ty to be exonerated and to be able to get on with his life."

"We share that goal," I said.

Other cars started arriving, including a few in which team members were crowded in together. It reminded me of those small circus cars from which a dozen people seem to emerge. They poured out one after the other, their attire spanning the range from neat, conservative outfits to baggy shorts, oversize T-shirts, and sandals. Carter Menzies was one of the better-dressed players, especially in contrast to the catcher, Billy Murphy, who looked as though he was wearing pajama bottoms topped by a sleeveless white undershirt.

"How did you manage to get the team here on such short notice?" Jack asked. "With the season over, these guys don't have any obligation to show up."

"Oh, but I think they do, Jack, especially when their bosses, the team owner and its manager, put out the word."

"How did you know they'd be doing that?" he asked.

"I asked them to."

"Will you please tell me—"

"All in due time," I said. "Let's get inside and join them."

As we left Jack's car and walked toward the players' entrance, Buddy Washington pulled up.

"Hello, Buddy," we said as the manager got out of

his car and paused to hitch up his trousers over his sizable girth.

"Hello to you," Buddy said.

"How's your wife?" I asked.

"Doing better," he replied, a smile crossing his face. "It looks like the treatments are working. She's gaining strength every day, and her spirits are improving, too."

"That's wonderful news," I said.

"It sure is," Buddy said. "So, here I am. H.B. put out the word and we all jump."

"That's nothing new, is it?" Jack said.

"I suppose not. What brings you here tonight, Mrs. Fletcher?" Buddy asked. "Do you have a locker to clean out, too?"

I laughed. "No, I don't, but if I did, I'm not sure I'd want anyone to know what's in it. I remember what you said at the team dinner about being able to know a lot about a player's entire life by what's in his locker."

Buddy chuckled. "It's true," he said. "I should have had them back here to clean them out sooner, but with all that's been going on, the wife's situation and the murder and all, I just never got around to it. What I can't figure out is why H.B. decided we had to do it now. He called and said he had something important to say to the team and wanted the lockers cleaned at the same time. Anybody know what it's all about?"

"I assume we'll find out soon enough," I said.

A particularly loud clap of thunder caused us all to wince and look up into the increasingly threatening sky. I felt a raindrop on my nose. "I think it's time we got inside," I said.

As we approached the entrance, I stopped and pointed to a Dumpster thirty feet away. A few stray pieces of yellow crime scene tape fluttered from it in the breeze. "That must be where the murder weapon was found," I said. "The aluminum bat."

"That's right," Buddy said. "The cover must have broken off. They'd better get it fixed before garbage piles up and flows over the top. Great for the birds, though," he said with a chuckle.

Those who'd already arrived were mingling in the team's locker room when we walked in. A row of benches fronted the lockers and some of the players were already seated. Murph stood by his locker, twirling the dial of his combination lock. The president of the Rattlers' fan club, whom I knew only by his first name, Lou—surely Dweeb wasn't his last name—had grabbed a seat at the end of one bench in the midst of the players. He had his signature Hawaiian shirt on and a Rattlers baseball hat worn backwards, the fashion of the day with young people.

Harrison Bennett waited near the door. He was immaculately dressed, as usual, a patrician figure lording over his domain. He was alone, and despite all that had transpired over the past few days, I felt a certain sympathy for him. No matter how much money he'd managed to accumulate, and regardless of the power he generated in the community and within his own family, this was a man who would always be alone, isolated from those human qualities that bring us love and respect, and inclusion in the human race. Even though they owed their minor-league jobs to H.B., the Rattlers players, who undoubtedly feared his wrath, were scornful of the man in private. A sad legacy.

"I don't see Sylvester Cole," I said to Jack, as we took an empty bench. "Did you call him?"

"I did exactly what you asked me to do, Jess. I told him there was going to be a team meeting here and asked him to meet me. He said he would."

"I assume he asked why you wanted him here."

"Sure. He asked, but I said I'd explain it to him later. Of course, I'd be more comfortable knowing *why* I asked him to meet me."

"He might have some light to shed on what happened to Junior Bennett," I said.

"You think he knows something that would point to the real killer?"

"Yes," I said. "I think he does."

Buddy Washington clapped his hands and asked for everyone's attention. There was a lot of shuffling and quips between the players, but they eventually settled down. Buddy turned to Bennett. "Want to start us off, Mr. Bennett?" he said.

Bennett looked at me, turned to his manager and said, "Not at the moment. You go ahead, Buddy."

"Okay then," Buddy said, "listen up. Mr. Bennett called this meeting. I got some announcements for you, like where to send your off-season addresses if you want to find out if we want you back. Then H.B. wants everyone's lockers cleaned out. No dawdling on this."

"Now?" Carter asked, amid rumbles of complaint from his teammates.

"Couldn't we do this tomorrow?" Sam said. "I've got a date tonight."

His teammates whooped. "What's this date look like?" Murph shouted.

"She must need glasses if she wants to go out with him," said Nassani.

"Or a guide dog," another player put in.

"Very funny. Very funny," Sam said.

"I know, I know," Buddy said, holding his hands in a defensive position. "But let's just get it done and—"

Carter leaned forward to talk to Jack. "You here to empty out Ty's locker, Judge?" he asked.

Jack nodded.

"I could have done that for you. You didn't have to come yourself."

"And I wanted to see what a baseball locker room looked like," I said. "The judge said this was a good time."

Carter turned back to Buddy, who was making announcements, just as Sylvester Cole walked into the room.

"Hello, Sylvester," Buddy said. "Didn't expect to see you."

"Didn't expect to be here myself," Cole said, taking a seat next to Jack and leaning close to his ear to say something. Jack wiggled his fingers, a nonverbal response that indicated they'd talk later.

Buddy glanced at his boss, as if waiting for him to take over the meeting before he released the players to clean out their lockers. Buddy's expression mirrored his confusion. The same question he'd posed outside was obviously on his mind at this moment: Why had H.B. called this last-minute meeting? The owner had told Buddy he wanted to address the team about some issue. What was it? Had it been a ploy by Bennett just to get the locker room cleaned out? What was going on here?

Some of the players began to talk among themselves, darting glances at Buddy and H.B.

Bennett cleared his throat and came to Buddy's side. "What I have to say," he said haltingly, "has to do with my son's death."

The voices in the locker room hushed immediately.

"I know that none of you like me, and probably most of you didn't give a damn about Junior or the way he died. But I think Mrs. Fletcher might change a few minds."

All eyes turned in my direction.

"I want you to listen carefully to what she has to say." Bennett nodded at me and stepped back. I stood, straightened my skirt, and went to the front of the room.

"Thank you for coming here on such short notice," I said. "I wouldn't have asked Mr. Bennett to call this meeting unless there was a very good reason for it, and murder, I think, ranks high on any list of good reasons. Junior Bennett's murder was a tragedy that didn't have to happen. It's devastated his family, and has had an impact on everyone in this room." I allowed my gaze to wander over the assembled, stopping briefly at each face, each set of eyes, finally coming to rest on Carter Menzies. He looked away and shifted in his chair.

"Junior Bennett was killed with an aluminum baseball bat," I said. "You, Carter, were the last person to have one in your possession at the Crazy Coyote, yet when I asked you if you'd seen it that night, you said no."

He looked right and left at his teammates, none of whom said anything. "Um, I don't remember."

I pointed at the president of the Rattlers' fan club. "Lou, who seems to live and die for the Rattlers, might remember. He'd brought a bat to the Crazy Coyote. Want to tell us why, Lou?"

Lou pushed himself up off the bench. "You know, I love this team," he said. "I'm your biggest fan, even when you're not nice to me. I know a lot of you make fun of me behind my back."

Many of the players looked away, uncomfortable.

"But I don't care. I just like hanging out with you guys. You're the greatest. Even when you don't win. But you did. We're the champs!" He pumped a fist in the air, hoping for a cheer. No one responded.

"Lou," I said. "Tell us about the bat."

"Oh, okay. Sorry. I, um, brought my bat to the Coyote for Junior and all you guys to sign. But Junior didn't want to do it just then. He would have done it later. I know he would. He was just in a bad mood. He was having a fight with his girlfriend. Anyhow, Carter took the bat and said he'd get Junior and the rest of you to sign it for me. You're the best, Carter."

Carter sat with his forearms resting on his knees, eyes trained on the floor. He swiveled his head to look at Lou. "Thanks, Lou."

"And Lou," I said, "was it an aluminum bat?"

"Yeah."

"Carter." I fixed the handsome young outfielder in my stare. "When I asked you and some of your teammates if anyone had seen the bat, you all said no. Was that true, Carter? Is Lou lying?"

Carter started to speak, stopped, shook his head. Finally he looked up at me. "No, Mrs. Fletcher. I saw the bat."

"So you did take the bat from Lou and promise to get Junior to sign it. Isn't that right, Carter?"

"That's about right," he said. "Yeah, that happened."

"Which could mean you were the last person to have possession of that bat—the bat that turned out to be the weapon that killed Junior."

His teammates began whispering to each other.

"Wait a minute," Carter said. "Are you accusing me—?"

"I'm not accusing anyone right now. Don't jump to conclusions. I'm simply tracing the possession of an aluminum bat."

"Did Junior sign it?" Billy Nassani asked Carter.

"No," Carter said. "I mean, I wanted to get Junior to sign it for the dweeb but—"

There were snickers around the room.

"I think you mean Lou, don't you?" I said.

Carter blushed. "Yeah, sorry. I wanted to get Junior to sign it for Lou, but he wasn't around."

"What did you do with the bat?" I asked.

"Shoot. I don't know. Oh, wait a minute. I remember all the guys running outside, so I went outside, too, and I brought it with me. That's when I saw Ty deck Junior. I just left it propped up against the building and went to stop the fight."

"And that's the last time you saw it?" I asked.

"Yes. Right. Absolutely. I never saw it again."

Billy Murphy, the team's catcher, guffawed.

"What's that supposed to mean?" Carter asked angrily.

"Nothing, man. Chill."

"It means," I said, "that anyone who went into the parking lot to watch the fight between Junior and Ty—any one of you—could have picked up that bat."

The ballplayers squirmed in their seats, eyes darting around the room.

I turned my attention to Lou, the fan club president. "Did you ever see the bat again, Lou?" I asked.

He shook his head. "No, ma'am, I never did."

"But someone did," I said. "Whoever killed Junior found that bat outside the bar and used it as a murder weapon."

There were nods and verbal sounds of agreement.

Sam spoke up. "I bet it was his girlfriend, that reporter, Karen Locke. She was fighting with him all night."

"Speedster's right," Murph called out.

"Did any of you witness that fight?"

"I saw them argue," Nassani said, "but I don't know what it was about."

"That's right," someone else said. "She and Junior didn't get along. They were always fighting. Man, I never knew what he saw in her."

I wondered whether Karen could hear this exchange through the walls of the locker room. I'd called her after returning to the Duffys' home, told her of the meeting that was planned, and suggested she might want to come to the stadium.

"Stay out of sight until I call you," I'd told her. Was she outside at that moment? I hoped so.

"This is ridiculous," Carter said. "The way I always figured it, somebody happened on Junior that night outside the bar and robbed him. Junior fought back and got killed. There were lots of people in the Coyote that night, not just us."

"I'm afraid that doesn't hold water, Carter," I said. "The police report indicates that nothing was missing from Junior that night. His wallet and cash were on his person."

Cole stood up to leave. "Hey, listen, this is a nice intellectual exercise, Mrs. Fletcher, but I don't see why it concerns me or Judge Duffy." He turned to Jack. "Why don't we talk outside?"

I shifted my attention to the back of the room. "I appreciate your coming here this evening, Sylvester," I said.

"Fine," he said, "but none of this means anything to me. Sure, I hope Junior's killer gets caught and punished, but I came here to talk business with Judge Duffy. We just got caught up in this meeting, right, Judge?"

"Actually, Sylvester, I asked for you to be here," I said.

"I can't imagine what for. And I've got better things to do right now. So I'll say ciao."

"Maybe you can answer a few questions before you leave."

"I don't see the need to answer any questions. I've already spoken to the police. With all due respect, you're not a policeman, Mrs. Fletcher."

"But I am," came a voice from the door. Sheriff Hualga was leaning against the jamb, his arms folded across his chest.

I heaved a small sigh of relief. I'd informed him of my plans for the meeting and he'd been skeptical. But I'd prevailed upon him to be available in the event things got out of hand. We weren't at that point yet, thank goodness. But I was grateful to see that he'd arrived.

"I don't think you'll be leaving, Mr. Cole," I said.

Cole appeared unsure of what action to take next.

"You might as well sit down again," I said. "As you can see, you're not going anywhere until I've finished what I have to say."

He gave me a hateful look but walked back to the bench. "Are you involved in this?" he snarled at Jack Duffy.

Jack smiled and indicated with his hand Cole's empty chair. "I'm not sure where this is going," Jack said, "but it sounds like it's about to get interesting."

Cole sat as I prepared to continue. But he popped up again and said in a loud voice, "This is crazy. Are you accusing me of killing Junior Bennett? Because if you are, I want to know it. I want to know why I'm being singled out here."

I said nothing in response.

"Well," he said, "if you are, you've gone off the deep end, Mrs. Fletcher. Maybe you've been reading too many of your own mystery novels." He looked at the others in the room for a sign of support, but instead received blank stares.

"Hey," he said to the players, who'd turned in their seats to watch, "I'm no murderer. I'm a sports agent. I'm on your side. I love you guys. We work together, and I make my living from getting you the best deals possible."

"Is that why you killed Junior?" I asked matter-of-factly.

"What are you talking about? Sheriff, she's nuts," he shouted, red-faced. "I wasn't interested in representing Junior. I had nothing to do with Junior. Ask Mr. Bennett. Ty Ramos was the one I wanted to sign."

"Exactly," I said.

Cole took a deep breath, then shook his head and winked at the players, as if he were humoring an addled aunt. He shrugged his shoulders and flashed that winning smile he used to charm many a prospective client. "Look, I'm sure there's been some misunderstanding. You know me. I wouldn't hurt a fly. I'm a good guy." He made eye contact with each man, one at a time. "Does anybody here think I'd let Ty Ramos take the rap for something I did? I love that kid like he is my own brother. I want to see him make it to the Big Show, become a superstar. We can make millions together. Together! Remember, I don't make anything if he's sitting in jail. I'm the last guy who'd want to see him end up in prison for the rest of his life for something he didn't do."

"Very convincing, Mr. Cole," I said, "but you don't have to be an expert in psychology to know that self-preservation is a primary instinct, more important even than making money. You didn't think about that when killing Junior, did you? All you thought about was protecting an investment."

He made a couple of false starts, sputtering, looking from person to person for understanding. Receiving none, he said, "You've got it all wrong, Mrs. Fletcher."

"I don't think so," I said. "Under different circumstances, what you say would be true. Ty Ramos would have been your meal ticket. Signing him could have pulled you out of bankruptcy."

"What are you talking about?" he barked, but the blood had drained from his face.

"I'm talking about your gambling debts and how betting has put you in an untenable financial position."

Jack stiffened in his seat, glanced at me, and slowly shook his head, probably more in upset at having been taken in by the smooth-talking agent than shock at learning the truth about the murderer.

Cole pulled himself up to full height and assumed a defiant expression and posture. "A recent temporary setback," he said. "Just a bump in the road. Everyone has them. How would killing Junior Bennett help that?"

"Junior threatened your investment," I said. "He was obsessed with destroying Ty's chances to make it into the major leagues. He was spreading lies about him, vicious lies that when coupled with aspects of Ty's background could well have sunk his chances to ever become a major-leaguer. He had you convinced, didn't he, Mr. Bennett? You asked the league to look into Ty's activities—you told me that yourself. Did they find anything?"

"Not yet," H.B. said, scowling. "Go on."

I turned back to Cole. "You had to stop Junior, didn't you, to protect Ty's career, but you never imagined that Ty would be accused in your stead."

Cole now appeared ready to bolt. But Carter, Murph, and the other players stood up to block all possible exits from the room. I looked to Harrison Bennett for any angry reaction to what I'd just said about his deceased son. There was none. He sat ramrod straight in a chair, one leg crossed over the other, his face devoid of any telltale emotions. "Anything else, Mrs. Fletcher?"

"Yes," I said, looking at Cole. "You called Judge Duffy to inform him about the murder weapon being found."

"That's right. So?"

"You said the police found the bat in an open Dumpster outside this stadium. You heard it on the radio. Yet the police report said nothing about the

Dumpster being open, so the radio couldn't have reported it that way. It's not open usually. Buddy Washington was surprised to see it that way tonight. All the others are closed. But the person who wiped the bat clean and threw it away would have known this Dumpster was missing a top."

He started to respond, but no words came.

"You also spoke of Mr. Bennett's new Mercedes. It was green, you said. You hate the color green. Yet I believe H.B. had it delivered from the dealer the morning of the murder. He never even drove it himself. You couldn't have known it was green unless you'd seen it—unless you were at the Crazy Coyote the night Junior was killed."

"Mrs. Fletcher, I—"

"The police found a lot of footprints near Junior's body. Sheriff Hualga, you may want your officers to check out Mr. Cole's shoes. I'm confident the photographs of footprints from the crime scene contained in the police report will match up nicely with a pair of his shoes."

There was a deathly stillness in the room.

Cole's sudden smile was wide and engaging. "You're one smart lady, Mrs. Fletcher. I really have to hand it to you. The only problem is, you've got it all wrong."

"If I'm wrong," I said, "I'll be the first to apologize to you and to everyone else who heard my accusation."

"Yes, I was there, but I didn't murder Junior Bennett," he said. He looked around at the men in the room, his eyes bright.

"No?"

"No. It was self-defense."

"He attacked you?"

"That's right. That's right," he said, panting. "I went to that dive to ask him to lay off Ty, to stop trying to ruin Ramos's career. You were right about me being broke. That's why Ty was so important. I haven't shared this with the judge or Ty, but my sources tell me that there are two major-league teams eager and ready to sign him to a lucrative contract." He faced Jack. "See? That's why you have to sign the contract right now. A year in Triple-A ball and he'll be a starter at shortstop for either team. I'm talking serious money, Jack, enough to set the kid up for life."

"That may be," I said, "but let's get back to what happened that night."

"Okay," he said, swinging in my direction. "Like I said, I went to that bar to try and talk sense into Junior." His words came pouring out, in staccato, his breathing audible. "I was, I was even going to offer to cut Junior in on some of my commission if he'd leave Ty alone. I had pulled into the lot right after the fight. I saw all the guys in the parking lot filing back into the Coyote. Carter was dragging Ty away. Junior got to his feet and grabbed the bat someone left by the door, the one Carter Menzies said he left out there, the one the fan club kid gave him."

Carter was staring at Sylvester, his hands fisted in his lap.

"Junior had a bloody nose. I got out my handkerchief to give him, but he was swinging the bat, saying he was going to kill Ty with it—'smash his skull in' was how he put it. Junior was nuts, off the wall. I was trying to *prevent* a murder, don't you see?"

"You were trying to protect your investment is what I think," H.B. said.

"Right," Cole said, seeming unconcerned that he was talking to his victim's father. "Ty was my ticket to financial health. I didn't want him to get a bashed-in skull. I wrestled Junior for the bat and I got it away from him. All I intended to do was walk away with it. He jumped me. I swung the bat and caught him in the side of the head. I didn't mean to kill him. It just happened."

"If it was accidental," I said, "you should have called the police yourself. Instead, you wiped off the murder weapon with your handkerchief, threw the bat in the Dumpster, and let Ty get arrested for what you did."

I checked with Sheriff Hualga, who had a tight smile on his face. He cocked his head at me, eyebrows raised. "Gentlemen," he said. All the men swiveled to look at him. "I'd appreciate it if you all left the room right now. Not you, Mr. Cole."

H.B. rose from his chair and strode out the door. The Rattlers filed out after him, Buddy Washington waving them through the door until they were all out of the locker room. He closed the door himself as he left.

The sheriff stepped outside, too.

Jack stood, his movements slow and stiff. "You'll

have a decent defense in court," Jack said to Cole. "But it doesn't change things for me. What's important is that the authorities know that you were responsible for Junior's death, and that Ty can now go free."

"Judge, I think we need to talk," Cole said.

"I don't want to talk with you anymore," Jack said, and crossed the room to where Hualga stood.

"You're forgetting one thing, Mrs. Fletcher," Cole said, his voice urgent. "How could you do this to Ty? I thought the Duffys were your friends." He clucked his tongue as if he were chastising a student.

"What do you mean?"

"Ty's future. I'm the one with the contacts with those two teams I mentioned. They know I'm acting as Ty's agent. I can kill those deals just like this." He snapped his fingers.

"I doubt whether either of those teams—or any major-league team for that matter—will want to do business with a convicted felon, even if it results in no more than a manslaughter conviction."

"Exactly. That's the whole point, Mrs. Fletcher. So this is what I think you should do. You tell the sheriff that we spoke, and you made a big mistake, and I'll put the deal together for Ty."

"Jack just told you he's not interested in talking to you."

"The judge will come around once I have the deal in my pocket. Otherwise, think about this: You'll be responsible for ruining Ty's baseball career."

I was tempted to laugh, as regretful as it was. His

twisted logic and perverted view of his situation, and how to salvage it, was staggering.

"That sounds like an extortion threat on top of your other problems, Mr. Cole," I said.

"Hey, Mrs. Fletcher, not only are you a smart lady, I have the feeling you're a pragmatic one, too. This is what a good deal is all about. I'm off the hook for killing Junior—hell, if anybody deserved to die, it was Junior—and Ty Ramos gets to live his dream. What do you say? Do we have a deal?"

"Not only do we not have a deal, Mr. Cole, you don't have my respect or my sympathy. You try to tell your story to Sheriff Hualga. And you can also tell it to the media. I believe Karen Locke and a camera crew are waiting outside for an exclusive interview."

I walked away from him.

"I'll beat this," he called to my back.

Sheriff Hualga came back into the locker room. He shook my hand, and I left.

Outside the locker room, the Rattlers were loitering in the stadium hallway. A few players began clapping, which quickly became sustained applause. Karen Locke's cameraman switched on his light and filmed the ovation.

Karen approached me, her hand holding the microphone by her side. "Care to make a comment, Mrs. Fletcher?"

"Not now, if you don't mind."

"Sure. I understand."

We smiled at each other.

My eyes searched the crowd for Jack Duffy. I

found him standing beside Harrison Bennett and Buddy Washington.

I extended my hand to Bennett. "I'm sorry about your son," I said. "You did the right thing by helping gather everyone here tonight. I'm sure it must have been painful for you."

"I'm just glad it's over," he said.

I said to Jack Duffy, "Let's go, Judge. Meg and Ty will want to know the good news, and I'm suddenly very tired."

Chapter Nineteen

I accompanied the Duffys and Ty to court for Judge McQuaid's formal dismissal of the charges against Ty.

"I must say," McQuaid said from the bench, "that I take personal pleasure in releasing you, Ty Ramos. Your foster father, Judge Duffy, and your foster mother, Meg Duffy, are the sort of people who give humanity a good name. And I would be remiss if I didn't mention your friend from back East, Jessica Fletcher, who I understand moved heaven and earth to prove your innocence. Despite what cynics might say, good things do happen to good people, and I am delighted to be in the position to wish you well in your baseball career."

We were all standing during Judge McQuaid's comments.

"Put your troubled past behind you, young man." A wide grin crossed McQuaid's face. "And pound the tar out of that baseball. Case dismissed!"

I stayed in Mesa a few extra days to get in that

sunrise hot-air-balloon ride, although I never did add to my pilot's logbook. That would have to wait for a more opportune moment.

Jack, Meg, and Ty drove me to the Phoenix airport for my flight to Boston, where a charter service would deliver me to Cabot Cove. Ty, minus his court-ordered ankle bracelet, was as happy as you might expect a young man who'd faced a lifetime in prison and was now exonerated of all charges to be. We said our good-byes.

As I disembarked the charter flight, it felt good to be home.

Seth was wearing his Diamondbacks cap when we went to dinner at Maureen and Mort Metzger's home.

"We're trying out this new recipe," Maureen said. "You're the first ones to taste it, so be honest. If it isn't good, tell me."

Mort carried in a platter of barbecued chicken fresh off the grill and placed it on the table next to the salad and rice. "Here we go, folks. A taste of Mexico in Maine."

"I've been modifying the recipe," Maureen said.

"Yeah, the first time she made it, I had to use the garden hose to cool down my throat," Mort said.

Seth and I glanced at each other.

"Well, I'm game," I said. I took a piece of chicken and cut off a tiny slice. I raised the fork to my mouth and looked up. Three pairs of eyes were trained on me. "Here goes," I said. I chewed slowly, all the while under the intense gaze of my friends. I put the fork down and took a sip of water.

"Well, Mrs. F, what do think?"

"Delicious!" I pronounced.

"The chipotle gives it a nice smoky flavor with a little bit of heat," Maureen said, sitting back with a smile.

"Now that you know how much to use," her husband added. "Doc, would you like to try it?"

"My pleasure," Seth said, spearing a drumstick. "Heard any news from the Duffys?" he asked me.

"As a matter of fact, I have," I said. "Ty has been signed by the Boston Red Sox and will be playing Triple-A ball for their top farm team."

"That's great, Mrs. F."

"Ayuh," Seth proclaimed. "Nice to heah that young man is getting his life straightened out again. Always thought he was a good one."

The Duffys and I had kept in touch recently through phone calls and e-mails. I shared their excitement as Jack read me the news release from the Red Sox office: "In signing this extremely talented shortstop, we feel the future for our ball club is in good hands. Ty Ramos is not only a gifted athlete, he comes to us as a young man of character and commitment. We welcome him to the Red Sox organization."

"It's thanks to you, Jessica," Meg said during the phone call that delivered this wonderful news.

"No," I said. "It's thanks to Ty for being the fine young person he is, and to you and Jack for being so generous and willing to share your life with a young man who needed a family."

Ty got on the phone. "Mrs. Fletcher, I'm so grateful. When I'm playing at Fenway Park, you'll always have a special box seat at every game."

"That's sweet of you, Ty, and I just might take advantage of it. By the way, something has been nagging at me and I hope you can settle my mind."

"Anything for you."

"The first time I saw the bookie outside the hotel at your team victory dinner, he said he was going to get money from you to give to a woman. That wasn't a bet on a game, was it?"

"No, Mrs. Fletcher," he replied. "I guess I can tell you now. I already told the Duffys. Jake used to help me send money to my mother in the Dominican Republic."

"So she hasn't 'disappeared.' "

"She did for a while, but we're in touch now. She was afraid if the authorities knew where she was, I would be sent back to the D.R. But, thanks to the judge, that didn't happen."

"That's wonderful," I said.

"Yeah, um, I mean, yes," he said. "She's real proud of me. Once I'm playing for the Sox, I'm going to bring her up so she can watch me play a game. She's never been away from home, but she said she'll make the trip to see me. The Duffys said she can stay with them."

"More chicken, Mrs. F?"

"I don't think I can manage another bite," I said. "Everything was wonderful."

"Meant to tell you. I got a call from Sheriff Hualga."

"I was going to ask you about him."

Sheriff Hualga had been keeping Mort up to date on what was happening in the Cole case. A jury had bought his plea of self-defense but didn't let him off the hook entirely. Rather than acquit him on that basis, they'd found him guilty of a lesser charge, aggravated manslaughter. He was sentenced to six years in prison, with the possibility of parole after serving two of those years.

"He said to tell you that Junior's father sold most of his businesses in Mesa, including the Rattlers baseball team, and retired to Costa Rica."

"I figured that's what would happen," I said. "He couldn't stay in baseball once news of his betting practices leaked out."

I had recently received a note from the formidable Harrison Bennett, Sr., familiarly known as H.B. Oddly, he had extended an invitation for me to visit him and his wife at their Costa Rican hacienda. I replied, of course, giving my regrets and wishing them well. Somehow, a week with the Bennetts was not high on my list of things to do.

But I did think a visit to Fenway Park should rank close to the top of that list. I was eager to see another baseball game.

Read on for an exciting sneak
peek at the next
Murder, She Wrote original mystery,

PANNING FOR MURDER

Coming from New American Library
in October 2007

Chapter One

"I feel uncomfortable flying first class, Kathy, and you being in coach."

"Don't be silly, Jessica," she replied. "You've had your reservations for a long time. Mine are last-minute. Don't even think about it."

When I made my reservation to fly from Boston to Seattle, I'd used some of my accumulated frequent-flier miles to upgrade to a first-class seat. Kathy, who seldom travels, didn't have that luxury and was booked in the coach section of the aircraft. I'd suggested changing my reservation to coach so that we could sit together, but she'd adamantly insisted that I not. "I'd feel terrible," she said. "Besides, I've brought two good books with me. I wouldn't be a talkative seat companion, anyway."

I did, however, bring her as my guest into the airline's first-class lounge, and we spent the two hours before our flight enjoying the club's amenities.

"I can't believe I'm going back to Alaska so soon,"

she said as we sat by a window overlooking one of the airport's active runways, from which a succession of aircraft landed and took off. "I was just there," she added, "and me being such a coward when it comes to flying."

"A lot safer than riding in a car to the airport," I said. "Have you heard anything further from the Alaska police about your sister?"

"No. Well, they did call to report that they haven't made any headway in their search for her. I just hope . . ."

"Hope what?"

"That she isn't off on some jaunt and putting everyone to so much trouble, especially the police."

"Frankly," I said, "if that *is* what happened, you'll be greatly relieved. It would mean that she's alive and well."

"I know," she said, nodding earnestly, "and I pray Willie is all right. But it would be so embarrassing if she's off having fun and the police have been knocking themselves out trying to find her."

"Let's wait and see," I suggested. "More coffee or tea?"

I refilled our cups and returned to her.

"I did get a call," she said, "from one of Willie's husbands."

"Oh? Which one?"

"The next to last." She laughed. "I used to joke with Willie that she should number her husbands, like baseball players. You know, like the old saying, you can't tell the players without a scorecard."

"Sounds like a sensible suggestion," I said, laughing along with her.

"Willie thought it was funny, too."

"What did this particular husband have to say when he called?"

"He said he'd been trying to contact Willie without success. He wanted to know if I knew where she was."

"Did you tell him that she's missing?"

"Oh, sure. He was shocked, very concerned."

"Had you met him?"

"No. I never met him—his name is Howard—or the husband who came after, her most recent. Both were very short marriages. I don't think either one lasted a year."

I couldn't help but shake my head. "Your sister has cut quite a swath, hasn't she?"

"I'm afraid so, Jessica. Sometimes I'm embarrassed about how Willie has lived her life, but I always remind myself that it's her life, not mine, and that she's entitled to live it any way she chooses. Still . . ."

"They'll be boarding our flight soon," I said. "The airlines are closing the doors earlier these days to try and maintain a better on-time record."

"Then we should go."

We grabbed our carry-on bags and headed for the departure gate. A few minutes later, the call was made for first-class passengers to board. I gave Kathy a hug and said, "See you in Seattle."

As I stood and gathered my belongings to join others in the line, Kathy said absently, as though talking to no one in particular, "It must be the gold."

Her words caused me to stop and turn back to her. "What gold?"

"The gold Willie is convinced the brothel madam might have left us."

"Brothel madam?"

"All first-class passengers should be on board," the agent at the boarding desk announced, sounding as though she meant it.

"Go on, Jess," Kathy said.

"Gold? Brothel madam?" I muttered to myself as I went to the gate, showed my boarding pass, and entered the plane to be seated in first class. *"Gold?"* I repeated aloud. *"Brothel madam?"*

"Pardon?" a flight attendant said.

"What? Oh, sorry," I said. "Just talking to myself."

She gave me a strange look but managed a smile as I settled into the large, comfortable seat. *Gold? Brothel madam?* It was virtually all I could think of for the duration of the six-hour flight to Seattle.

The weather was clear as we approached the Seattle-Tacoma airport, affording those of us on one side of the plane a splendid view of Mount Rainier. The thought of spending a few days in the city prior to departing on the cruise wiped away any fatigue I might have been experiencing. Seattle is less than 150 years old, and it's known as the Emerald City, or Jewel of the Northwest, worthy of either label in my opinion. I've always enjoyed my time there; the easy mix of people and the spectacular views in virtually every direction are a true spirit booster.

First-class passengers were the first to deplane. I waited until Kathy eventually came through the door.

"Nice flight," she said. "I wasn't nervous, except for all those strange noises before we landed."

"All normal," I said. "Landing gear being lowered and locked into place, flaps extended, routine things like that."

"That's right," she said as we headed in the direction of baggage claim. "You know all about planes."

"I know very little," I said. "Just enough to get myself in potential trouble when I'm flying."

A cab whisked us to the downtown area, where we checked into the lovely Fairmont Olympic Hotel. I'd stayed there a few times before. This princely hotel, located on the southern edge of the retail center, has been operating since the 1920s and has been luxuriously restored to its former splendor, with all the expected amenities befitting a four-star property. Our rooms, each a small suite, were adjoining.

It was midafternoon, and after unpacking we met up for a walk. The sun shone brightly, and there was a slight breeze off the water that surrounds the city. Seattle's reputation for excessive, almost unrelenting rain, is a myth. Its annual rainfall is actually less than that of any major city on the East Coast. What fuels its wet reputation is a tendency for cloudy, misty weather—not rainfall, just a pervasive dampness. But there are plenty of fair days, too, and this was one of them.

"When is your book signing?" Kathy asked as we

maintained a brisk pace to work out the kinks from having sat too long in the plane. Kathy is an inveterate walker, always seen around Cabot Cove in motion on her way someplace, arms swinging, legs moving in a regular rhythm, a determined expression on her face. She'd changed into a sweat suit and sturdy sneakers. Kathy is a short, chunky woman, perhaps a shade over five feet, two inches, with a full, round face, expressive blue eyes, and brunette hair worn simply. She often complains about being overweight, although she isn't. She's simply one of those compact, physically fit people without an ounce of excess flesh.

"Tomorrow, at noon."

"Is it all right if I come?"

"Of course it is. I'd love to have you there."

"I always come to your signings in Cabot Cove, and I went to that one in Boston a few years ago," she said as we paused to window-shop.

"Seattle is different," I offered, setting off again. "Maybe it's because of the generally overcast weather, but Seattle probably has more bookstores than any other comparable city in the country, and more book buyers per capita than anywhere else. They devour books here, which is good for us writers. By the way, I've made a dinner reservation for us tonight at Canlis. Hope you don't mind my not conferring with you."

"Why would I mind?" she said. "You know Seattle. Besides, I trust your palate, Jessica."

"I think you'll enjoy Canlis," I said. "It's set in the hills with wonderful views of the city and beyond."

"Sounds yummy. I'm suddenly hungry."

Canlis might possibly be the most beautiful restaurant in America. With stone columns soaring high above the dining room, and light and landscape flooding in through a translucent wall, the restaurant has an almost Zen-like atmosphere. We were seated at a prime table affording a fine view of the city as dusk began to settle. Because I'd raved about my last meal there, Kathy insisted that I order for us, which I did—Canlis chowder to start, rich with Dungeness crab, sea scallops, and prawns in a heavenly ginger-scented cream, and a sublime salad, followed by an entrée of wild Pacific king salmon with hazelnut-caper butter, and jumbo asparagus, all accompanied by a shared bottle of DeLille Cellars Chaleur Estate Blanc from Washington's Columbia Valley, recommended by our sommelier.

"Kathy," I said as we enjoyed our first sip of the wine, "you said at the airport that your sister's disappearance might have to do with gold and a brothel madam?"

"Just thinking out loud," she said.

"Thinking about gold and brothels?"

She nodded, laced her fingers around her glass, and stared down into it. "I'm embarrassed that I even brought it up."

"But now that you have, you can't keep me dangling like this. What gold? What brothel madam?"

She turned to look at me, exhaled loudly, and said, "Dolly Arthur."

"Who's she?"

"She's—well, she was the most famous madam in Alaska's history."

"I'll take your word for it, Kathy. But what does it have to do with Wilimena?"

"It's a very long story."

"We have all evening. Could it possibly have to do with Wilimena's disappearance?"

"Maybe. How do I begin?"

"At the beginning, Kathy. At the very beginning."

By the time our coffee and dessert had been served—peanut butter mousse with a chocolate cookie crust and caramelized banana—we were both sated and somewhat drowsy. But while the Canlis dining experience had taken center stage, the conversation was equally satisfying, and provocative. Kathy had spun a tale of gold and madams in detail for me, and quite a tale it was.